Serendipity
Samantha M Thomas

Contents

To long distance relationships:
You suck, but damn are you worth it sometimes.

And to my husband.
Our own long distance love story was a wild one, but we made it through and
created something incredible together.

Chapter 1
sydney

"It's already done. There's a room with your name on it for two weeks. Go. Enjoy. And if you send an email during that time, I'll fire you," Pierce Vanstone says in my ear.

"You won't fire me." I roll my eyes at my demanding boss and resort mogul as I shuffle through paperwork on my desk.

"Sydney, please. The fact that I have to beg you to take a vacation is ridiculous. All of corporate is closed over the holiday. There's nothing for you to do. Wouldn't you rather relax by a fire and look at the Tetons? Catch up on your reading?"

Pierce from three years ago would never have sent me on vacation, let alone take one. The difference is like night and day, and it's still something I'm getting used to. Jane changed the way he not only works but lives. Now, apparently, he's forcing his new way of life on me.

"I'm not a reader," I deadpan.

"I'll call Jane..." he threatens.

"Dirty play." Calling his wife and telling her I'm refusing to take a vacation is possibly the one thing that'll get me to do what he says.

"If you weren't so damn stubborn, I wouldn't have to. Seriously, Sydney, the general managers have things under control. There will be no one at the Austin office. What are you planning to work on for two weeks?" he asks, exasperated.

"Contracts. Looking for new property. The New Year's Eve party. The usual," I rush out. He doesn't need to know that work is the only thing that keeps my brain sane. Being alone with my thoughts is far scarier than his wife's wrath.

"Sydney..."

I drop the paperwork back onto my desk and sigh. "Fine. I'll go to Idaho. Happy?"

"Very. It's Christmas; you shouldn't be working eighty-hour weeks. Hell, you shouldn't be working that much anyway, but I'm not having this conversation with you again." It's like I can actually see him shaking his head in disapproval.

"Nope, we sure aren't." I smirk even though he can't see it. "When am I leaving?"

"Monday. I have the jet set to take you there around nine in the morning."

"Four days? Jesus, Pierce, a little notice would have been nice," I grumble.

"Well, if I gave you too much notice, you'd find a way to put more work on your shoulders and not actually go."

"We've known each other too long."

"It does come in handy when I'm trying to get you to do something," he muses.

"I'm hanging up now since my tyrant of a boss decided I can't work in four days. I need to wrap up a bunch of stuff before then," I taunt.

In reality, Pierce is the best boss. When I started working for him over ten years ago, he was a grade A asshole with daddy issues, but he was damn good at running hotels and resorts. Now, he lives life at a slower pace, choosing to focus on the resort side of his business and really building his luxury brand. It's been fun to see the evolution and continue to take on more responsibilities as he steps back into the husband and father role.

"Details are in your email. Enjoy the time off, and have a great holiday. Call me on the flight back." He hangs up without preamble as I slump back in my office chair.

Fucking Pierce. An overwhelming feeling of dread thrums through my body.

What the hell am I going to do for two weeks with just myself as company? I haven't celebrated the holiday since I was a kid, and even then, it was nothing to write home about. My mom passed away when I was in college, and I never knew my sperm donor. Once my mom was gone, the holiday season fell by the wayside along with her. It's never bothered me before, but now Pierce is forcing

Christmas joy on me. *Lovely.*

Looking through the glass wall that offers a view of most of our corporate office, I see only a handful of people still working. I didn't even notice the lack of employees in the building, too lost in my work to realize the holiday season was already upon us.

That's probably not a good thing to admit.

Observing the piles of work on my desk, I tell myself I'll work through it all in the next four days, then focus on relaxing the best I can.

***

It's nine twenty in the morning, and I'm racing up the tarmac, frazzled and annoyed. Parking my car at the little private airport, I pop open my trunk before fumbling out the door and grabbing my luggage.

I see the pilot waiting by Pierce's private plane, and guilt hits me in the gut.

"I'm so sorry! I lost track of time and got carried away at work wrapping up the last of the contracts I needed to read through."

He walks over to grab my suitcase. "No need to apologize, Ms. Johnson."

"Sydney, please. I'm just never late, and I know you have plans to keep to, Dave." My breathing is labored as I follow him up the steps.

"Guess that's the nice perk of having access to a private plane, then. We leave when you get here." He smirks at me over his shoulder.

Since I'm Pierce's executive assistant, Dave and I have spoken so much over the years that we've developed a sort of friendship. At the very least, we bust each other's balls about how the other half lives, not that either of us have anything to complain about.

It doesn't take long to get us up in the air, and by the time we're at cruising altitude, my heart rate has settled and the stress over being late has dissipated. Now, the realization of too much free time is creeping in.

What the fuck am I going to do for two weeks?

I'm trying to run through ideas, and every single thing I come up with gets me more and more annoyed. I'm not a reader. I'm not outdoorsy. I dislike the cold. All the things this resort in Idaho is perfect for, yet I have no interest in.

Why did Pierce pick this resort? He has a million other ones in the most beautiful tropical locations. At least at one of them, I could lie on the beach, drink a mojito, and maybe go for a swim.

I'm going to start a list of grievances to give to him when I get back, so he'll never send me on one of these so-called vacations again.

Sighing, I lean back in the comfortable chair, and before I know it, my eyes start to droop and I'm asleep for the duration of the flight.

A jolt and a bounce startle me awake. Looking out the window, I see the tarmac and realize we're landing. At least I was able to take a nap instead of overthinking for the entire flight.

Dave stops in our designated area before his voice sounds over the intercom. "Welcome to Idaho. It's a warm two degrees outside today, so I hope you packed your bathing suit."

I chuckle at that one.

"Give me five minutes to wrap everything up here, and then I'll grab your bags."

I start gathering my purse and tote, which has a bunch of miscellaneous crap I thought would keep me busy on the flight in it. Standing up, I stretch out my back and neck, and contemplate my life's choices.

Two degrees is not my idea of a good time. Being the executive assistant to a luxury resort chain owner has its perks, but this particular one is feeling less and less luxurious by the second.

Dave meets me by the door, leading the way to a tinted SUV that will take me to the resort. You can't say Pierce doesn't cover all his bases while traveling.

In the two minutes it takes us to walk to the SUV, my face hurts from the sheer force of the cold. Adding that to my mental list of things to bitch about to Pierce, I bundle up as the car starts.

The good news is it's only about an hour drive to the resort—as long as the weather holds up—then I can camp out in my room or at the bar, and not have to deal with the cold.

The drive is nice enough. Lots of snow, lots of mountain peaks, but all I feel is dread for the next two weeks. By the time we make it to the sprawling mountain resort, I'm sufficiently worked up and need a drink.

"Thank you so much. Be safe going back," I tell the driver as I grab my things and head to the lobby. I'm immediately greeted by the concierge, who takes my bags and leads me to the elevator.

The top floor has all the big suites, and it's no surprise that's where Pierce set me up for the next two weeks. There are only a handful of rooms up here, so at least I won't have to deal with people if I don't want to.

After the concierge walks me through the suite and makes sure I'm all set, he departs without a trace, leaving me in the blissful quiet. Walking over to the floor-to-ceiling windows, I look out over the Grand Tetons in wonder. I've been to this resort once, and that was when we opened it. I wasn't paying attention to the view, too busy making sure everything was running smoothly and handling any fuckups that popped up. Now? Looking at the mountain range makes me feel small, unimportant. It's unnerving, and that drink sounds perfect right now.

The bar is busy when I get there, full of families excited for the holiday, singles splurging on the resort, and bored executives killing time before their next meeting or ignoring the family they left at home. After finding an empty chair at the end of the bar, I sit down and flag down the bartender.

"Good afternoon. What can I get for ya?"

"Gin and tonic, top shelf. Whatever you have," I clip.

He nods, turning to quickly make my drink.

The rustic wood bar top lets me focus on something. I trace the grain, desperate for something to do with my hands.

My drink is placed in front of me with a wink, and I barely hold back my eye roll. There's not a moment in our interactions that would lead him to believe I want any form of flirtation from him. In fact, I'm pretty sure I have a "don't talk to me" stamp on my forehead.

I down half my drink in one swallow then sigh as I put it down.

"No one should sigh over top-shelf gin," the man next to me says.

Turning to look at him, I'm struck by his profile. The perfect Roman nose sits on smooth skin and a square jaw. His chestnut hair has some wave to it and rests just on his collar. His eyes aren't looking at me; instead, they're staring down at his drink, which looks to be whiskey or maybe bourbon.

"Thanks for the tip," I snark then down the rest of my drink. I dig into my wallet and toss some cash on the bar top before leaving. The last thing I want to do today is deal with people, especially in any form of small talk.

The walk back to my room is uneventful, and I order my weight in food from room service, including drinks. No highly attractive man to butt in where he isn't needed. No bartender winking to get a better tip. Just me and all my favorites as I watch a snowstorm roll in over the mountains.

Chapter 2
Beck

So far, I've stayed under the radar. It's our winter break after the end of the Formula 1 season, and I decided to go somewhere off the beaten path or what's expected of me, to get away from it all. All the pressure, all the media, and all the expectations.

So far, it seems to be working. No one's outwardly recognized me, and I'm grateful. I wasn't sure what to expect with this resort, but I've been pleasantly surprised. Not to mention, the suite is nice as hell, comparable to where I usually stay in more high-profile cities.

I've been sitting at the bar, nursing my one glass of whiskey, for far longer than I should. Lost in thoughts about the future, about racing, about everything I wanted to get away from.

My wayward thoughts are stymied when a woman sits down in the seat next to me and orders her drink in a no-nonsense tone. When the bartender not-so-subtly tries to flirt with her, I can feel her annoyance. It tips up the side of my lips into a smirk.

She's a spitfire.

The sigh that leaves her after she downs half her glass makes me want to test my theory.

"No one should sigh over top-shelf gin," I interject. I don't look at her, content to watch her reaction from the corner of my eye.

She turns to look at me; I feel her eyes take me in but can't get a strong read on her.

"Thanks for the tip," she snips before downing the rest of her drink, tossing some cash down, and leaving.

I shift in my chair so I can watch her leave. Her fast clip is anything but seductive. Her hair is piled up on top of her head, like she doesn't care about the opinion of anyone in this hotel. She's not putting on a front, not hiding her feelings to appease others.

It's admirable, really, to be able to just *be* without consequences or some journalist taking everything you do or say out of context to fit a narrative. I'm envious.

I can't remember the last time I ever felt that free to do what I want. Instead, I'm Beck Davis, broody F1 driver and most hated man on the grid. One who was a superstar but has recently been struggling. It's a persona created from one interview, nine years ago, when I just came up into Formula 1. I was pissed at the invasive questions and took it out on the journalist, thus creating an image I've never been free of since. The really sad part is I don't even know if I can separate myself from the persona anymore, so used to being the villain, the grump who's eternally pessimistic.

I down my whiskey and decide to call it a night. The alcohol won't help my mood, and catching up on some sleep sounds amazing. It's better than thinking about things I can't currently change.

The short trip to the top floor has my thoughts alternating between the spitfire in the bar and how little time I have to prepare for the new season. As I get older, the three months between seasons seem to get shorter and shorter. I have to work harder and harder to prove I still belong while acting like it's as easy as walking.

Frankly, it's getting exhausting, but I also don't have a backup plan. This is all I know. It's all I've known since I was four and started karting. So, I'll take the next two weeks to pretend like my life isn't my own, then I'll go back to training until March when I'll be Beck Davis once more.

***

Rolling over, I look at the clock on the nightstand. Ten fifty-two in the morning. I can't remember the last time I slept this long, but the blackout curtains certainly contributed.

My days usually consist of waking up with the sun so I'm able to get ahead on the day. Sometimes, I go to Legacy headquarters, and sometimes my trainer and I work out all fucking day. None of it is thrilling; all of it is hard work.

I'm not even sure what to do with myself right now. I'm not really a skier. Don't really want to do any of the activities the resort offers. Maybe it was foolish to think I could spend two weeks here and relax. It's day two, and I'm already struggling.

My stomach at least helps and makes the decision for me. A loud, hungry growl interrupts my musings. I swing my legs over the side of the bed then stand up and walk to the bathroom. Once I'm done pissing, I stare at myself in the mirror. My hair is overly long, and I hate it, but the PR team said the female audience goes wild for it, so I can't change it. I shove back the locks on my right side and look at the scar close to my hairline—a reminder of how dangerous the sport I've committed my life to is.

My normally vibrant hazel eyes look dull and weary. Rolling them, I turn on my heel and go to my suitcase. When I get back from breakfast—or rather lunch, I guess—I can unpack while I figure out how I want the next two weeks to go. On the trek down to one of the restaurants, my mind wanders to the woman at the bar last night. From what I saw, she was fucking gorgeous. Maybe I could get to know her better while I'm here.

Jesus, Beck, thinking with your cock will not help anything. You're supposed to be figuring out your shit, not getting your dick wet like you just signed your first big contract.

Shaking my head at myself, I push the mystery woman to the back of my mind. I'll probably never see her again anyway. This resort is way too damn big to run into someone all that often.

"Good morning, sir. Table for brunch?" a hostess asks.

Awesome. I don't even have to make a decision between breakfast and lunch this way. "Uh, yeah, that would be great."

I'm seated and put my order in. My grapefruit juice is delivered almost immediately, and I take a sip as I look around. The place is pretty full, and there isn't a table free; it's mostly couples and some families, which just proves I'm the oddball loner. Nate Murphy—my trainer, best friend, life coach, general jack of all trades—offered to come, but I declined, saying I wanted the alone time. Now, I'm not so sure.

"I'm sorry, ma'am. There's going to be at least a half an hour wait," the hostess says louder than she probably should, drawing the attention of the entire restaurant.

I look over to the stand, which isn't too far from me, and spot the woman from last night.

"Are you fucking kidding me right now? Should have just stayed in my damn room," she grumbles just loud enough for me to hear.

In the light of day, I can see her features much better. Her brown hair is still piled on her head, but now I can see her forest-green eyes, and I'm drawn to them. She's wearing leggings and an oversized sweater—a sharp contrast to the attire of almost everyone else in the restaurant, but she doesn't seem bothered in the least.

"I'm sorry. If you leave your number, I can call you when I have a table ready for you," the hostess says with a tinge of annoyance, which is the polar opposite of how she acted around me.

"I'm good, thanks." The woman goes to turn around, and I act on instinct.

"Excuse me," I call out as I shove my chair back and stand.

The mystery woman stops in her tracks, and the hostess turns to look at me with unconcealed jealousy.

Yikes. No, thank you.

"I'm by myself today and have a chair open, if you'd like to join me," I offer. "Would save you the time," I add in hopes it makes me look like less of a creep and more of a nice guy.

She looks me up and down, and recognition hits her eyes, making me hold my breath for the inevitable callout. Except it doesn't happen.

"Is top-shelf gin involved?" she asks with an arched eyebrow.

"It can be." I smirk.

We hold each other's stare for a moment before I see her shoulders slump as she sighs. "That'd be nice, actually. Thank you." She walks past the hostess giving her a dirty look and sits in the chair opposite me before I have time to pull it out for her.

I settle back into my chair. The waiter appears out of nowhere, handing the mystery woman a menu, and then disappears just as fast.

"So, is this your first time at The Vanstone?" she asks, not bothering to look at the menu.

"It is, actually. How about you?"

"Nope." She snags the glass of water on the table—*my* water—and downs a healthy gulp before smiling. "Although, I haven't been to this one in a long while." She looks around.

My brows furrow at her words, but I don't get a chance to ask her more because the waiter stops by to take her order. She orders like a seasoned patron, making me more curious by the second.

Awkward silence fills the space as I try to find something to say. Although I couldn't get this woman out of my head, I find it hard to come up with something to talk about. I want to ask her more about herself, but that comes with reciprocation and risking my anonymity.

The waiter sets down her drink. She thanks him then takes a sip, moaning, and tips her head back, savoring the taste.

My hand grips my juice, the knuckles turning white as my breath stalls. *If you want to be alone for the next two weeks, the time to abort this brunch is now.*

But my stupid ass doesn't. No, instead, I dive in head first. "That's how you should sound drinking top-shelf gin."

Her eyes meet mine, a glint of mischief in them. Oh, she's trouble.

"You have an awful lot of opinions on how top-shelf gin should be drunk. Let me guess, you're a distiller? No, that's too easy." She shakes her head in jest. "Maybe a bartender?" Her eyebrow arches. "Doubtful, judging by the Rolex." She nods at my wrist. "Or maybe you're just after something other than how one sounds while drinking gin. Maybe something a little more seductive. Salacious, if you will?" She smirks.

Goddamn, her wit and bluntness are doing it for me. "Seems I'm not the only one with grandiose opinions."

"Oh, big word choice. Sunday crossword?" Her smirk grows.

"Sure, we'll go with that," I concede.

"And what are you drinking this morning, oh knowledgeable one?"

"Grapefruit juice," I deadpan, picking up my glass and taking a sip. My eyes never leave hers.

Her eyebrows shoot up. "Well, that's … not that I was expecting." She chuckles right as the waiter delivers our food.

I wasn't expecting the ease of banter with this woman. I don't even know her name.

The waiter leaves, and I stick my hand out over the table. "Name's Beckett." I'm not sure why I give her my full name, the one I haven't gone by in years. She doesn't seem to know who I am, and Beckett is a lot more common than Beck is. It's an extra layer of cover that I hope sticks.

She looks into my eyes and then down to my hand, cautiously bringing hers to mine. "Sydney."

"Thanks for joining me for brunch, Sydney." Her name rolls off my tongue, and I'm thinking all sorts of dirty things I could say in conjunction with it.

Nope. That's not why you're here. You will not hook up with the gorgeous woman who seems to match you tit for tat.

She clears her throat before releasing my hand and digging into her pancakes. Before I can blink, it seems, we're finishing up our meal and the time comes to part ways.

I know if I hang out with this woman more, I'm in danger of pushing the boundaries, and that's not my goal. I need these two weeks so I can get my head on straight and refocus on my career and my future.

Chapter 3
SYDNEY

*B*eckett.

Somehow, the name both fits him and doesn't. It's been four days since our impromptu brunch, and he's been on my mind a little too often. He's intriguing, and I've been on the verge of seeking him out more times than I want to admit, even if it's just to test our sexual chemistry.

Hooking up on vacation is not something I do, especially not at one of the properties I help run. The staff may not know my face, but they know my name. That's why I haven't been flaunting it because, for once, I want to just be *me*, not work and have people intimidated by my title or put me in this category of importance because of who my boss is. For once, I'm grateful to be anonymous.

Maybe Pierce was onto something here. I won't ever tell him that, though. Can't let him have too much credit.

I'm too lost in my head, not paying attention to anything around me, when I bump into a hard body.

"Woah, you okay? I called your name." Beckett's voice finally registers.

"Yep, totally fine. Sorry, was lost in my head."

I look at him, realizing he's not super tall. He's only about a half a head taller than me. This is the first time I've seen his full height because I've hustled out of every situation before he could even stand up. I clearly wasn't paying attention at brunch when I walked up to his table.

"All good. What are you up to today?" He shoves his hands into his jeans' pockets.

"Oh, umm, no real plans. Maybe read, who knows." As I say it, I realize how little I've done so far and how antsy it's making me. I'm used to being on the go all day, every day, but with nothing to do, I'm going stir-crazy already.

"Well, I was about to have one of the concierges drive me up to the Tetons and explore a little. Would you like to join me?" His eyes—not quite green, not quite brown—are a mixture of hopeful and weary, like he's afraid to push too far.

"Uh…"

"No pressure. Just something to do," he quickly adds.

I think about what I would do if I declined, and I find my options severely lacking. But a drive to the mountains, and then God knows what else, with a man I can't get out of my head spells trouble.

Fuck, either option is problematic.

I peer up at him again, making a decision for the rest of my time here in Idaho: it's time to take advantage of this anonymity and jump into some fun.

"I'm in."

The smile that stretches across his face lights up the whole damn lobby. His mostly straight teeth draw my eye, and I wonder what kind of a kisser he is.

Slow it down, Syd. You're just taking a day trip with him, not screwing his brains out. I doubt he even wants that. But damn if that doesn't sound tempting.

"Yeah?" he asks in a boyish tone that's adorable.

"Yeah. I need to go run up to my room and change real quick, though." I look down at my leggings and oversized long-sleeve T-shirt and cringe.

"Not a problem. I needed to stop by my room because I forgot to grab my … jacket."

My eyes drop down to the one in his hand, and I raise an eyebrow at him.

"A thicker one," he rushes out. A tinge of pink dusting his cheeks makes him strangely endearing.

This one's trouble for sure.

We're both quiet as we make our way to the elevator.

"So, how long are you here for?" he asks as we step inside.

"Two weeks, apparently. My boss set this up for me. A forced-vacation situation. So, I've got a little over a week left."

"Generous boss," he remarks.

I ignore him because, although he's right, I don't really want to talk about Pierce today.

"What about you?"

"About the same. I need to get back to ... work ... as well, sadly."

The way he hesitates on the word "work" has me curious. It's not that I think he's hiding something; it's more that there's probably more to the story than he's letting on. I know he has money—you can't stay at a resort like this without it—but that doesn't narrow down things at all. Pierce and I have seen it all at the resorts. Tech geniuses, TV personalities, and every kind of famous person you can think of.

"Sounds ... interesting." And I sound lame because I can't come up with an actual conversation. Unlike our banter at brunch, this feels stilted and I'm not sure why.

It's probably best to just head back to my room and let whatever this is between Beckett and me fizzle before it ever gets a chance to start. Learning more about him will just make me want to dig deeper, and Lord knows I don't have time for any form of a relationship in my life. *After the trip to the Tetons,* I tell myself. I'll distance myself when we get back.

Beckett's laughter erupts from his chest, sending shivers down my spine. It's deep and raspy and so damn sexy.

I hit the button for the top floor and arch an eyebrow at him in question.

"It's not interesting at all, but I appreciate the thought. Lots of repetition and not a lot of free time." His tone turns melancholy in a second, and the urge to comfort him and ask for more details is overwhelming.

No need to dig deeper. You'll never see him past this vacation, I struggle to remind myself.

I briefly wonder what he could do for a living again, but he doesn't seem very forthright.

The elevator doors open, and I walk out on the top floor. He follows after me, and I abruptly stop in my tracks.

"Uh, are you just going to wait out here?" I ask.

"I was going to trade out jackets," he says slowly with a furrowed brow.

"But my room is here," I say dumbly. Duh, why else would I get off the elevator.

"As is mine, it seems." His small smirk lights up his eyes, and in an instant, I know I'm screwed. Having him on the same floor as me will be too damn tempting.

"Of course it is," I mumble under my breath and stomp to my room.

Unlike all of our other properties, this one has real keys to hone in on that cabin-like charm of the area. Now, it just means that it takes me too long to get my damn door open as the attractive anomaly watches me in mirth.

With far too much effort, I'm finally in my room, and I collapse against my door.

This is a terrible idea, but what else am I going to do for the next week? I've done all the *relaxing* I can handle. Outside of eating my weight in food every day and walking around the property, which just makes me want to work, I'm coming up empty.

If Beckett is into it, would it really be so wrong to spend the rest of the week in his bed? It's been ... long enough that I can't even remember since I've had sex with anything other than my vibrator. This could be good for me.

Am I really thinking about hooking up with Beckett?

A knock on my door startles me. My hand comes up to my racing heart as I clear my throat.

"Yeah?" I croak out.

"You ready to go?" Beckett asks.

"Umm, almost. Give me just another minute," I yell as I run to my room and start stripping in the process. Thick jeans, a long-sleeve wool sweater, and waterproof boots are on in less than a minute. I snag my snow jacket as I race out of my room and go to the front door. "Okay, I'm ready," I huff, trying to catch my breath.

Beckett's lips roll inward as he looks down my body. "I think I liked the leggings better."

Bold. Maybe he is into me.

"Then, next time, don't plan a mountain trip." I tilt my head.

"Next time, huh?" His blinding smile hits again.

Movie star. With that smile? Definitely a movie star.

"It's an option." I brush past him, shutting and locking my door as I do. The feel of his hard body, even through the layers, makes me think this wild idea of mine could work.

"I like options." He walks toward the elevator, not waiting for me to follow, and I'm glad for the moment to gather my head.

***

Two hours later, we're sipping hot chocolate and looking out the window of the little coffee shop we found that overlooks the valley below. We've talked about everything and nothing. It feels like we've known each other for years, not just hours.

"Is it sad to admit that's the most fun I've had in ... a really long time?" I cringe at the truth in my words. It makes me sound boring, and in truth, I am. Work is my life, and that's never been more evident than it is now.

"Not really. I can't remember the last time I just stopped thinking about life. About the responsibilities and the obligations. I couldn't tell you the last time I was just present in the moment." His voice is soft. Thoughtful.

"That's very reflective," I muse. "But a great way to put it. It's strange to be so far in my life and feel like I haven't had time to slow down and appreciate it."

"Exactly! For me, it's more that I haven't been able to make more of my own decisions to go along with that. Forget slowing down; this makes me realize how little control I really have."

Well, that's sad.

"How do we change that? For both of us, you think?"

"At this point in our life, can we really change it?" he asks.

"God, I hope so." I laugh humorlessly.

I feel the heat of his gaze on the side of my face, but I'm scared to turn my head. I'm scared of what I'll see reflected back at me. Of the truth of our quiet words spoken in this bubble of time.

"Come back to my room tonight. We can do dinner, room service, or whatever, and we can ... change our lives." His voice is soft but clear.

This time, I do look at him. His hazel eyes are brimming with so much hope that I know is shining in mine as well. I don't expect an impromptu Christmas vacation to change my life, but fuck if I don't want to cling to the idea that it could.

"Tomorrow is Christmas Eve," I say stupidly instead of the "hell yes" my head is screaming.

"It is." That's it—no inflection, no concern that we're practically strangers potentially spending the holiday together.

"And you don't have family or anyone you'd rather spend the holiday with?"

"Do you?" he counters.

"Nope. Hence why my boss had to force the vacation on me in the first place. I just don't want you to feel like you need to spend time with me because I don't have anyone." I don't want pity and I'm probably overreacting, but I'd rather give him the out if he really wants it.

"Well, unless I want to call up my trainer, I'm alone as well. And if I have to pick, I'd sure as hell rather spend it with you."

We haven't talked about our jobs. It's the one thing that we've left unsaid, and I don't hate it. But his hint of having a trainer has my head puzzling things together. *Athlete of some sort?*

I look deep into his eyes, really taking in his words while deciding what I really want. It won't hurt me to say no, but I think I would regret it if I didn't say yes. Logically, I know we don't have to do anything but be together, but realistically, I know it won't stop at that. I'm too attracted to him. To his mind, his whole demeanor—all of it is so enticing.

Change our lives.

Do I think this one interaction could change the course of my life? Doubtful, but damn do I want it to. I want to feel, to be spontaneous for once.

A lightning bolt of clarity hits me.

"Okay," I whisper. "I'll come to your room tonight."

Chapter 4

BECK

What the fuck am I doing?

As I pace my suite, I wonder, not for the first time, if I've lost my damn mind. I barely know Sydney, and yet I can't imagine spending the next week with anyone else. There's something about her. She understands me like no one else does, without knowing every detail of my life.

So often, I feel like my life isn't my own. I have a million people telling me how to breathe daily. Sydney is a breath of fresh air that I desperately need. It doesn't hurt that she's so fucking gorgeous. It's like looking into the sun.

I've had more fun today than I have in so long. I knew if I had the chance to spend more time with her, I would take it. Now, I'm waiting for her to cross the hallway and join me for dinner with the hope of more. Who knows if she even wants more, but the realization that tomorrow is Christmas Eve gave me an urgency to not be alone for once.

I'm very distant from my family. Over the years, they've proven that they only want to be in my life for the money I make. My brother even more so, so I just chose not to communicate with them anymore. Although I feel all the better for it, it doesn't minimize the loneliness, especially around the holidays.

A knock on the door disrupts my thoughts, and I'm grateful for the reprieve. No need to think about the rest of the Davis clan.

Four steps are all it takes to bring me to the woman I can't get out of my head. Four steps to cure loneliness, if only for a blip in time.

"Hi." I smile as I open the door.

"Hi." She's changed since our excursion. A pair of gray leggings wrap around her muscled legs, and the tight T-shirt with Santa on the front and the words

Where my ho's at? on it makes me laugh.

"I like the shirt." I nod down her body.

Her cheeks turn pink. "I'm not very good at being festive. It's really all I have, and it was a gag gift from my boss's wife."

I gesture down my own body. "I'm not festive at all, so you've one-upped me." I'm in a pair of joggers and a plain workout shirt, both from one of my sponsors. I was careful to not wear any Legacy—my racing team—gear.

She stares a little too long before jolting her head up. "So ... you gonna let me in?" she snarks to hide her embarrassment, the overly confident and borderline grumpy woman nowhere to be found. In its place is a shy, hesitant Sydney who's alluring as hell.

"Of course." I hold open the door and move to the side so she can come in.

She walks in like she's been here before. I know this particular resort prides itself on having all of the top floor suites different, so my curiosity is piqued. I won't ask her, though; our jobs seem to be off-limits, and I'm not willing to be the one who changes that.

"I was thinking we could just do room service, maybe put on a movie," I suggest as I join her in the living room.

"Love it. Are we doing full-on Christmas movies?"

"I was thinking *Die Hard*," I offer, holding my breath.

The smile she gives me makes my heart beat faster.

"I knew I liked you," she says.

"I'm glad we're in agreement." I grab the remote off the table and turn on the streaming service I already have set up.

She plops down on the couch like she lives here, and all the tension and stress I've felt for too long dissipate. I hit play and sit next to her, pulling up the room service menu on my phone and handing it to her. She navigates it with ease before handing it back to me.

I see she's ordered a rib eye with all the fixings. The fact that she isn't afraid to go big and get what she really wants is sexy as hell. I'm used to models and movie stars who starve themselves for their jobs, barely eating most days so they can keep their coveted bodies. I'd much rather have a woman like Sydney. Strong and capable, she has something to grab onto when I show her what I can do to her body.

I drop my phone down to my lap in an attempt to hide my dick. These joggers do very little to help my situation, but hopefully, she's too focused on the movie to notice.

With our room service order sent, my mind starts wandering to what will actually happen tonight. I'll let Sydney take the lead because I don't want to push any boundaries, but I'd be lying if I said I'm not hoping for a sleepover.

"I can hear your mind working overtime." Her voice startles me.

"Sorry, got lost for a second." I turn to look at the concern on her face.

My eyes flicker between hers, the concern morphing into heat, and I stop thinking altogether.

Change our lives.

My hand moves to her cheek at the same time she leans in closer. We hesitate for only a moment before the band between us snaps. The pressure of her lips sends my head spinning. This isn't just a kiss; this is a fucking earthquake to my system. In a split second, it feels like my life's axis has shifted.

Her tongue peeks out, brushing along my bottom lip before nipping it. I keep her cheek cupped in my one hand as the other grips her ass and pulls her onto my lap. A whimper of need escapes her lips and makes my dick even harder, if that's possible.

My lips take on a mind of their own, trailing from hers to nip at her ear then down her neck. Her fingers tangle in my hair, keeping me as close as possible. She doesn't have to worry, though. I'm not going anywhere. I feel so alive, even more so than when I'm racing at two hundred kilometers per hour.

Her hips start moving against me, and I'm about to flip her on her back, when there's a knock on the door.

"Room service!"

Sydney drops her forehead to my shoulder as her frame shakes with laughter.

"Of fucking course it's room service," I grumble.

"It's probably good timing. I have a feeling we're going to need our energy."

I pull back to look at her fully. "Are we now?"

"Um, hell yes. I'm not stopping at a tease. You owe me now." She winks then stands off my lap and heads to the door.

Blowing out a steady stream of air, I try to rein in my thoughts of just saying "fuck the food." She's right. If the slideshow of images in my head is anything to go by, we'll both need our energy. I plan to keep her wet and needy through the whole damn holiday if I can.

"Thank you so much," she says before I hear the door shut. She wheels the whole cart into the living room and uses the coffee table in front of us as a makeshift dining room table.

I've scarfed down my steak by the time she's halfway through. I can barely focus on anything other than getting my hands back on this woman.

So, I do just that.

She puts her fork down to wipe her mouth, and I take advantage of it. Leaning over, I grip her hip and drag her over into my lap.

"I wasn't done eating!" she squeaks.

"I know, but I need my hands on you." I bring her plate to my side and pick up a piece of steak. Bringing it to her lips, I arch an eyebrow and wait for her to take a bite.

She does so, gingerly, unsure of where I'm going with this. To be honest, I have no clue; I just know that I need her in my space, and if that means feeding her the last of her dinner, so be it. I'm too keyed up to be patient. And the feel of her in my lap is just ... *right.*

"Is this a kink you're into?" she asks with mischief in her eyes.

"If that kink is you, then yes." I give her another bite of steak.

"What is happening?" she whispers once she's eaten her steak.

"Can we just go with it and not think about it too much?" I don't want to delve too deeply because this may be fast—hell, this may end up just being a hookup—but it feels too fucking good, and I don't want to stop.

"I think I can do that."

I move her plate onto the table as she moves her leg to straddle me. *Die Hard* is long over, but who needs background music when I'm about to hear what this woman sounds like mid-orgasm.

"Good." I stand up with her ass cupped in my hands. If we're doing this, we're doing it right, not on the fucking couch like teenagers.

"Jesus, you're going to hurt yourself," Sydney grumbles.

"Yeah, we're not acting like I can't manhandle you into any position I want you in. I can do it, I *will* do it, and you'll love every second of it. Carrying you is just the start."

She pulls back and looks into my eyes. Her pupils are blown wide, and for once, I wish I had a smaller room so it didn't take so damn long to walk to the bedroom.

Within a few strides, I toss her onto my bed and reach back to rip my shirt off.

"Holy hell, you weren't kidding about that trainer, were you?"

I look down at my body that's not overly muscled but defined—a hazard of the job when the name of the game is adding less weight to the car. Every ounce counts and can affect your race. I've never really cared about it much since I don't have time to mingle with the ladies. But seeing the way my body lights up Sydney? Well worth the hours and pain it takes to stay in this kind of shape.

"Get naked, woman," I grunt instead of responding.

She smirks as she strips her T-shirt off. Her leggings come next; she expertly shucks them and throws them at my face, which is mesmerized by every inch of skin she exposes. I don't miss a beat, tossing them down on the floor at the exact moment she unhooks her bra and slides it down her arms.

Perfection.

She's not stick thin and her more-than-a-handful breasts make me salivate to get my hands on them.

Sydney leans back on her elbows and arches that damn eyebrow at me—a challenge I'm all too willing to step up to. Untying my joggers, I hook my thumbs into the waistband, making sure I catch into my boxer briefs too.

"Take the panties off."

That fucking smirk grows as she starts sliding her panties down. I follow her movements, pushing my pants down my legs at the same pace she does.

"Fuck, why is that so sexy?" she groans, her eyes never leaving my lower half.

By the time we're both naked, just watching each other has us both so keyed up that I know this first time has the potential to be embarrassing. It's a good thing I can't wait to get my mouth on her and feel her with my fingers before I need to worry about that.

"Jesus, Beckett, you're killing me here," she whimpers, her hand sliding down her body to put pressure on her clit. The trimmed triangle of hair on her pussy looks so fucking good as her fingers take control of her own pleasure.

Her confidence fuels my own. Licking my bottom lip, I grip my cock so tight it steals my breath. My imagination is going overboard thinking about how she'll feel around me. The tightness in my balls is a tell of my urgency, so I take my hand off and kneel on the bed in front of her, watching as her fingers dip down, pumping inside of her before dragging back up to her clit.

"Feel good, baby?" I murmur as I watch her. I scoot in closer, my hands trailing up her legs.

Goose bumps prickle her skin, and she shivers at my touch. "Higher." She moans, making me smile at how desperate she is.

I wanted her wet and needy, and here she is, like a willing, greedy present waiting for me to open it.

My thumbs brush along the crease of her thighs as they drop open for me. I can feel the precum leaking from my tip, but I couldn't care less about me right now. Keeping my hands there, I smirk as I lean forward, my eyes still on her face.

She follows my movements, lifting her head up. The confusion written on her face turns to a gasp when I lick her from her pussy to those fingers that are still circling her clit.

Fuck, her taste is a drug. One I want every single fucking day.

The hand that was working up her pleasure moves to my overgrown hair, gripping it so tight I wonder if she'll yank some strands out. I'd welcome the pain. It would give me something to focus on, so I don't blow my load all over the sheets.

"Oh my God." She hisses as I pulse her clit between my lips.

She's making me feel like a god, like all my life's problems can be solved with the taste of her on my lips and the feel of her around my fingers. As I think it,

I trace around her opening, not entering her like her desperate hips are telling me she wants. I release her clit, taking one long stroke before I circle it again and slide a finger inside of her.

Her back arches off the bed as her moan gets louder. My hips grind against the bed unconsciously. The need to be inside of her is getting harder and harder to ignore, but she clenches tight around my finger and twitches against my lips.

"Holy fuuuck, don't stop," she whimpers.

I pull my finger out almost all the way before adding another to mix, matching the rhythm her hips are grinding against my face.

"Beckett!" she screams out my name as she comes.

The pulsing against my lips and fingers has me barely hanging on, but I make sure to draw out her orgasm before disengaging. I clumsily reach over to the nightstand, feeling around for the condoms I placed there before she came over. I meant what I said about just hanging out, but let's say I was hopeful for more.

As I crawl up her body, I rip one open with my teeth and quickly put it on. My hands grasp for every inch of skin I can find as my lips wrap around one of her nipples. It's like I can't get enough of her, can't stop touching her enough to speak words, let alone dirty talk. I need every inch of my body touching hers, and then maybe I'll feel content.

Notching at her entrance, I slide my hand down her leg, gripping her ankle and putting it on my shoulder, opening her up completely for me. I want to be so fucking deep she'll feel me when we leave to go back to our real lives.

Her other leg wraps around my waist as I finally let her nipple go and kiss her. Her hips undulate underneath me, trying to push me inside of her, but my willpower is strong as hell. She doesn't know that yet, but she will.

Pulling back, I look down at where we're barely connected. "You have no idea how much I fucking want you. How much I've wanted you since the first time I saw you in the bar."

"Beckett, I swear to God, you better put your fucking cock inside of me now before I flip you over and take what I need."

My eyes jolt up to hers. "Is that a promise?"

Her eyes light up with lust, and I know exactly what round two is going to look like. But not this time. No, this time, I'm doing what I've pictured since the moment she shot that gin.

Holding eye contact, I push forward, steady and smooth. I give her time to adjust but not time to get used to me. I may not have a ton of height on me, but I'd like to think my thick cock makes up for it a little.

"Holy shit, holy shit, holy shit," she chants, eyes wide as I seat myself fully inside of her.

"Next time, you can have all the control you want, baby, but tonight you're mine," I growl as I start to thrust.

My eyes go back to where we're connected; seeing her stretched wide to take me has my pace picking up. Gripping her ankle on my shoulder, I push it off and up to her chest, which gives me the best fucking view I've ever seen.

Her moans and whimpers aren't even coherent anymore. She's getting close, and I'm dangerously on edge myself. The hand not holding her ankle moves to her stomach, applying pressure, and I drop my thumb to her clit.

"Come on, Sydney. Give it to me," I grunt, trying to hold back the tingling in my spine.

Her stomach contracts under my palm, and her pussy pulses tight around me, making me lose all control. I collapse on top of her as my hips move at an erratic pace until fire shoots through me and I come inside of her.

Panting against her neck, still holding her body open for me, I try to catch my breath as she does the same.

"Where the fuck did you come from?" she whispers through her pants.

I can't answer her, but I wonder the exact same thing.

Chapter 5
SYDNEY

I'm wide awake, watching the snow fall as I feel puffs of breath on my neck—a sign that Beckett is still sound asleep. I don't blame him; I should be sleeping too with all the activities we've done in the last two days, but I can't.

It's Christmas day. A day I should be excited to spend with a man like Beckett, and yet I'm so conflicted.

The sex... Holy shit, the sex is phenomenal, but spending a major holiday with him seems bigger somehow. In just a few days, we'll both leave here and go back to our normal lives. This blip in time will be just that, a fond memory to think about on lonely nights.

And I'm scared because I'm starting to not want it to just be a blip in time.

"Do I need to make you come again?" Beckett's raspy voice sends a chill up my spine.

I send my wayward thoughts to the back of my mind and submit to the man who is starting to know my body better than I do.

"What a way to wake up on Christmas morning." I smile. "A white Christmas and an orgasm, is there anything better?"

His hand slides over my hip to my ready and willing pussy. I don't think we've gotten dressed in two days. Ordering room service and hiding out in the bathroom when they deliver it has been our routine. It's a fantasy I could surely get used to.

His fingers circle my clit, and I breathe deep and focus on this feeling. On staying in the moment and not thinking about the after. I'll have plenty of time for that when I leave.

"God, you get so fucking wet for me," he groans into my neck.

All thoughts disappear. His touch combined with the feeling of his hard cock pushing up against me is the biggest turn-on I've ever experienced. He's never unsure of himself, confident yet attentive. He's an anomaly that my body is constantly wanting.

"Why are you up, anyway?" he whispers into my ear.

"My brain wouldn't shut off." I whimper as he adds a little more pressure.

He tsks me and dips a digit low before pushing it inside of me. I arch against him as his other hand slides up my stomach, his fingers tweaking my nipple.

"Fuck," I curse as my orgasm floats to the surface.

I come on a silent scream, gripping his wrist as he eases me through it. The crazy part? He presses a kiss to my shoulder before rolling over and walking to the bathroom. No push for more, no need to get off, just giving me an orgasm before doing his morning routine.

It's wild to me. I've never had a man who cared more about my pleasure than his own, and it's making my already conflicted thoughts worse.

An idea burrows itself in my head as I listen to him brush his teeth. It's Christmas Day. Neither of us are celebrating if sex doesn't count, and it makes me want to do something for him. I know—I *know*—it's a stupid idea. We won't matter to each other the second we leave for the airport, but it doesn't stop me from running with it. The need to make him a priority, just like he's made me, is too strong.

"Hey, I'm going to run downstairs real quick. Will you order some breakfast?" I call out as I pop up from the bed and start to throw on some sweats. I did manage to snag a very basic wardrobe from my suite, just in case.

"Yeah, where are you going?" His head pops out of the bathroom.

"Just to get some…" My mind races to come up with something. "Condoms," I damn near shout. *Jesus, I'm so bad at this covert shit.*

His eyebrow arches. "I can have a concierge bring some up."

"Nah, I'll just run down there." I'm already halfway to the door.

The click of the door sounds behind me, and the tightening of my chest loosens a little. Getting Beckett a Christmas present feels right, even if it's making me scared that I'm pushing things too far. If I keep telling myself that, maybe I'll be less manic about it all.

The elevator ride down to the lobby is fast, and before I'm mentally prepared, the doors open and I step out.

This resort has a pretty large gift shop. Since the Grand Tetons are such a tourist attraction, Pierce thought it would be good to add in a large area with all sorts of branded shit and Grand Tetons swag— our PR person's words, not mine— and today, I'm grateful for the vast selection. It also helps that it's Christmas Day, so the chance of finding an actual present should be high.

"Merry Christmas. Can I help you find anything?" the sales associate asks as I walk in.

"Nope, just browsing. Thank you, though."

I see a stand of ornaments and head toward them. A beautiful hand-blown glass ball in a white shade that looks just like the snow on the mountains pulls me in. When I spin the tag around, I see it's not just a price tag but a wooden decorative tag that has our location and the year on it. It's not ostentatious but simple, with a subtle tree background behind the words. He may not have anywhere to spend Christmas regularly, but this screams the perfect present to give him today. Something to remember this year, and me, by.

Grabbing it, I head to the counter before looking to the side and seeing the condoms. Might as well stay true to my word; we do actually need more if we continue our pattern.

"Find everything you need?" The woman starts ringing up my purchases.

"I did, thank you. Is there a way to get that wrapped?" I point to the ornament.

"Of course." She boxes up the blown glass in an equally gorgeous wooden box, then turns around to the wrapping station I didn't even notice.

Maybe we should have all of our gift shops set up this way; it's a great service. As I think it, I pull out my phone to make a note to bring it up at our next meeting.

"All right, here you go. I put it in the bag with your other purchase."

I look at her name tag—Nikki—and make a mental note to talk to the general manager here about her wonderful service. She deserves to be recognized.

"Thank you so much." I pay and then head back to the elevators.

Worry starts to take hold as I climb to the top floor. What if he hates it? What if I took this a step too far?

If that's the case, then I'll just head back to my suite and act like nothing ever happened. Avoid him like the plague and leave in a few days to pretend we haven't been fucking each other senseless for the past couple of days. I'm not usually an anxious person, but Beckett is making me second-guess my every decision, and I'm starting to hate it. Gone is the sure woman who helps run a resort empire.

I stand outside of his suite for a minute, trying to calm myself down, when the door opens to reveal the man himself.

"Hi," he says shyly.

"Hi."

"I did something, and if you hate it, I'll get rid of it," he rushes out.

"Umm, okay?"

His nervousness is so fucking endearing; I just want to kiss him. He's always so confident that this new, shy version of him just makes me want to know more about him.

He moves to the side and holds the door open for me to walk through. There, in the living room, is a small Christmas tree, simply decorated but nonetheless gorgeous. A tray of smores sits on the table next to the fireplace, mugs of hot chocolate next to them.

"You did all of this while I was gone?" It couldn't have taken me more than half an hour to get what I needed and be back up here.

"All I did was call the front desk and ask if we could make it happen. They did the rest."

I look over at him; that shyness he's never had before is written all over his face.

"I can take it all down," he rushes out, doubt in every word.

"Please don't. It's so perfect," I whisper as I walk closer to it.

I reach into the bag I'm still carrying and pull out the present. Placing it under the tree, all my doubts about whether this was a good idea or not vanish in a second. I can deal with the fallout later, but right now? I want to enjoy

Christmas for once, with a man who apparently wants to do the same.

"What did you do?" he asks, his eyes hyper-focused on the package now sitting under the tree.

"It's Christmas." I shrug. "It seems we both had a similar idea about actually celebrating it."

"Sydney..." He draws out my name like he can't quite believe I would do something as simple as get him a present.

"I promise it's not that big of a deal." Do I wish it was a big deal? That things could potentially turn into something more? Absolutely. But fantasy is rarely based in reality.

"I can't remember the last time anyone got me a Christmas present," he whispers, cracking my heart just a little more.

Time to deflect and refocus on what we agreed on.

"Well..." I walk up to him before dropping to my knees. "Why don't you open it while I give you another gift."

His eyebrow arches as a wicked smirk spreads across his face. "You drive a hard bargain, baby."

I hand him the wrapped box before hooking my fingers into his joggers and pulling them just low enough for his dick to pop out. Wrapping my hand around him, I slowly pump as I watch his head tip back as he blows out a steady stream of air through his pursed lips.

"Open the present, Beckett." I grin.

Having this effect on a man who's this fucking attractive sends my confidence through the roof. It's one of my favorite things about this time with him. He makes me feel like a goddess who can do anything in the bedroom.

I continue to run my hand up and down his shaft as he struggles with the wrapping paper. Once he finally gets it off, I run my tongue along the underside of him. My eyes never leave him.

His hand reaches out and tangles in my hair, pulling me off of him. "I swear to God, I will never pull you off my cock again, but if I want to get this open, you have to stop. I can't fucking focus with your hot mouth on me."

His words make me chuckle as I sit back on my heels, waiting for him to open the impromptu gift.

He rotates the wooden box before finding the part that slides out. Once it's open, he gingerly pulls out the ornament. "Sydney..." His voice trails off, and worry hits my gut hard.

"It was just a quick grab from the gift shop—" I start to overexplain it before he cuts me off.

"I fucking love it." He sets it down on the coffee table and hoists me up off my knees. I wrap my legs around his waist while he cups my cheek in his palm.

"I just wanted to thank you for keeping me company during a time I usually hate with a passion. It's been ... really nice." The words don't match how I'm truly feeling, but I can't go there after only a couple of days with this man. It's the lust, the attraction, that's messing with my head, so keeping things simple is how it needs to be.

"I came here to get away from my life. To be unknown and think about my future. Instead, I found a little slice of peace I didn't even think was possible. Thank you for bringing me that; it's meant more than I can tell you." He presses a kiss to my cheek as the pressure in my eyes tells me my emotions are running haywire.

I will not cry because I'm so touch starved that the man currently helping with that saying nice things to me is making me overly emotional. I'm an emotionless badass and need to reel myself back in. I'm getting way too attached, which only spells trouble for me in the end.

Reaching my hand down in between us, I grip his still-hard cock, teasing him with the promise of more.

"I see what you're doing, and I'll let it slide. But know that I see you." His eyes look too deep into mine, like he's searching for deeper meaning, and I know I need to pull away from it.

His agile body holds me close to him as he kneels down and lays me on the blanket he had set up in front of the tree. Wasting no time, he grips the waist of my sweats and rips them down my legs as he kicks his off at the same time. His multitasking is truly impressive.

As he reaches up toward the tree, my brows knit together in confusion at what he's going for. When he pulls a condom out from the middle of the tree, I burst out laughing.

His grin is adorable as he rips it open and slides it on. "I figured we'd take advantage of the atmosphere at some point, unless I really fucked the whole thing up."

"Planning ahead is always a good move. There's some in my bag too." I giggle.

"Smart woman. I'll be sure we use every single one."

His fingers trail down my sweatshirt-covered body before they reach my pelvis. As I've come to know him, he wastes no time circling my clit and getting me close before he pushes two fingers inside of me, slamming my body with an orgasm only he can expertly bring me.

We spend the rest of Christmas day watching the snow fall, in between countless rounds of sex.

Even though I'm in dangerous territory with this man, it's the best Christmas I've ever had. As I fall asleep, wrapped in his warmth, I hope that I can spend the rest of my time here with Beckett before I have to head back to the real world.

Chapter 6

BECK

I've been up for hours.

Today, Sydney and I leave Idaho and each other to go back to our regularly scheduled programming, and I'm not ready. It feels apropos that we're both scheduled to leave on the same day. Both from the executive airport, adding more to the mystery of who she is.

But I won't ask her. I won't dig deeper because she didn't ask for more. We agreed to spend our time here together as relief to our loneliness, and we accomplished that in spades. Now it's time to go, and I have to accept that.

It's not like I won't have plenty of distraction once I'm back in England at our training facility. My days will be spent working my ass off to get into driving shape and keep up with the kids coming into the field. The doubts associated with my name at the end of last season are why I ended up in Idaho of all places. A place to be nobody. A place without pressure.

A place where I made Sydney come every single way I know how and then some.

Yeah, I'm screwed with this woman. But we've pointedly avoided any conversation past this trip, and I have to respect that. She's in the driver's seat, and I won't push her regardless of how I'm feeling.

"It's too early to be thinking that hard. My alarm hasn't even gone off yet." Sydney groans as she rolls over and cuddles into my side.

"You are absolutely right. Sorry I woke you up." I press a kiss to the crown of her head.

Her heavy sigh clenches my heart tight. "You didn't. Just thinking about everything I need to do before I leave."

"Same," I whisper.

It feels like we're breaking the spell of this place, and I hate every second of it. But time waits for no one, especially a Formula 1 driver who is on borrowed time in his career as it is.

"What time do you need to leave?" she asks. Her fingers are tracing the spot where my heart is.

"Ten a.m. at the latest." The long flight to London, followed up by a meeting with the team tomorrow, means I don't have a lot of leeway on when I leave. "What about you?" "Well, I have a big New Year's shindig I need to finalize all the last-minute stuff for, so around the same. I'm not giving myself a lot of time with only three days until New Year's Eve."

Maybe she's a party planner. I've been making guesses in my head all week, but none of them feel right.

I peek at the clock on the nightstand and see it's just past seven. With an hour's drive to the airport, we don't have much time at all to gather our things and pack before needing to head out.

"Do you want to share a ride to the airport since we're going at the same time?" her timid voice asks.

I'd do a hell of a lot to spend more time with this woman, even if it's in a car for an hour. "I'd love to. How much do you have to pack?"

"Not much, honestly. I didn't really unpack, and since I've met you, I've been either naked, in your T-shirts, or in my sweats." Her lips tip up against my chest.

"I don't hear a complaint."

"And you won't hear one. Besides the endless orgasms, not having to pack up a ton of shit is a real bonus."

I poke her side, which makes her giggle.

Fuck, I'm going to miss her. A lot.

"Shower with me before we need to start getting ready." It's not an ask. I need this last little bit of closeness before I lose it all.

"Just showering. Lord knows when you get going, we'll be there longer than an hour," she warns.

It's amazing how well it feels like we know each other already. It's not the mundane shit, like our favorite color or movie preferences. It's this inherent knowledge of each other's reactions and responses. I've never had that with another person outside of my trainer, Nate, whom I spend almost every waking moment with. Never with a woman.

"We'll see." I smirk as we both get out of bed.

Within minutes, we're under the spray, quickly getting washed up.

She's about to walk out when I grab her hand and pull her to me. Her arms wrap around my middle as mine do the same. Resting my cheek against her head, I hold her close.

Under the spray of the shower in a luxury resort in Idaho, I soak in the last minutes of closeness and real companionship I'll have for far longer than I'm willing to admit right now. Sydney is everything I could want in a woman, at the worst possible time to even consider it.

My contract is up this year, and I'm driving to stay in the sport that's taken up all the best years of my life. I'm not ready to retire. I feel that I have years left in me, even at the ripe age of thirty-five, but I need to prove it on the track. A girlfriend—hell, even a friend with benefits—is out of the question. It'd just be a distraction I can't afford right now.

But Sydney makes me want to say "fuck it" and see where life takes us.

"All right, I really do need to pack." She steps back and opens the shower door.

A chill that has nothing to do with the cold air rushing in runs up my spine. One I fear I'll have to deal with for the foreseeable future without Sydney in my life. She brings a warmth I didn't realize I was even missing.

I watch her walk out of the bathroom, staying in the shower long after I hear the front door close. Turning the water to as cold as I can get it, I welcome the icy blast. It seeps into my bones, reaffirming the fact that I have bigger things to focus on for the next twelve months.

Sometimes, I wonder what life would look like if I didn't get to this point within racing. Only the top twenty drivers get to drive every year. Out of all the people who try, who train, who give up so much of their lives to make it, only twenty reach elite status. It's hard to remember that some days.

The chill turns to shivers, and I know I need to get my ass in gear. I need to pack, and delaying won't make leaving this place—and Sydney— any easier.

Running on autopilot, I load up my luggage, double-checking the entire suite before stopping by the coffee table and picking up the wooden box containing the best present I've possibly ever received. The thoughtfulness is something I'll hold close, and wherever I end up for Christmas in the future, I'll be bringing this along to hang on my tree.

I take one last look at the little tree by the fireplace, one last snapshot of Sydney lying next to it naked, before I head out the door.

The drive to the airport is stilted at best. I'm not sure what's going through Sydney's mind, but I'm trying to figure out if it's a good idea to get her number. Hell, any contact information. By the time we reach the airport, I've been so lost in my thoughts that the opportunity to get her information is all but gone. As the car parks, I shift toward her. One last chance to take whatever this is into the real world, even if it's just occasional contact.

But she's already out the door.

I scramble to join her as her pilot takes her luggage to the plane next to us. The jet my team, Legacy Racing, uses is sitting next to hers, but I don't make a move over to it.

"So..."

"I've had such an amazing time with you," I say.

"Beckett... Let's just keep the good memories and not draw this out, okay?" Her voice is tiny like she's trying to keep her emotions in check.

The second I hear it, I back off. I could never cause her any kind of hurt even if it's unintended. Prolonging things is clearly not what she wants. It doesn't matter if I want to keep in contact, no matter how delusional it is, when I have every reason to distance myself from her. What matters is respecting what she wants, what she needs right now.

I lean in, gripping her upper arm gently as I press a kiss to her cheek. "Thank you for the most incredible week," I whisper before I pull away.

I don't wait for a response. I don't look into her eyes to see what she's feeling. Instead, I walk to the trunk and grab my luggage. I wait for a minute before I peek around and watch her walk up the stairs. She doesn't turn around or hesitate, and once she's inside, the pilot shuts the door behind her.

Gone.

Without a way to contact her. Without a last name or any details to find her.

Taking a deep breath, I grab my suitcase and walk over to the jet.

"Good morning, Mr. Davis. Ready for the long flight?" The pilot takes my luggage from my hand.

"Yep. Can't wait." I drag my ass to the back, plopping down onto one of the recliners and staring out the window as her plane taxis.

However logical, however she feels, my head and my heart say leaving here is a mistake.

We're halfway over the Atlantic when I finally come to terms with not having a way to contact her and the fact that my focus needs to be completely on racing and not on a woman I knew for a week.

I'll always remember this time when I'm lonely at night. When I need the comfort I rarely get during the season or need to release all the tension, Sydney is who I'll think about.

A memory is better than never knowing her, never experiencing her body or her mind. At least that's what I tell myself as we land, and when Nate picks me up and goes over my schedule for the entire week. That's what I tell myself when I'm sitting in the meeting with the whole crew, discussing what we hope the next year looks like. It's what I tell myself when the team principal pulls me aside to discuss my future and what he needs to see from me this year.

But when I go home that night, her memory is a poor substitute for the real thing, and I realize just how much I fucked up by not getting any identifying information about her.

I have many regrets in my life, but only having Sydney for a week may go down as one of my biggest.

Chapter 7
SYDNEY

"What is sitting on my desk?' I say into the phone as I hold up a lanyard with a big-ass VIP tag on it.

"Do you even watch television? Go on Instagram and scroll to see what's popular?" Pierce's voice is grating on my nerves.

"No, but I'm glad to know you have time to do so. I've been a little busy opening up two new resorts while keeping the others up and running," I snap before sighing and slumping back into my office chair.

"I deserved that," Pierce says. "The lanyard is a VIP ticket to the Formula 1 race coming up this week at Circuit of the Americas. One of the owners offered up tickets and I took them, but I'm unable to use them."

"So, you're a sports fan now? A car racing one at that? Not very luxury brand of you," I needle him. To be honest, I know nothing about sports or their inner workings. It's never been my thing, and I can't imagine watching cars going around a track will be all that.

"I think you'll have a good time seeing how luxury Formula 1 is." He chuckles.

"You're annoying. Why don't you take Jane and make it a date? I'll even watch the kids." An offer I rarely make, but I don't know if I have it in me to wine and dine rich bastards this week.

"Tempting, but I'm taking her on surprise trip to the new Italy resort."

Ugly jealousy rages through my body. I've never, in as long as they've been together, been jealous of Pierce and Jane. Envious? A little unfulfilled with my own life? Absolutely, but that's mostly because they're soulmates. Who doesn't want that for themselves?

But this is different. It's been different ever since Idaho all those months ago.

Shaking my head, I shove those thoughts down. It won't do me any good. I know that by now. It's only taken me ten months to figure it out.

"She'll love it. It's beyond beautiful."

Italy was the first resort that Pierce wasn't on premise for any part of opening it. He put it all on me for the first time, and I'm damn proud of it.

"You did a great job on it. When we get back, you and I need to have a meeting."

Ominous. But Pierce doesn't scare me. If it was something bad, he wouldn't warn me about it. We've worked together long enough that I assume it's a new property he's eyeballing.

"Sounds good. So, what all do I need to do at this sports thing?" I toss the lanyard on my desk and grab a pen to write the details down.

"You technically have two tickets, so bring whomever you want. There are two days of practice and qualifiers before the actual race on Sunday. Your ticket gets you into the VIP areas on all days. I think you'll be above the paddock, but either way, you'll have a great view of the action."

"Sounds ... loud," I say.

"You'll probably be able to go into the pit lane, where the cars are, and meet the drivers. There's supposed to be a bunch of celebrities there. Should be a small circus." He chuckles.

Awesome. Exactly what I don't want to deal with.

"Yeah, I won't be doing that. I'll show up for the weekend to make you look good, but I'm not going above and beyond to kiss anyone's ass, especially not a man's who drives a car for a living."

His laughter is booming. "You never know, you might meet someone."

"Sure, boss. Can't wait." I don't even try to hide the sarcasm.

"Just take it for what it is—a break from working all the time." He sighs.

We've had this conversation too often lately, but he doesn't understand that working is the only thing that keeps my mind occupied. That distracts me from thinking about a certain man I'll never see again.

***

VIP at a Formula 1 race means VIP. I've never gotten such special treatment before in my life, outside of general managers going overboard whenever Pierce and I show up at a resort. But that's because they're trying to make the best impression. Here, I don't even register as the one thousandth most interesting person. I'm a fly on the wall in an environment I don't belong in.

I brought Daisy, my assistant, with me. She's the closest thing to a friend I have outside of Pierce and Jane. And she was free, so it was a no-brainer.

Unlike me, Daisy is an extrovert and knows a thing or two about sports. The entire drive here, she was telling me names of the drivers and what team they drove for. I'll be honest, I didn't retain any of it, which is unlike me, but I just don't have it in me today.

As we walk up to the track, we tap our lanyards against a post that lets us in. After being directed to an area above the paddock that houses a metric ton of catering and an equal number of celebrities, we settle into a table in the corner that offers a decent view of the track and the pit lanes, or so I've learned.

I had no idea so many people enjoyed this type of thing, but I'm quickly realizing it's way more popular than I assumed. And the sheer amount of money here? It rivals anything I've seen at our resorts.

"Wow, this is where you need to come to find a man." Daisy runs her hands together.

I take a giant sip of my gin and tonic while rolling my eyes. "Not everything is about meeting men."

"It is if they are this loaded."

"Do I not pay you enough? Are you hurting for money?" I chuckle.

I know I pay her well. I've given her a raise every year she's been with me, and her salary is at the top end of her pay bracket. Peirce gave me full rein with her, and it's been nice to be able to reward her whenever I want without having to get Pierce's approval.

"You know you do, but who doesn't love the idea of a sugar daddy?" She giggles.

"Me." I groan as I take another gulp.

"We need to get you out more. There are so many attractive men here, and you're acting like we're at the dentist." She tsks.

The problem is, none of them are the man I want but can't have. I had my chance, and instead of growing some balls, I turned my back on him without a way to contact each other. It's what I thought he wanted, but over the last ten months, I've gone over that decision in great detail many, many times. Regret is a heady thing. Compounded by the amount of hours I work regularly, it's forced me to do some serious thinking lately.

"Oh! Look, here come the drivers!" Daisy all but squeals, pointing to the track.

There's a train of pickup trucks with people in the back, waving to fans. It's all a bit much, a bit showy, but apparently, people love it if the cheers are anything to go by.

"And who are we rooting for?" I pick the cucumber from my drink and take a bite.

"Well, Sawyer Joseph and Beck Davis are the only Americans, so I would say them, but have you seen Luka Tomic?" She fans herself.

"Can't say I have."

"Luka is gorgeous, so I'm rooting for him," she says in a daze.

I roll my eyes but turn my attention to the trucks pulling into the paddock area. Daisy explains it's the pit lane, but I know I won't remember that. She's listing drivers as they go by, but I'm not really paying attention.

Until I see longer light-brown hair in a familiar cut—one I see when I close my eyes most night.

What the fuck?

I stand up and walk closer to the edge. Lots of men have that haircut. I'm just still so hung up on him that I'm imagining him at the slightest similarities. That has to be it.

"Beck Davis. Not a bad choice at all," Daisy says from beside me, and I freeze.

Beck. *Beckett.* That can't be coincidental, can it?

I keep my eyes on him as he messes around with the other drivers. When he steps away, rolls his neck, and takes a deep breath before looking to the sky, my own breath stalls and my heart stops.

Holy shit, it's him.

I step back from the railing to the area hidden in the corner. A place I can watch him, but he can't see me.

"What just happened?" Daisy asks, joining me at the table.

"Remember when I came back from Idaho, and I told you—very vaguely—about the guy I had met but it didn't work out?"

"Yep. The one you were trying too hard to act like was nothing but was really something because you've never told me about a man before."

"I'm not even going to comment on that," I grumble. "Anyway ... it's him."

"Him who?"

"The guy. It's Beckett— I mean Beck. Davis. He's Beck Davis," I rush out in a jumble of words I'm not even sure make sense.

"What the fuck?" Daisy calls out loudly.

"Shh, what the hell?" I chastise.

"I'm sorry. I just found out that my boss, who literally does nothing but work too much, hooked up with a guy on a forced Christmas vacation, and couldn't stop thinking about him because she fucked up and didn't have a way to communicate with him. And now I learn she actually hooked up with a fucking Formula 1 driver. Like, how did you do it? Do you have notes on how I could replicate it?"

"Jesus, Daisy." I rub my temples.

"Sorry, I'm still a little shocked," she says plainly.

"No shit. Imagine how I feel."

She's tapping away on her phone as I try to regain my footing. Or hell, just wrap my head around the fact that a very famous athlete, if I'm to believe all the hype around this race, is a man who helped me have one of the best Christmases I've ever had in my life. Not to mention the orgasms. God, I miss the orgasms.

"Oh shit," Daisy whispers.

"What?" My head jolts up to look at her. The cringe on her face makes me think I don't want to know what she's looking at.

"You know what? It's none of our business. You don't need to know this unless you plan on finding a way to talk to him."

"What do you mean?"

"Nothing."

"Daisy. What did you find?"

She holds my gaze before her shoulders slump. "He's been photographed with Vivian Locke. Multiple sources say they are dating."

My chest feels like it's caving in on itself. It's stupid. Of course he's dating someone. He's too amazing not to be taken. It's been ten months since Idaho, so did I really expect him to be single? What was I expecting? For us to magically find our way back to each other and still be single in order to act on it? Of course not. He's dating a fucking super model. I never had a chance.

Delusional, room for one please.

But *fuck*, it crushes me.

"I'm sorry, Syd," Daisy whispers.

"Nope. Nothing to be sorry about."

"We can leave," she offers.

"Absolutely not. We're going to stay, come back all weekend, and watch Luke— What's his name?"

"Luka," Daisy adds helpfully.

"We'll watch Luka kick some ass. Watch some cars go around in a circle, eat and drink until we can't anymore, and have fun," I tell her with determination.

"In that case, let me get us new drinks." She hops up with excitement, but I can see the pity in her eyes.

I never expected to run into him again, let alone at his job. And I never expected him to be in a relationship. In some fairytale world, I expected him to be as hung up on me as I am on him, but it's not meant to be. I just have to accept that. By watching him all weekend as punishment for not taking the chance when I should have.

It's a hard lesson. Even at thirty-one, it makes you realize how much you still believe in the fantasy of it all. Pierce and Jane are the exception. To find that kind of connection at the perfect time so it turns into a life together isn't what most people find. They're the lucky ones.

By the end of day one, I'm drunk and ready to sleep. Luckily, we grabbed a hotel close by, so we can rideshare there and not have to worry about actually making it back home, although we could just as easily do so since it's only about half an hour away.

On day two, my raging hangover prevents me from drowning my sadness in more liquor, but that's probably a good thing. Daisy does exactly what she's good at: talking all day about anything and everything, but nothing Beckett—no, Beck—related. God bless her.

By the time race day rolls around, I'm actually having fun. Daisy has created a million scenarios where she hooks up with Luka and he falls madly in love with her. Some are simple situations, some so outlandish I have to laugh. My favorite is her somehow getting onto the track and him saving her from certain death. She's kept me laughing and mostly distracted the entire weekend, and I couldn't be more grateful for her.

It's made me realize how closed off I've made myself to anything outside of work. I haven't cultured friendships or made myself available as a shoulder to lean on—a point of change I hope to work on in the future.

The weekend ends with Luka winning and Beck coming in second.

When we finally leave Circuit of the Americas, it's with renewed purpose and a fresh mind. Will I still think about Beckett, not Beck, on the lonely nights? Most likely, but I hope it will be with less pain. And a lot less hope.

"Thank you for coming with me this weekend. I really had so much fun," I tell Daisy as we drive home.

"Thanks for inviting me. I will now closely be following my imaginary boyfriend's career, so thank you for that." She giggles.

"Glad I could help you." I smile over at her. "We'll have to do drinks again soon."

She looks over at me with her eyebrows raised high. "Yeah?"

"Yeah. We work hard; we should let loose once in a while."

"I'd like that," she murmurs.

The weekend may have been full of sadness and disappointment, but at least

I'm ending it on a high. With a friendship that always should have been.

Chapter 8
sydney

I've never been an impulsive person, yet standing in the lobby of our Idaho resort on a last-minute decision three days before Christmas proves different this year.

Maybe I'm a glutton for punishment, but ever since that damn race weekend, my mild obsession with Beckett has turned into full-blown internet stalking of Beck Davis during all of my free time. It's scary what you can find on the internet about people in the spotlight. I tried to steer clear of pictures of his dates with Vivian, but they were everywhere.

Maybe I came here to just *feel* an ounce of what I felt last year when I was with him. Curb the loneliness and the chill that only he seemed to be able to cure.

"Good morning, Miss Johnson, so lovely of you to join us again. Mr. Vanstone called us earlier, and we have your suite all set up and ready whenever you are," our GM, Stephan, says.

The anonymity of last year is gone, but I'm not as desperate for it as I was then.

"Thanks. I'm just going to hit the gift shop before I head up." I offer him a smile. They've already taken my luggage up and handed me the key.

As I enter the gift shop, a sense of déjà vu hits me. It has the exact same setup as a year ago, and I walk straight to the ornaments. A small selection of the hand-blown glass orbs are sitting front and center. A flash of what happened last time I was here enters my mind before I can shake it off.

Coming here was a bad idea.

But then an ornament in a gold shade catches my eye. The wooden tag has a fireplace in the background, and I grab it immediately.

I looked up the company when I got home last year. I don't know what I was hoping to find, but I look at their website periodically to see if something speaks to me. This is the first one that has, and it's back in the place I met Beckett.

I've started separating them in my head. Beck Davis is the famous driver, the playboy with a girlfriend. Beckett is mine. The man I've thought about too often and who made me rethink my priorities over the last year.

It doesn't hurt that Pierce promoted me to co-CEO with him after that fateful Formula 1 race. Now, we split the load, with the intention of both of our schedules lightening up tenfold, and me working far less hours. It's something I don't have a grasp on yet. He's made changes within the company, allowing both of us to thrive without adding more to our plates. He actually apologized for not promoting me sooner. I laughed in his face because I started as a lowly assistant, never expecting it to turn into anything more. Now I'm the co-CEO of a billion-dollar luxury resort company. Some days, it's hard to believe this is my life.

But as I hold the ornament in my hand, the stark reality that I don't have it all hits me in the gut. Another year, another Christmas by myself.

After checking out, I head up to my room. Luckily, it's not the one I stayed in last year or Beckett's. I don't think I could have handled that. My emotions are already going haywire by being here. I must have sounded like a snob requesting a certain room.

Unlocking the door with the key, I walk in and am greeted by a gorgeous, already decorated Christmas tree, with a couple of presents underneath.

Pierce.

Pulling out my phone, I snap a picture and send it to him.

Me:

It's gorgeous. You shouldn't have.

Pierce:

I should have done it last year. Enjoy your stay, and if you want to stay longer, the suite is yours until after the new year.

I won't lie, there are major perks to this job.

Walking over to the tree, I pull my new ornament out of its wooden box and hang it front and center on the tree.

I'm not sure what my goal is for coming here again, but maybe it's just to be at peace with the fact that I can't have Beckett. That my chance at something with him ended the second I got on that plane with no way to contact him. This is just my fucked-up way to move on.

Collapsing back on the couch, I watch the snow fall. Tomorrow, I'll walk around and maybe eat at one of the restaurants, but today, I just want to sit here and reflect on a milestone year.

***

This really has become one of my favorite resorts the company owns. Sure, we have more high-end ones, a lot of them on private beaches with all sorts of cool features, but there's something about the charm here that makes me happy. The real keys, the fireplaces everywhere, and the stunning view of the Tetons are so different from our normal resorts.

I'm sitting at the bar right off the lobby, people-watching and sipping a gin and tonic. Families exhausted from all the mountain excursions, couples spending time in a picturesque setting for a holiday together... All of it makes me proud of what we've accomplished here.

Tossing some cash on the bar once I finish my drink, I ready myself to spend Christmas Eve night in front of the fire with room service. It may not be exciting, but I think it's exactly what I need.

I'm checking my email on my phone when I walk into someone.

"Oh my God, I'm so sorry. This is why I don't check my—" My words freeze in my throat.

There's no way.

"Hey, baby," he says softly with a small smile on his face.

"What the fuck are you doing here?" I hiss, all of my calm gone in a flash. This ugly anger stems from seeing him and Vivian together for the past two months.

His smile drops as he takes a step back. "Can we go somewhere quiet and talk maybe?"

"No. I don't know." I sigh. I may have come back here for some misplaced sense of closure, but never did I expect to run into him again. "Do you want to come back to my room?" I offer.

I don't know why he's here or if he even has a room, but it seems like the best option. It gives me a sense of familiarity, at the very least.

"I'd love to."

The elevator ride is tense. I'm not sure if it's just me, but the combination of shock, annoyance, and fear over him being here has my head in shambles. I don't think I could make small talk if you lit a fire under my ass right now.

I struggle to get the key in my door, but once I do, I walk to the couch, needing to sit down before I collapse. I'm not ready for whatever he has to say. I'm not ready to let him know I know who he is. This wasn't supposed to happen, and now I'm not sure how I'm supposed to react.

He has a fucking girlfriend. Just the thought fuels my stubborn anger.

"Why are you here, Beckett?"

Chapter 9
BECK

Definitely not the reception I was expecting. Hell, I wasn't expecting her to actually be here. But now she's looking at me like I've wrecked her entire plan.

Shit, what if she's here with someone?

My fist clenches tight as I breathe through my nose. If she's here with someone, I'll bow out. It would kill me, but it's the right thing to do.

Three hundred and sixty days I've waited for the chance to see her again. Through one of the most challenging years I've ever survived, the only thing that kept me pushing, that made me do things that would help my career in the long run, was this woman. And she's staring at me like I'm the bad guy.

"I'm here for you. I came here on the very far-off chance that you would come back here too."

"And what about Vivian?" she asks, completely throwing me off kilter.

"Vivian?" I ask dumbly. If she's asking about her, that means she knows who I am. "When did you figure out who I was?"

The when doesn't really matter. It's the jealousy and anger radiating off of her that tell me I may still have a chance here.

"At COTA. My boss gave me VIP tickets, so I went. Imagine my surprise when you pulled up in a truck feet away from me."

She was feet away from me just a couple of months ago, and I missed her.

"And then you looked me up," I say, connecting the dots.

"Hard not to when you're some racing superstar." Beyond the anger is hurt.

I see it now. The reason she's here now is the same reason I am, but she thinks I'm with Vivian.

"Hardly a superstar. Vivian is—"

"Listen. It doesn't really matter. I'm just here to enjoy the white Christmas and get a break from work before it becomes really busy." She stands up and walks to the door. Opening it up, she stands to the side, effectively telling me to leave.

Crushing disappointment hits me hard, almost bringing me to my knees. But I understand where she's coming from. For now, I'll let her have a little bit of space, give her time to come to terms with me being here. And then I'll try again. And again, until she hears me out.

"It was great to see you, Sydney." I tell her as I pass her and head down the hallway.

***

I've been pacing for hours.

With the season over, there was only one thing I wanted to do: come to Idaho for Christmas and hope against hope that Sydney had the same idea. I haven't stopped thinking about her in the year since we last saw each other. It wasn't just the sex that stuck with me, although I'd be lying through my teeth if I said I didn't think about it every single time I got myself off. No, Sydney stuck with me because she's the first woman who treated me like a person. Not an entity, not a business deal, not a social deal to boost visibility. Just a man.

I craved that feeling again. I craved her, and that's why I'm here.

Her knowing who I am throws a wrench into everything, though. Not only do I need to explain my hectic life and what all it entails, but I need to explain Vivian and how Sydney is more of my girlfriend than she is.

I knew agreeing to that stupid fucking "date" would bite me in the ass. What started as a favor to our CEO turned into fake dating rumors that Vivian said to just go with. I don't keep up with the tabloids, so I never care what they say about me, but I didn't anticipate Sydney having to see it all. I can't imagine how she felt seeing the pictures, the stories I'm sure were saying all sorts of things about us that weren't true. I think about if the roles were reversed, and I want to break the fictious asshole's face apart.

Shit. What if she doesn't hear me out? What if she doesn't believe me? It's not like I can call Vivian and have her vouch for me. I can't trust her as far as I can throw her.

I walk to the bedroom and fall back onto the bed, looking at the ceiling.

This is not how I thought things would go. I thought I would have time to ease her into the idea of my name and what comes along with it. She makes me want to be just Beckett, but that's not my reality. Especially after last season.

Last year, I was contemplating my future. My contract was up, and I needed to prove I could still hang with the new guys coming up. I did so in spades by securing a four-year contract with Legacy and quite a pay bump. But it comes with a price. I'm under a microscope now. With social media being what it is, I can't go to most places without someone snapping a picture or getting a video. I have to always be on my game, never stepping a foot out of line. Some guys love it and actually thrive on the attention. Not me. I hate every second of it. But I love driving, and this is the trade-off to make that happen.

But Sydney makes me want to be able to separate the two. In my downtime, I can just be Beckett, hopefully with her. I can stay away from the content-hungry fans and pretend to be normal for a while.

Now, the problem is getting her to believe me. It's hard to imagine playing along with a dating headline in any other world, so I'm not sure how to convince her yet. But I will.

I doze off sometime during the night. When I wake up, it's because the morning sun bouncing off the fresh snow is so bright. Groaning, I roll over, rubbing my eyes, and think about Sydney.

She looked good—*too* fucking good—last night. Her oversized green sweater didn't stop my imagination from running wild. Add in the tight jeans and heeled boots, and I'm glad I have some self-control, because, *damn,* she looks phenomenal.

The year had been good to her. She seemed lighter and happier, until she ran into me.

A knock on my door has me bolting upright. Once I'm there, I open it without a thought; it displays Sydney in all her gorgeous glory.

Her eyebrows almost hit her hairline as her eyes trail down my body. "Umm, clothing might be a good option when you open the door next time."

Looking down in confusion, I realize I'm in just my boxers with a very obvious erection.

"Shit," I curse and leave the door open to put on a pair of joggers and a T-shirt.

By the time I'm dressed, I've heard the door close. I wonder briefly if she just walked straight back to her room. No one needs to be accosted by dick unwillingly this early in the morning.

Luckily, when I walk out of my bedroom, she's sitting on the edge of the couch.

"Hi."

Her head snaps up to mine. "Hi." Her voice is so soft, so unsure.

The need to find a way to undo the damage the fucking media and I have done is so strong.

"How'd you find my room?" I ask instead of dropping to my knees like an idiot and begging to be heard out.

"Perk of the job." She smirks.

"The job?"

"I'm co-CEO of Vanstone Properties." She says it so simply like it's just another job, not that she runs the most popular and highly spoken of luxury resort brand in the world.

"Holy shit," I whisper. "And I just drive a car. Talk about out of my league."

"Be serious," she scolds, the tip of her lip lifting because she knows she's a badass.

"I am serious." I laugh.

"Well, I just used my position to illegally obtain your room number, so I can't be all that intelligent."

"I won't tell." If it got her to my room, I'd do a hell of a lot more than keep a secret.

"I figured as much. I only came so I could hear you out and not regret just walking away. I'm working on that— the regrets in my life." She stares at the wall. "And I knew leaving here without at least having a conversation with you would be a regret."

"Can I get you some coffee? Order breakfast?"

"Coffee would be lovely."

I walk to the open kitchen and make some coffee for us. I'm really biding my time in order to figure out how to explain things in a way that keeps her here. I've come up with nothing by the time I set our coffee on the table and sit in the chair across from her.

"I'm not dating Vivian," I blurt out.

She chokes on the sip of coffee she just took.

"Shit, sorry." I cringe.

"It's fine." She coughs.

Sighing, I lean forward, putting my elbows on my knees.

"You have to deal with a lot of celebrities, I assume."

She nods.

"The CEO of Legacy, the team I race for, thought it would be nice for the team and my image if I took a date to this event that gets a lot of attention. They set me up with Vivian on the premise that it was just for image and nothing else. It was great publicity for us both, but she didn't want the spotlight to end. I'll be honest, I don't ever look at tabloids, so it didn't really affect me at all. We would go to dinner, talk about random people in the business, and then go our separate ways. It was never anything more than that. A few weeks ago, I told her I was done. It was a drag, and if I'm honest and albeit probably a dick, the conversation wasn't all that great. I signed my new contract, and it was no longer something I needed to keep doing in order to make the bosses happy."

God, just saying that makes me feel like an asshole.

I look up at her, but her attention is out the window at the snow falling.

"Congrats on the new contract."

"Thank you."

She finally turns her head to look at me. "I ... I don't really know what to make out of all of this. And I genuinely feel bad about that. I'm not one to believe tabloids, by any means. Lord knows I've shooed enough of them away from our properties. But I can't disconnect the image of the two of you together in my brain. I don't even know if that makes sense." She shakes her head.

"It does." I scrub my overgrown hair with a huff. "You know, all of this could have been avoided if I had just manned up last year and gotten any form of contact information from you."

Her sad chuckle has my stomach twisting in knots.

"Possibly. There were two of us, though, and I'm just as much to blame on that."

We sit and stare at each other for a long moment. I see the second she takes a step back from me in her mind.

My heart sinks. Explaining wasn't enough, and I can't even blame her. How do you watch stories about someone you like with another woman on repeat for months? I know I would have lost my absolute mind.

"I think I just need time to wrap my head around all of that. Thank you for taking the time to explain it, though."

"Door's always open. I'll be here until the twenty-ninth." There's no use pushing for more right now. She needs time to think, and I need time to come up with a better plan to, at the very least, keep in touch with her.

"Thank you for the coffee and for being honest." She stands up, pausing before she heads to the door like she wants to say something.

I open my mouth then promptly close it because anything I say right now will be pushing her for more than she's ready for.

She nods then walks out the door, leaving me alone with too many thoughts in my head and no solutions to be found.

Chapter 10
SYDNEY

I've been in this world of celebrities and people with far too much money for long enough to know everything that Beckett told me is most likely the truth.

There are countless times I've been contacted to be discreet about someone showing up to our resorts, knowing that the media is portraying them with another partner. It's messed up and something I still think is wild to even have to do, but it happens.

And I hate that it happened with Beckett—*Beck.* I'm still conflicted on what to call him. Hell, I'm conflicted about everything. A time to get closure, to figure out how to move past this fixation I have on the man, has turned into contemplating a way to move forward with him.

Is that even possible when two people have such hectic schedules? I mean, he races nine months out of the year. I'm now taking on bigger responsibilities at work that have me traveling a lot more as well. How does that turn into any form of relationship? Is that even what I want?

I'm antsy, confused, and alone—the worst possible combination for me.

Pulling out my phone, I pace around the suite as I pull up a new group chat with Daisy and Jane. I'll take all the help I can get right now.

My verbal diarrhea is horrendous, but I can't even think clearly right now to apologize.

Daisy:

> Woah, slow down.

Jane:

> Okay, so I clearly missed some things. He's the Formula 1 driver, correct? I know you were done with him after the race here, but you didn't tell me why.

Me:

> When Daisy and I put things together, she googled him and we found a ton of pictures, posts, and magazine covers of him and Vivian together. You name it, they had a story about them together.

Jane:

> Oh shit.

You know it's serious when Jane curses.

Daisy:

> But what did he say about it?

Me:

> Right. He said it was a publicity stunt, basically. Started as a date to an event for his team, then it just didn't stop. He said he wasn't into her and that nothing happened and … I want to believe him. But that's so stupid, right? Who trusts a guy after there is irrevocable proof that he was in a relationship?

Jane:

> I'm going for tough love right now… You know the world that you and Pierce are in, that Beckett is in. You know that this isn't uncommon, however dumb it is. Seriously, when will people learn that publicly dating for PR is just stupid? I digress. Your gut is obviously telling you to believe him. So, believe him. You're both extremely busy people, but there is no rule that says you need to jump into anything serious. Maybe just … keep in touch, as friends, before you make any drastic decisions. Learn about each other and then go from there.

Daisy:

> It's kind of weird to have my boss's wife in a girls' chat, but I just want to say that you are woman goals. Holy shit. Laying down the law while still being so nice about it… Adopt me please. Teach me your ways. Hell, mentor me; I don't care.

I can't help it. Daisy is so ridiculous that I have to laugh. It breaks the severe tension in my body enough to take some deep breaths and really take in what Jane's saying.

She's right. I don't need to make a decision to be with him, to start a relationship right this minute. Lord knows I'm still getting settled into my new position and my new normal within it. Jumping into a relationship isn't the be-all and end-all. We can keep in touch, see if we really are compatible outside of the bedroom, before moving forward.

My cheeks heat just thinking about the man in bed. *That*, I have missed. Desperately. But it would absolutely send the wrong message if friendship is the direction I'm going.

Jane:

> Uh, thanks? You should meet my best friends. I'm the nice, timid one in the group.

Daisy:

Is that an invitation? *Fangirls so hard I'm about to pass out.*

Me:

Daisy's met Bea and Pen for sure, maybe not Larkin. I think she has a major girl crush on your friend group.

Jane:

Well then, you'll definitely have to come to brunch one day. You too, Sydney, and I won't take no for an answer.

Me:

You'll have to talk to your husband about making me available for whatever weekend, then.

Jane:

Yeah, that won't be an issue. Back to your drama. Take a walk, go lie in the snow and reset yourself, and then think about what you really want. You don't owe him anything you aren't comfortable giving, and that includes conversation.

Me:

You're right. I have to leave here the day after Christmas anyway to get some work done. That leaves me … two days to figure things out.

Jane:

Totally doable. And is Pierce making you work? I'll withhold sex if he is.

Me:

Jesus, Jane. Please don't… We've had this conversation too many times. I don't want to know about his sex life in any form. I will just dig my own grave and put myself out of my misery.

Jane:

But is he?

Me:

No. One of the properties is struggling with morale, so I'm throwing a New Year's party for the employees. The logistics are complicated because I can't just shut the damn place down to let everyone have time off, so I need time to get it all figured out.

Jane:

Well, that's a wonderful idea. If you need help, call me.

Me:

I will not be doing that. Thank you, though. And thank you for talking me off the ledge.

Me:

Daisy, are you okay?

She's been too quiet. She's never this quiet.

Daisy:

Oh, good. Great. Just hyperventilated because I got invited to *the* brunch. I'm totally good.

I can hear the panic in her text. Not much rattles Daisy, but she's idolized Jane and her best friends for as long as I can remember. It's adorable, really, and makes me realize our age difference shows in situations like this.

Jane:

Is our brunch notorious now? Is it because of Larkin? She's so loud when she talks about the sexcapades. Come to think of it, Bea's just as bad lately. How many people in the company know about our brunch dates?

Me:

Literally everyone. I think your wedding solidified it as legend within the company.

Jane:

We weren't that bad at the wedding.

Me:

Sure, babe, keep telling yourself that. Or maybe you just forgot because you were puking your guts out with baby Henry on board.

Daisy:

Is this what winning the lottery feels like? I'll bring you your favorite coffee every single day for including me in this group chat, Sydney.

Me:

No thanks needed. But I am going to bundle up and walk around the property to figure out what to do next. Thank you, lovely humans, for being here when I need you.

Jane:

Love you! Call me later!

***

The walk around the large mountain cabin property the next morning does clear my head. It also turned my lips blue, so I'm in the process of stripping down and jumping into the large shower as I solidify my decision.

Jane's right. Jumping into a relationship right now would probably make me stressed to the max. Pierce and I are in the early stages of figuring out our new normal going forward as co-CEOs, and while I expect it to calm down in the future, that time is not now. I wouldn't be able to give my all to a person, and that's not fair to either of us.

But I was able to unwind my thoughts about Beckett and Vivian. I believe him, truly, and if we get into a relationship at some point, I'd be seeing stories like that all the time. It's something I need to learn to trust him on if there's any hope in the future.

That brings me to what I think I'm capable of right now. And right now, I think I can only commit to friendship. I barely have time to grab lunch with Jane or Daisy, and I see Daisy every single day. It's not realistic to think I'd be able to keep up with my job and not only handle but thrive in a long-distance relationship.

Am I getting ahead of myself? Totally, but I'm thirty-two, and dating for shits and giggles isn't it anymore. If I'm going to date someone, it's because I can see a potential future there. I owe my partner nothing less.

As the spray hits my back, I let the disappointment wash away. This isn't giving up on things with Beckett. It's giving us time to figure out if something more is even possible. People underestimate the challenge of distance, the loneliness and the doubts that will surely arise. I've lived lonely, and with Beckett, I'd have to be prepared to live with a new version of that. I'm not sure I'm ready for it.

Once I'm done in the shower, I get dressed in jeans and a long-sleeve Henley before walking to Beckett's room.

Chapter 11

BECK

The knock at my door startles me.

In my borderline depression, I ordered my weight in greasy comfort food I never eat. It just happened to get here a lot faster than I was expecting.

I'm under no illusion that Sydney will come knocking within a day, but it is disappointing nonetheless when it hasn't happened yet. Hence, the comfort food binge. I definitely won't be telling Nate about any of this.

I struggle to get off the couch but finally make it to the door to open it.

"Hey, sorry it took so—"

It's not my food. No, it's a hundred times better than food.

"Expecting someone else?" Her voice takes on a flirty tone, and my shoulders release their tension.

"Food." My voice barely gets out, so I clear my throat. "I ordered food. Would you like to come in?"

"I'd like that very much." She walks in, makes her way to the living room, and sits in one of the chairs.

I can't take my eyes off her. I'm not sure if this is a good talk or a bad one, but I'm just grateful she's here.

I sit across from her on the couch and wait her out. I don't want to stick my foot in my mouth and make things worse. This is the safest option.

"I'm sorry about my reaction yesterday. I didn't expect to see you, let alone talk to you," she starts. "I'll be honest, seeing you at the Austin race was… shocking. When my friend searched you, we found all the pictures and stories about you and … yeah. I may not be a celebrity, but I've delt with enough of them to know things like that happen all the time, so first, I want to say I believe you."

My relief is palpable. Whatever else she has to say, I can work with, because her believing me about Vivian was far and away the largest obstacle.

"Second, it's Christmas Eve and I didn't want you to spend it alone. Last year was ... nice, and I don't really want to spend it alone either."

Her gentle confession lights a fire in me.

"But..."

Shit, it was too good to be true.

"I'm not sure I can offer anything except friendship at the moment. I'd like to talk about it more—maybe over food and watching the snow fall, throw in a movie perhaps—but I also understand if you'd rather call it a wash."

"I don't want to call it a wash," I say instantly. "I'd love for you to stick around, and we can talk all day." Desperate much? But honestly, I couldn't care less how it comes off. I don't want her to think that I am hesitant at all with her.

"Actually, I was wondering if you'd like to come to my room this time. My boss set up a whole tree complete with presents. It's really beautiful." Her shy voice tells me she's unsure about a lot of things right now, but she doesn't need to worry.

"I would love that. Let me call down and tell them to bring the food to your room, if that's okay. Or I can cancel it."

"Please don't cancel it. I'll call down and change the delivery to my place. I'm in room 932; just come by when you're ready, but take your time," she adds.

I tilt my head in question before looking down at my clothes. It's then that I realize I'm in my boxers and a T-shirt. My hair is all over the place as I didn't even bother combing it when I woke up, just tossed on a shirt and moved to the couch before ordering food.

"Well shit," I murmur.

"It's not bad. I promise."

"Yep, totally not bad. Just look like I rolled out of bed and didn't do shit except order my weight in food then laze on the couch."

"I mean, it's technically what you did, I assume. And that's not bad." She holds her hands up. "I've seen worse. Hell, I've been worse. Way worse." She cringes.

"That's a story I'd like to hear."

"Teenage hormones mixed with wannabe love is not a great combo."

"Definitely need to hear it now. Just give me ten minutes, and I'll head over."

"Sounds good." She stands to leave, stops for a second like she's going to say something, but then continues to the door.

I watch her leave with my heart pounding in my chest. I may only get one shot at this, so I better make it count.

***

I knock on her door twelve minutes later. I had to take a detour, but I think it was worth it.

"Hi," she says with a bright smile on her face as she opens the door.

"Hi." I stand there just looking at her.

She's so damn beautiful. It was a mistake not to get contact information from her last year. While I may not have been obsessively thinking about her every single day in the past year, she's popped into my head more often than not. And I'll maybe confess to looking up little things I've remembered about her to try to find her, on occasion. I've never had a woman affect me like this. I've been career focused, and besides some hookups and short-lived relationships, a woman has never taken over the top spot in my head.

Until Sydney.

My mind flashes to her underneath me, writhing as I fuck her hard.

Shit. Nope. Absolutely cannot go there right now.

"Beckett?" Sydney's concerned voice refocuses me.

"Sorry. I—" What? Was imagining taking her to bed? Want to see her face as I bring her to orgasm again and again? She drew a hard boundary at friendship, and I need to respect that. If I don't, I might as well turn around and walk out of her life. "I got distracted, sorry," I relent instead. It's as honest as I can get, and judging by the look in her eyes, she understands exactly where my head was at.

"Come on in. The kitchen said food should be here in a few minutes."

Her suite might be the nicest in the resort. We both don't have the same rooms as before, and this one is complete with a balcony off the living space and what looks to be a hot tub. The floor-to-ceiling windows cover two sides of the space to give you an endless view of the mountain range. It's fucking gorgeous.

"Holy shit," I whisper. I've been in nice places—hell, my apartment in Monaco could rival this, just with a different view—but there's a home-like feel here while still being the pinnacle of luxury. It's a testament to the brand, and she plays a very large role in that, apparently.

"This is one of my favorite rooms in all of our resorts," she says from behind me.

"I can see why." I turn and spot the Christmas tree she was talking about. It's simple but no less stunning. Its effortless decorations make it look like the picture-perfect tree. And there are a couple presents underneath that remind me of what took me the extra minutes to get here.

Walking up to it, I place the wrapped present underneath to join the others.

"You shouldn't have done anything." she says quietly.

"I should have done more, but I was tight on time." I smirk.

She doesn't relay my smile, though. Her eyes shift back and forth between mine, and I can see the conflict.

We obviously have the physical attraction, but our lives create a problem for acting on it. When we thought it was just a vacation fling, things were less complicated. Now? Now, it's time to step back and see if things are feasible between us, if the feelings are still there.

A well-timed knock followed by a curt "Room service" breaks whatever thoughts we both were having, though.

She quickly turns around and opens the door with a kind smile. When I see how much food is being brought in, embarrassment hits me hard.

Jesus, wallowing is not a good look for me.

Once everything is laid out at the dining room table, we're left alone again while I try to find a way to explain the sheer amount of food I ordered.

"Don't order food when you're hungry. It always bites you in the ass." She smiles over at me as she starts lifting cloches to see what all there is.

"I wish I could fault just being hungry. I was throwing a pity party." I give her a self-deprecating smile.

"I'm sorry." She cringes.

"It's one hundred percent not your fault," I tell her as I watch her pick up a piece of bacon off a plate and take a bite.

"Let me grab some plates and we can load up, set up a Christmas movie, and then ... go from there?" She tilts her head in question.

Nodding, I will myself to snap out of this haze of contrition and be present with Sydney.

We're halfway through the movie and about the same through the food as I stand up to put everything in the refrigerator to heat up later. What there hasn't been is a lot of talking. My stilted brain can't come up with a good conversation starter to save my life.

"So, media doesn't say how long Formula 1 contracts are. How long is your contract?" she asks.

Normally, this is something I wouldn't answer to anyone that wasn't already involved in my career. The length of our contracts aren't secret, but money and all the other details usually are. Our contracts are notoriously vague in the media, and I won't be the one to break that cycle. But again, Sydney is different. I think she always will be.

"It's four years and will probably be my last one." It's something I had to come to terms with when I signed it. I'm not getting any younger, and the kids that are coming up through the F1 Academy and Formula 2 and 3 are really fucking good. I went with length of contract, not so much the actual amount, although it's nothing to turn your head at.

"Bittersweet?"

"Kind of. It's part of why I came here last year. I needed to really hone in on what I wanted to do. If I wanted to push for more years or step back completely. Maybe even race for one of the smaller teams."

"But you're with the top team on the grid with a lengthy contract," she observes.

"I am. And you've done some homework on the lingo."

Her cheeks tinge pink, and it's possibly the most adorable thing I've seen on her.

"Call it a glutton for punishment. I may have thought you were with Vivian the whole time, but it didn't stop me from keeping up with your team and watching the rest of the races."

Her admission makes my heart pound in my chest.

"And what about you? How did you get promoted to co-CEO? What does that even entail?" I can't even imagine keeping track of the number of resorts under the Vanstone umbrella. She may have followed my career after Austin, but all of this information is brand new for me.

"Great question." She laughs. "We're figuring it out at the moment. My boss—I guess, not so much boss anymore—is restructuring the company more than he already did a few years ago, and part of that entails lessening his load. I've been his assistant for over a decade. The title has changed over the years, but I've been his right hand for a long time. He offered me the job, and it was a natural progression for me. I was doing a lot of it already. But I won't lie and say it's terrible. I think I'm working less hours than I have in years while making … a lot more. Although, I'm traveling more."

"So, your boss is a good guy?" I don't know why I ask, but this need to make sure that she's treated well takes over. It's an instinct I can't fight.

"He's the best." She sighs wistfully, and jealousy rages in my stomach. "He was a grade-A asshole before he met his wife. Never to me, just with business in general. Now, he's a pushover who tries to figure out ways to spend more time with her and the kids. It's been entertaining to witness." She smiles, and it makes me relax back into the couch.

"Good," I murmur, unable to say anything else or it will give away that I had thoughts of the two of them together, however insane it is.

Jesus, I'm so twisted up over this woman.

"At the moment, it's a lot of travel. We're trying to split the properties so he has all the ones closer to home, so he travels less, and I take everything else, but we're also not actively looking at more properties to bring to the brand."

"Where is home base?"

"Austin, Texas. Pierce, my boss or whatever, had tickets from Legacy actually, and he was out of town, so he gave them to me. I took my friend and assistant, Daisy. She's the exact opposite of me and would have gotten your number, your home address, and your entire schedule before we left here last year." She chuckles, but there's a sad overcast in her eyes. "Where's home for you?"

"Originally, Phoenix, Arizona. Currently, Monaco."

"Oh, fancy pants now." Her eyes twinkle.

"Half the grid lives there. It's like a home base for everyone. Legacy is based in the UK, though, so I have a place there too because I'm there so often."

It's strange to meet a woman who probably travels more than I do and isn't a model or actress. Sydney also probably works as much as I do, if not more, and I'm starting to understand her reluctance. How would we even find time for each other? She's a CEO of a luxury resort company; she can't just drop whatever she's doing to come to a race weekend with me. And I have to keep up training in between races, so I can't drop everything either. Nine months out of the year, we would most likely see each other once a month if we're lucky.

"I've only been to Monaco once a long time ago. Pierce was trying to see if he wanted to break into the market there but decided against it and to hit lesser-known spots, not quite so packed with resorts already."

"It's really gorgeous. I never thought in a million years it would be my life, but I try not to take it for granted." It's the truth, and I've tried hard to keep my roots with me always.

Chapter 12
Sydney

Beckett—*Beck*—is nothing like I expected.

"Do you go by Beck normally? I know that's what they call you on television, but you introduced yourself to me as Beckett," I blurt out.

It's an interruption in conversation, but I'm sick of having him as two different people in my head. Now that we've been talking for a while, the distinction between the two is blurring.

His smile is blinding. Straight teeth with the scruff growing on his jaw might just be my downfall.

"Beck is what most people call me. It's edgier, according to all the PR gurus out there." He rolls his eyes. "But…" The twinkle in his eyes returns. "I like that you're the only one who calls me Beckett."

The way he catches me off guard with one sentence is scary. No one person should affect me like this, and yet here we are.

"Beckett it is, then." I nod. "So, what does a typical season look like for you? Do you stay in one place in between races? Go to cities early and just hang out? I'll admit, having two weeks between most races on your schedule confuses me." I laugh. "I'm usually somewhere a couple of days to a week, and then I move on to the next place or go back to Austin."

"It depends on the race week, honestly, but mostly I go back to Monaco with my trainer, Nate, and he kicks my ass on the off time. Work doesn't really end during the week. If anything, it's harder work than the actual driving."

I can see the exhaustion on his face. Even though the season ended a couple of weeks ago, he's still feeling the effects of it.

"I can't imagine." I shake my head.

"It sounds like you travel more than I do, which is quite the feat," he observes.

"The past three years have been … busy. Pierce got married and they immediately had a baby, so that's been his priority, and I've been happy to pick up any slack. It feels like I see my house maybe once a month on average. Since the promotion, it's slowed down a decent amount. We've been focused on the properties we have rather than picking up more. It's a huge shift within the business, so I'm not sure what the future looks like. I hope less travel, honestly. I'm not getting any younger, and it's just exhausting sometimes. Not that I don't have the best places to stay." I smirk.

"Not going to lie, if you're going to travel that much, you have the best home away from homes. If there's a Vanstone where we're racing, I stay there now."

My heart warms. Pierce has created a place everyone loves. That I've played a part in it and will continue to do so in the future makes me feel fulfilled for the first time in a long time. Being an assistant makes you think about your career in the long term, even with someone like Pierce as your boss.

"Thank you for that."

"This is still my favorite place, though." He looks out at the mountain view.

Mine too, I think. I don't say that, though, because it's letting him see too much.

My thoughts turn back to last year. So much has changed since, and yet being with him now feels just as comfortable as it did then. Only with a lack of sex. Not that I don't want that, but I know there are too many challenges now. If we hooked up tonight, it wouldn't just be a random hookup. I'm starting to like him too much, and I can't risk my heart on a man who doesn't really have a home base nine months out of the year. Hell, between both of our travel, I doubt we would see each other for very long chunks of time. And that's not how I picture a relationship, however selfish that may be.

"Same," I whisper. It doesn't change the fact that being together isn't in the cards for us, but he has made this place special to me.

"So... You have some presents to open. Tonight or tomorrow?" He refocuses on me.

I have a choice. If I say tomorrow, I know I'll let him stay. I'll let him hold me, kiss me, and make me feel something special. And I want that, but I also don't think I can handle it. If we do it tonight, there's a very real chance we don't see each other again before I have to leave.

Fuck, I don't know if there is a right answer.

Clearing my throat, I hold his eyes. "Tonight, I think."

The sad smile he gives me tells me he knows my conflict and that tonight is probably it for us. He gets up and grabs the present he brought in along with the other three that Pierce sent here. Laying them in front of me, he sits next to me and waits patiently.

I'm nervous. Not for whatever Pierce sent, because I'd put money down that the kids made me something and then Jane picked out the rest, but for whatever is in the package Beckett brought. It could be anything. Something funny, something sweet, or maybe it's sentimental. Who knows.

I open one of Pierce's first. As I unwrap it, I see a homemade stocking filled with all my favorite things: Lindt truffles, corn nuts, a new pack of stationery, and some shower steamers from my favorite local place. I smile at the mess of color on the stocking. Squiggles and an attempt at a Christmas tree are there, but I love that the babies made it for me, so it wouldn't matter how much of a mess it was.

"That's adorable," Beckett remarks.

"Pierce's kids. They always make me something. It's the best." I smile.

Next, I open the smaller of the other two from the Vanstone family. This one is a pair of earrings that look like starbursts. They're gorgeous, and because I know Pierce and Jane, I know these are real diamonds, which is ridiculous. I put them to the side, picking up the last one as Beckett takes a peek at the earrings.

It's strange opening up presents from my boss and friend in front of Beckett. He doesn't know enough about me to know if I love this stuff, or if I do, why. Explaining things feels too artificial.

"So, you like sun things?" he asks in confusion.

I laugh at his description. "It's a sunburst. I started collecting them randomly when I was in college. This sense of a symbol of the world or eternity, something never ending, intrigued me. I just like the idea that things come full circle, that life somehow continues long after we're gone."

"I like that," he murmurs.

The next gift is a card, and when I open it, I see a spa day package. Reading the note from Jane, I crack up.

"Jane, Pierce's wife, wrote: We're ditching P-man. Pick a day, and let's go relax."

"They sound like a great family."

"They're the best. I didn't think we'd ever be so close, but I'm glad for our friendship." I don't say how my only two real friends are my assistant and my boss's wife. It makes it very obvious how my life revolves around work.

"That's Nate for me. Okay, so if you hate this, just tell me." He hands me his gift, full of uncertainty and hesitation.

"I won't hate it," I whisper.

As I open it, a familiar wooden box is revealed, and my heart is in my throat. Once I get the box open, the gorgeous blown glass comes into view, but it's not an ornament. No, it's so much better.

"Oh my God, it's beautiful," I mutter as I pull out the snow globe. Flakes of snow fall on the mountain range they somehow put inside of the glass ball.

"The whole thing is glass, minus the base."

"That's unbelievable." I move it at every angle, trying to figure out how they did it. "Thank you so much. It's perfect." I look up at him.

"It's nothing crazy," he deflects.

"It's reflective of this place, and I love that I have something to always remember it by now."

It almost brings tears to my eyes. Something about this moment, this gift, makes me think this could be the last time I see this man, and I *hate* it.

With that in mind, I make a rash decision. "What do you say about exchanging numbers?"

Owlish eyes meet mine, and I know I threw him for a loop. Hell, I did it to myself too.

"I would love that. I mostly use WhatsApp since I'm in a million different time zones."

"Same." I smile.

He fumbles to get his phone out of his pocket, and in a matter of minutes, numbers are given and I officially have a way to contact him. It's stupid, really, irresponsible to my heart, and yet I'm thrilled to have a way to talk to him.

The rest of the evening is filled with more eating, talking, and movie watching. It's low-key and utterly perfect. When it's time to say goodbye, I feel less dread than I felt the entire day. All because I took a chance to keep in touch.

Who knows what that will look like. Friendship at the bare minimum, I assume. Maybe more if we're really lucky. I won't hold my breath, though. The whole reason I don't think this will work is because of our hectic schedules, so I don't expect to hear from him often.

When Christmas day rolls around, the pressure and doubt about the future don't seem so dire. Even this New Year's party I need to figure out doesn't fill me with dread anymore.

As I carefully pack up my new ornament and snow globe, I send Beckett a message without the fear that it's too much.

Me:

> Thank you for yesterday. It was ... wonderful to get to know you, and I hope you have a lovely Christmas here. Maybe we can turn this into a tradition.

Beckett:

> I think we already have. Be safe traveling tomorrow, and I'll talk to you again soon.

Chapter 13

January 1

Monaco/Bahamas

Beckett 2:47pm CEST (UTC +2)

Happy New Year, Sydney. Hope you have a great start to the year.

Sydney 11:45 am EDT (UTC -4)

Hey! You too. It's been hectic as hell here, but I'm finally in my hotel room and eating my weight in fries, so I'm happy.

Beckett 5:53 pm CEST (UTC +2)

Don't forget to order dessert. That's always a necessity on hard days.

Sydney 12:03 pm EDT (UTC -4)

Seven-layer chocolate cake is sitting on the table waiting for me.

Beckett 6:05 pm CEST (UTC +2)

And I'm eating chicken and rice...

Sydney 12:07 pm EDT (UTC -4)

Sucks to be an elite athlete, huh?

Beckett 6:08 pm CEST (UTC +2)

It really does sometimes…

January 22

London/Austin

Sydney 1:15 pm CDT (UTC -5)

I'm home for the first time since before Christmas, and while the beds in the Vanstone are nice, they don't beat my own bed.

Beckett 7:18 pm GMT (UTC +0)

It does have perks to have apartments in the two locations I spend the most time in. Traveling that much just sucks anyway. Jet lag sucks. Flying sucks.

Beckett 1:20 pm CDT (UTC -5)

I used to be so excited to fly all the time. Go new places on the boss's dime. It lost its shine after about a year of heavy travel.

Beckett 7:20 pm BST (GMT +0)

It was sad when I lost the excitement of travel. I remember very vividly being on a plane and just wanting to go home. I wanted to call my mom, but we don't have a good relationship and never talk, so yeah.

Beckett 7:21pm BST (GMT +0)

And that was a lot of depressing information that you probably don't care about.

Sydney 1:22 pm CDT (UTC -5)

Of course I care! And I understand it. You just hit the point where you want the familiarity of something. I'm sorry to hear about your mom, too. Not having that easy comfort is difficult sometimes.

Beckett 7:23 pm BST (GMT +0)

I appreciate it. That's exactly it, though. The familiarity… I think I still search for that most days even though my family has proven themselves to be the opposite of that.

Sydney 1:24 pm CDT (UTC -5)

When does the new season start up? Sorry, I'm a new F1 watcher, so I'm absolutely clueless. Expect tons of random questions.

Beckett 7:25 pm BST (GMT +0)

Ask away. Season starts on March 3. Legacy is unveiling the newest car in two weeks, so I'll be at their home base for the foreseeable future.

Sydney 1:25 pm CDT (UTC -5)

So, you get a brand-new car every year and you don't know shit about it until two weeks before you need to go race it in a real race that counts for your point totals or whatever? That makes no sense.

Beckett 7:26 pm BST (GMT +0)

I've never thought of it like that. It's just how it is, so I've never questioned it, but yeah. We don't get a ton of time with it before it's showtime. Keeps the adrenaline pumping, though.

Sydney 1:27 pm CDT (UTC -5)

You adrenaline junkies are wild. No, thank you.

March 3

Bahrain/Austin

Sydney 2:00 am CDT (UTC -5)

Tell Luka he's a dickhead.

Beckett 12:30 pm AST (UTC +3)

Done. I also may have twisted his nipple for running me off course. And punched his dick.

Sydney 7:08 am CDT (UTC -5)

Good. He deserved it.

Beckett 4:10 pm AST (UTC +3)

Jesus, did you get any sleep? Almost everywhere is on the opposite side of the world from me right now.

Sydney 7:15 am CDT (UTC -5)

I am running on a functional four hours of sleep, thank you very much. Honestly, I thought I could watch a majority of the races live but … yeah, that's not going to happen, sorry. I'll be dragging ass all day today.

Beckett 4:16 pm AST (UTC +3)

I didn't expect you to watch any of them, so thank you. But also, please don't stay up to watch them. I promise, we are not that important.

Sydney 7:17 am CDT (UTC -5)

Noted. But if Luka tries some shit again, I'm going to have words.

May 3

Miami/Austin

Sydney 12:00 pm CDT (UTC-5)

Heads up… Daisy, my assistant, is there this weekend.

Beckett 1:01 pm EDT (UTC -4)

So, funny story…

Sydney 12:02 pm CDT (UTC-5)

Ugh. Do I need to fly out there and bail her out?

Beckett 1:03 pm EDT (UTC -4)

No, but Luka may need to be bailed out if he sees anyone checking her out.

Sydney 12:04 pm CDT (UTC-5)

GASP No! Have they actually met? Or did he just see her? How do you know who she is? I have so many fucking questions.

Beckett 1:05 pm EDT (UTC -4)

She had a VIP pass, was on the grid during some of our downtime before a practice session, and she went up to him immediately. A woman on a mission. She said she worked for you, so Luka asked me about it because I may or may not have mentioned you at some point, and now he can't keep his eyes off of her.

Sydney 12:06 pm CDT (UTC-5)

Hold please.

Sydney 12:08 pm CDT (UTC-5)

THEY'RE GOING ON A DATE?! What the actual fuck is going on in Miami?

Beckett 1:09 pm EDT (UTC -4)

Glad we're just going to breeze past me oversharing. I didn't know they were going on a date. Luka's a decent guy, so I wouldn't worry.

Sydney 12:10 pm CDT (UTC-5)

We're not. I'm just focused on Daisy right now. What do you mean *decent*? He needs to be a hell of a lot more than decent to go out with my girl.

Beckett 1:12 pm EDT (UTC -4)

He's a good guy. A little high maintenance and thrives in our lifestyle, but he won't be an asshole to her.

Sydney 12:13 pm CDT (UTC-5)

I'm holding you to that if he breaks her heart. Now, you've been talking about me?

Beckett 1:14 pm EDT (UTC -4)

I mean… Shit…

Beckett 1:15 pm EDT (UTC -4)

We talk a lot. The guys notice, especially during the season. It just naturally came out and now … the whole grid knows that we're … friends.

Sydney 12:16 pm CDT (UTC-5)

You're kind of adorable when you're flustered.

Beckett 1:17 pm EDT (UTC -4)

No one in my life has ever accused me of being adorable.

Sydney 12:18 pm CDT (UTC-5)

Oh, I saw your interview after the race. That was definitely not adorable. I thought you were going to punch out that reporter.

Beckett 1:19 pm EDT (UTC -4)

Ask stupid questions, get stupid answers. That's not my fault.

Sydney 12:20 pm CDT (UTC-5)

Good luck in qualifiers, *Beck*. I can't watch live tomorrow, but I'll be watching the race with a lovely mango gin and tonic.

Beckett 1:21 pm EDT (UTC -4)

Thanks, Sydney. I think I'll need it this weekend.

May 5

Miami/Austin

Sydney 3:21 pm CDT (UTC-5)

HOLY SHIT! WHAT A WIN!

Beckett 5:12 pm EDT (UTC -4)

Thank you very much. It was hard fought, but I'm happy with the outcome.

Sydney 4:14 pm CDT (UTC-5)

You can cut the PR canned response with me.

Beckett 5:15 pm EDT (UTC -4)

I'm so fucking tired. Almost crashed, was almost hit, and tweaked my back. But I still have a ton of press work to do before I can go back to my room. I am staying at a Vanstone, though, so that's a positive.

Sydney 4:16 pm CDT (UTC-5)

Shit, I'm sorry. Do you have some time off after this? Or is it straight back on the grind?

Beckett 5:18 pm EDT (UTC -4)

Technically, back on the grind, but I'm giving myself a couple of days of a break. I've learned that once I hit this level of exhaustion, I need to take the break while I have the time. Otherwise, I don't make it to the end of the season.

Sydney 4:19 pm CDT (UTC-5)

I can't even imagine. If you need anything tonight, just tell the front desk it's on me.

Beckett 5:21 pm EDT (UTC -4)

Absolutely not, but thank you for the thought. I do need to go do some interviews, though, so I'll talk to you later.

Beckett 9:18 pm EDT (UTC -4)

Sydney Johnson!

Sydney 8:20 pm CDT (UTC-5)

Uh-oh, getting full-named is never a good thing.

Beckett 9:21 pm EDT (UTC -4)

The room service, the bath basket, the Biofreeze... I just... I'm speechless. Thank you isn't enough.

Sydney 8:22 pm CDT (UTC-5)

It isn't a big deal. I just put in a call, that's all.

Beckett 9:23 pm EDT (UTC -4)

It's a huge deal. And I wish I wasn't about to collapse into bed immediately, so I could really express that.

Sydney 8:25 pm CDT (UTC-5)

Don't think twice about it. Get some sleep, Beckett. I'll talk to you later.

JULY 7

Cook Island

Sydney 8:25 pm CKT (UTC-10)

Tough day. I'm sorry.

JULY 8

London/Cook Island

Beckett 8:30 am BST (UTC +1)

Sorry I went quiet. I'm not good at losing and even worse at not finishing a race.

Sydney 9:32 pm CKT (UTC-10)

Zero reason to apologize. I get it. Just wanted to check in and see how you were doing. There's no expectation.

Beckett 8:34 am BST (UTC +1)

Thank you for that.

AUGUST 12

Monaco/Austin

Sydney 8:41am CDT (UTC-5)

Umm … what the hell is going on with Luka and Daisy??

Beckett 3:45 pm CEST (UTC +2)

I have no clue. I just got back to Monaco, and he's droning on and on about how far he's gone for her, and I've never seen him like this.

Sydney 8:47 am CDT (UTC-5)

She called out for vacation, so I called her to see if she needed anything, and she's literally headed to Monaco to spend the week there with him before you guys are off of break.

Beckett 3:49 pm CEST (UTC +2)

He's doing something big. I just talked to him, and he's taking her to Paris.

Sydney 8:50 am CDT (UTC-5)

Holy shit.

AUGUST 14

Monaco/Austin

Sydney 4:26 pm CDT (UTC-5)

HE PROPOSED?!

Beckett 11:26 pm CEST (UTC +2)

What the fuck? Luka?

Sydney 4:27 pm CDT (UTC-5)

Yes Luka! I didn't think they were serious!

Beckett 11:28 pm CEST (UTC +2)

Yeah, I didn't either.

Sydney 4:29 pm CDT (UTC-5)

> How the hell were they able to even be together often enough to be that serious? All they do is travel. How … how did they do it?

Beckett 11:30 pm CEST (UTC +2)

I suppose if you really want someone, you make anything happen.

septembeR 5

Monaco/Bahamas

Beckett 10:02 pm CEST (UTC +2)

So, a Christmas wedding. In Idaho…

Sydney 6:19 am EDT (UTC-4)

> These time zone differences are fucking killing me. Who's getting married?

Beckett 12:20 pm CEST (UTC +2)

Luka and Daisy. Want to spend another year together? Keep our tradition going?

Sydney 6:22 am EDT (UTC-4)

> I think I'd like that very much.

OCTOBeR 18

Austin

Sydney 4:08 pm CDT (UTC-5)

I'm so dang proud of you, and even if it was from far away, it was so good to see you again. Way to kick ass!

Beckett 4:15 pm CDT (UTC-5)

You couldn't stay?

Sydney 4:20 pm CDT (UTC-5)

I have to catch a flight out. I really wish I could have stayed, though.

Beckett 4:23 pm CDT (UTC-5)

I totally understand. No big deal. It would have been great to see you, maybe grab dinner, but duty calls. I'll definitely see you for the wedding, so at least we have that.

Sydney 4:24 pm CDT (UTC-5)

That, we do. Have fun celebrating your win.

NOVEMBER 21

Las Vegas/ Turkey

Beckett 2:39 pm PDT (UTC-7)

Were you able to make it to the Vegas race?

Sydney 6:56 am EESDT (UTC+3)

I tried so damn hard, but there's a problem at our Turkey property that I couldn't push off. I'm so sorry.

Beckett 8:58 pm PDT (UTC-7)

It's not a big deal, Syd. It would have been great to see you, but I understand. No worries, okay? T-minus one month until the wedding anyway.

Sydney 7:01 am EESDT (UTC+3)

It's not okay. I was looking forward to this for weeks. I'm sorry, Beckett. I really am.

Sydney 9:03 pm PDT (UTC-7)

I know, but we knew meeting up was always going to be complicated. It's not a big deal. Have fun in Turkey, Syd.

December 17

Idaho

Sydney 3:11 am MDT (UTC-6)

Just landed. Let the wedding festivities begin.

Chapter 14
BECKETT

My nerves are going haywire.

It's not like we haven't talked throughout the year, but we haven't seen each other since last Christmas day. I've gotten to know her better and we text each other when stupid shit reminds us of something random, but *seeing* her feels ... bigger.

I'm pacing the lobby as Luka watches me with amusement in his eyes.

"And I thought I was the only one gone." He smirks.

"What are you talking about?"

"You're pacing like it's your wedding in three days, not mine. Daisy said Sydney is just as antsy as you are."

"I'm not antsy. It's snowing, and I just want to make sure she gets here okay. It's just a safety concern," I lie.

There were many times during the last year we had planned to meet up, but something always came up. It reinforces our concerns about how complicated our schedules are individually, let alone together. It's been impossible to carve out time where both of us were free. And her promotion was supposed to give her more time. Ha, joke's on us.

"Sure, man, whatever you say. I need to go check in on Dais, but I'll catch you later. Set an alarm for the rehearsal dinner please. I don't need the two of you getting carried away and forgetting about it," he calls over his shoulder as he heads to the elevators.

I fucking wish we'd get carried away, but I know that won't be happening. The physical distance isn't the only distance we've contended with. As much as I want to throw caution to the wind, Sydney isn't just a hookup. She never has been, even if I didn't realize it at the time. Two years ago, I didn't realize the snarky woman at the bar would be a mainstay in my life, but here we are. I won't jeopardize that for a quick fuck.

"Good afternoon, Alan. How's everything looking?" Her voice is all business, and it makes the edge of my lip turn up.

I watch her work, talking to the general manager and ensuring that everything is perfect for the wedding. She hasn't seen me yet, which works to my advantage. It gives me time to take in her tight-fitting jeans. Her snow boots somehow still look like they belong with a fancy outfit even though they're functional, and her parka still hugs her shape. Her hair is down in long waves, making my hand itch to sink into. She's fucking gorgeous.

But she isn't mine.

I can admire her from a distance, but then I have to snap back into friend mode. It's better this way. Neither of us will have a broken heart at the end of the day.

Sydney grabs a notepad and pen from behind the front desk, quickly jotting down a note as the GM talks to her about something. I've never seen her working. Sure, we've talked about her job and everything she does, but I've never actually seen her on the job, and let me just say, it's sexy as hell. She's every bit the boss she portrays. You can feel the energy of her being in charge the second she walks into the lobby, but you can tell everyone respects her. The respect that she holds is incredible to watch.

Once she's done, she turns on her heel and looks around, instantly spotting me. The smile that takes over her face could light up Alaska in the dead of winter. It makes my heart pound in my chest that she's looking at *me* like that. Somehow, I've earned that smile, and I'll try everything to keep it.

"Well, hey there, stranger," she says as she walks up to me.

"Hey yourself. Flight okay?"

"Flight was good. Long as hell since I came from Costa Rica, but not terrible. How about you?"

"Not too bad. Slept most of it, so I'm feeling good."

"Good. Good. I know I told you after the race, but I'm sorry about how the season ended." Her voice is so full of empathy that I can't handle it.

"Nothing to be sorry about. Luka won, and now he's getting married. There are no hard feelings there, I promise."

"But it still stings. You guys were so close in the points. Just because you're friends doesn't mean it hurts any less."

"I'm good, I promise." I want to cut this conversation off as soon as humanly possible.

Am I happy Luka ended up winning the Drivers' Championship? Hell no. But that's the job. It stung more that I only lost by eight points, honestly. At the end of the day, it's on me to win. It's on me to put my best foot forward every single race, and I failed this year. I don't want to talk about it, though.

"Being a tough-ass about it won't diminish the shitty feeling of losing." She shoots a sad smile my way.

"Correct, but talking about it to death won't change the outcome," I snap back, immediately feeling like an asshole. "I'm sorry. It's all anyone wants to talk about, and I'm just tired."

"I get it. I just wanted to say it in person, but I'll leave it alone. I'm here if you want to talk, though." Her face changes from compassion to excitement in a heartbeat. "So, what room did they put you up in? I made sure Daisy and Luka got the best one but told them you were the next highest priority."

It's not normal to make just a friend a priority to this level when we're talking about another friend's wedding, right? That means something, right?

"Umm, I'm in the room you had the first year we met."

"Great room," she murmurs. "Well, I need to drop my shit off then check in with Daisy. Are you busy, or do you want to come with me?"

"I'll come." I don't even wait a half a second to respond. *Eager much? Jesus.*

"Awesome." She reaches for her suitcase, but I beat her too it, picking it up and heading toward the elevator.

The sounds of her boots follow me, and the anticipation of what the next couple of weeks hold is almost too much.

I want so much with her. I wish I could have more, but I'll take what I can get from this woman. Outside of Nate, she's my closest friend, and we've only seen each other once a year. We've never had extended time like this, and I can't wait to just *be* together, even if we aren't *together.*

The elevator ride is hard. The way I want her, with her only being a foot away from me in a tight space, is testing every ounce of self-control I have. I can't count how many times I've jacked off to this woman in the past year, and frankly, it would be embarrassing to count the times I haven't. Now, she's so close. The smell of laundry detergent mixed with the faint lingering of her perfume is about to do me in. She smells good. She looks fucking amazing. Hell, she's still in her parka, and I'd fuck her right here and now if she said yes.

But I can't. I know I can't. So instead, I'll torture myself with thoughts of what could be if our lives were different.

"I have the resort handling most of the wedding, but can you stay and help me walk through everything to make sure I didn't forget anything? I usually have Daisy help me, but I didn't want her lifting a finger for her wedding."

"I'm yours to use."

My words register, and I can feel my cheeks heat. The double meaning is lost on Sydney, but fuck if I would let her use me for anything she needed, including her pleasure. If I had known that the first year was the only time I had to touch her, to give her as many orgasms as possible, I would have made every excuse to make it last longer.

Wordlessly, she leaves the enclosed space once the doors open, and I follow with her suitcase, like a lonely puppy looking for crumbs. I'd feel more pathetic, but I'm happy to be in her atmosphere. I'm just thrilled our friends are getting married, so there's a chance we see each other more than once a year.

We get settled into her suite, which is conveniently right next to mine, and she makes a list of everything needed for the wedding. I sit next to her and listen, but her ass is so organized there's no way I can even pretend to bring anything to the table.

Before I know it, two hours have gone by, and I'm starting to get hungry.

"Room service or go down to the restaurant?" I ask.

"Umm, room service. I'm almost done here, but I don't really want to socialize ... or work. And if we go down there, I'll have to do both." Her shy smile lets me see more of her, of who she really is, and I love it.

She's long since taken off her parka, now donning a tight green sweater that looks so soft I want to run my hands all over her body.

Busying myself with ordering my food, I try to ignore the way my body heats around her. I try to ignore the little looks she keeps shooting my way.

After she tells me her order, I place it and watch as she walks to her bedroom. When she comes back out, I almost die right there on the spot. Gone are the jeans and professional sweater; in their place are joggers that are tight enough to see every curve of her hips and a tank top that leaves nothing to the imagination.

Shit, maybe I can't keep myself in check.

"Okay, so Daisy wanted to do a rehearsal dinner. I've got that all set up, but she didn't want to do a bachelorette party. Did Luka say anything about wanting a bachelor party?" She looks up at me.

"Uh." I clear my throat. "He said no party, so I didn't plan anything."

"Okay, good. That means less to keep track of. That leaves day-of festivities. I was going to do a whole girls' morning with pampering, spa treatments, and all that shit. Are the guys doing anything?" The pen in her hand is poised to take notes.

"Luka had talked about going for a hike, but it's supposed to snow, so we're up in the air. He wants something super low-key, which isn't like him, but I'm not arguing. I don't want to run around for the next week straight," I confess.

Luka has changed right before my eyes, all because of Daisy. More than once since they've gotten together, thoughts about how they're able to be a couple have sprung into my head. If they can have all of this, why can't Sydney and I? I come to the same conclusion every time. Sydney's job is more demanding. Sure, Daisy is her assistant, but Sydney told me she doesn't make her travel with her. As long as she has access to her work computer, Daisy can work from anywhere. There's also the fact that Luka is in race shape without even trying. His spare time can be committed to Daisy, whereas I barely have time once I'm done working out and doing simulations. Don't get me wrong, I'm thrilled for them both, but it feels like Sydney and I should be able to have the same thing. Except we don't. We can't.

"I'll see if I can get some snowmobiles open for y'all to explore if that would work better. If it snows, you can still go out."

I smirk at the hint of Texas coming through. I won't ever point it out, though, for fear she'll intentionally stop saying it.

"I'll check with Luka before you go through all that trouble."

"Okay, I can do that. What else, what else?" she mutters to herself as she walks the length of the living room.

"Syd." I stand in front of her to stop her pacing.

When she looks up at me, I see the stress in her eyes. Not stress about the wedding but about making sure that her friend is happy.

"Daisy will love everything. I don't know her well, but that woman has never had a bad time in her life. She's happy just about anywhere, and she'll appreciate all the work you put in to make her wedding perfect." My hands hold her shoulders, hoping she really hears me.

Her entire body slumps before she leans into my chest. "I just want to make sure it's perfect for her," she mumbles into my shirt.

"And it is. Running yourself to empty won't help anyone. You seriously came straight here from Costa Rica and started to work immediately. You deserve to slow down too."

The last year of texting with this woman has let me catch glimpses of just how busy she is. She once told me her load was supposed to lighten at work, but I don't think that's happened. I'd venture to say she's traveling more now.

"I don't think I know how to slow down."

Laughter bursts out of me at her words, making her head bounce against my chest. "Yeah, shockingly, I picked up on that."

She pulls back and smacks my chest. "You are the last person who should talk about not knowing how to slow down." Her smile is soft.

I fucking wish things were different for us.

But they aren't.

And this is all I get from her.

Chapter 15
Sydney

I'm dangerously close to caving on something I've told myself a million times not to in the last two days.

Beckett's warmth, his support, has made my head a complete mess. Yes, I'm worried about Daisy and Luka's wedding, but my anxiety is one hundred percent due to the man in front of me.

The stark comparison between Luka and Daisy and me and Beckett couldn't be clearer. Somehow, Luka and Daisy have made it work. And somehow, two years later, Beckett and I are exactly where we started—without the sex.

It's all been heavy on my mind since I boarded the plane to come here. Work's allowed me to push off all of these feelings. But now, standing in front of the only man I've wanted for a long time, I can no longer hide from it.

As we stare at each other, both realizing the distance between us feels more like the Grand Canyon than just a small bump in the road, my heart aches in my chest.

My eyes trail down his body. His lean frame is covered by a T-shirt and joggers from his sponsors, which do little to hide the strong muscle there. My mind flashes back to that fateful Christmas two years ago. To him stripping me naked and showing me just how fucking good he is in the bedroom.

Fuck. I told myself we can't be anything more than friends, because if we throw sex into the mix, I know I'll want more. I'll want it all. Every ounce of him he can give me, I'll crave it.

But I don't get to be that happy. I don't get to have the booming career and the amazing love life. I'm just not that lucky. Sometimes, you don't get to have it all even if it doesn't feel fair.

Shaking my head to clear the melancholy thoughts, I refocus on Beckett.

"Well, let's both make an attempt to slow down the next couple of weeks while we're here," he says.

Did I choose not to focus on the fact that we're both here for almost three weeks? Yes, because if I think about it too hard, depression that I can't have him sets in. That I have to spend an extended amount of time around him as only his friend.

"Friends" feels like a curse word now.

"I will ... try very hard," I concede.

We're cut off by a knocking at the door.

"Food's here," I whisper and take a giant step back as Beckett runs his hand through his hair.

"I'll get it," he mumbles.

I watch him go as I get a funny feeling in my chest.

Watching him walk away sucks. It's illogical; I know he's coming back with food, but it feels like this huge life metaphor that he's going to walk out of my life at some point and not come back. It's absolutely crushing to think about.

He sets up everything at the table as I stand stock-still. The realization that I'm spending a good chunk of the next three weeks with the man I can't have finally hits me dead in the chest.

How the hell am I supposed to keep my feelings and my fucking libido in check? Being friends with him when we're both on opposite sides of the world is relatively easy. Being friends with him when his hotel room is right next to mine? When we are both in the wedding for our good friends? There's no way I survive this.

"Food's getting cold. Hurry up," Beckett calls over his shoulder as he sits down.

I quickly join him, worrying the entire meal if any of this is a good idea. Or if my heart will be shattered by the time I leave Idaho.

***

Beckett left a couple of hours ago, and since then, I've been lying in bed wide awake.

Daisy and Luka are getting married in two days. After that, they're off to wherever Luka planned the honeymoon, and I'm here … with Beckett … and no buffer.

It seems like he's gotten more attractive in the last two years, but I know it's more likely that I haven't seen him in a year except on television. My attraction to him hasn't waned. No, getting to know him over the last year sure has amped it up, though. But neither of us is going to be less busy over the next year. Our situation and reasoning for not being together hasn't changed.

Knowing the layout of the rooms here, I know his bedroom backs up to mine. I place my palm against the wall and imagine him doing the same.

There's this natural, comfortable connection with him. Every time we've been together, every time we talk, it's just so *easy*. And yet, we can't prioritize being together. Well… I can't, mostly. Because as much as we can blame our jobs and the amount of travel we do, at the end of the day, it's because we haven't found a way to push each other to the forefront of our lives.

I kind of hate myself for it. But I also have no idea how to shift everything in my life to make space for him. I'm a total asshole for that.

Sighing, I bring my hand back down and shift to my side.

I've dwelled on it too long already. It's time to focus on the wedding and hope that I can make it through without getting more attached to this unattainable man.

Chapter 16

BECKETT

Daisy and Luka's wedding went off without a hitch, just like I knew it would because Sydney would never let anything go wrong.

The last three days have awarded me time to watch her in action, see her interactions with Daisy, and see her all sorts of dolled up. Holy hell, I think I've had a permanent hard-on for three days because she looks phenomenal in a dress. Keeping my hands to myself has been a huge challenge, but I've done it.

Things are winding down; half the guests have left, and the newlyweds look like they're about to leave before they rip each other's clothes off.

"Hey, stranger." Sydney's soft voice floats my way. She looks tired, making my hands itch to sweep her in my arms and take her back to my room. Her flowy dark-green dress wraps around her middle like a second skin, wreaking havoc on my system.

"Hey."

"Daisy and Luka are heading out. I told them I'd hang out until the last guests are gone," she says.

"Sounds good. I'll stay with you."

"You don't have to do that," she argues like she thinks it'll change my mind somehow.

It won't. I'm not leaving her to deal with this alone.

I slide out the chair next to me, gesturing for her to sit down. The sigh that leaves her makes me want to take care of her. Lord knows no one else seems to.

Her leg brushes against mine, sending a zing up my body, but I don't move my leg. Pathetic? Yes, but I'll take the little bit of contact like it's an addiction.

We watch as the last of the guests, drunk on too much free booze, stumble out of the room. My body is full of tension. Every touch, every brush of her skin on mine, has been sending me higher and higher until I'm pulled so tight I feel like I could snap.

"I'm just going to help—"

"I'm taking you upstairs," I cut her off.

"Beckett, I'm just going to help clean up."

"You absolutely are not. You literally paid people to do that. You've been on your feet all day, working nonstop since we got here, and now the wedding is over. It's time to relax."

"I can't just leave it all to them." She gestures to the waiters grabbing glasses that were left behind.

I don't think about my actions. I don't think about what they mean. It's pure instinct and annoyance that she just won't stop working. Rising to my feet, I bend down until her midsection is at my shoulder before standing with her on it.

"Oh my God! What are you doing? Put me down!" she squeals. Her legs flail wildly, but I lock them down with my arm.

"Getting you the fuck out of here. Jesus. I have to drag your ass out of here so you stop working."

"I would have come with you!" she argues.

I laugh. "You sure as shit wouldn't have."

"Well, now we'll never know."

"Guess not. What I do know is that you're going to stop working. You're going to try and shut your brain off, and finally relax like you were supposed to be doing all along."

We reach the elevator, and the people around us raise an eyebrow but otherwise leave us alone. Perk of being in a high-end resort? I doubt anyone would say anything.

Once the elevator doors close, some of the tension I've been feeling loosens up. "If I put you down, are you going to come with me? Or are you going to say you are and just go back downstairs to micromanage?"

"Beckett Davis, I do not micromanage!"

I squeeze her thigh that I'm still holding as she sighs with acceptance.

"Fine. I will come upstairs with you. Now, put me down, you caveman."

"I seem to remember you like me being a little bit of a caveman." *Shit.* It's out of my mouth before I can rein it in. We've strictly kept to not talking about us having sex, and I just broke that without a thought.

She slides down my body, touching as much of it as possible, including my hard dick. If she notices, she doesn't say anything, but there is a twinkle in her eye. Her eyes shift between mine, and the tension in the elevator feels like a heavy fog wrapping around us.

I try to hold back, I do. If you ask me in a month if I lost control, I'll deny it. But the second her eyes shift to my lips, it's over.

I step up to her, backing her into the wall as I wrap my arm around her waist and bring my other to the nape of her neck.

And then I'm kissing her.

With all the pent-up longing.

With all pressure releasing in my body.

With all the hope that this isn't just one time or a mistake in her eyes.

Her leg hikes up over my hip, notching me right at the apex of her thighs. My hips grind into her without conscious effort. I couldn't find it in me to pull back right now anyway.

Her tongue drags along my bottom lip, making me groan with need. I practically inhale her, unable to get close enough.

And then, the elevator doors open. I hear the ding, but I don't disconnect. Instead, I wrap her legs around me and carry her to my room. I fumble getting the key into the door, mumbling about how dumb it is to have real keys before I get the door open. I slam it shut before pushing her against it and kissing down her neck.

"Beck," she breathes. It's the first time she's called me that and the first time it doesn't annoy me.

No, from now on, every time I hear Beck, I'll remember this gorgeous woman in the throes of an orgasm.

"I tried, baby, I really did."

"Shut up and fuck me."

A mischievous smirk tips my lips. "Say please."

"Please, Beckett, fuck me with your incredible dick and make me see stars."

I look up and see her playful smile.

"You're gonna pay for that smart mouth tonight, Sydney."

"I'm counting on it, *Beckett*." Her exaggeration of my name puts me in motion.

I walk us over to my bedroom before tossing her on the bed. Stripping off my tux, I waste no time getting naked. She goes to her side to unzip her dress, but I stop her with a shake of my head.

"I want to look at you for a minute." I slide my hand down my abs to my cock, stroking while my eyes look at every inch of Sydney they can. She squirms as I squeeze the tip, and I pray I can have some semblance of stamina tonight.

Putting one knee on the bed, I trail my free palm up her exposed leg. Her skin is so damn soft that I want to nuzzle it like a damn cat. Her hips can't keep still, turning me on more if possible. She wants this as much as I do. *Thank God.*

Once I reach her hip, I slide my hand up a little further, expecting to find the seam of her panties. My head tilts when I find none.

"Who are you going commando for, baby?" My voice borders a growl, but the possessiveness I feel right now has me too worked up to tame it.

"Some waiter that's coming to my room later." She bites her lip to hide her smirk.

My eyebrows shoot up as my fingers shift to slide against the edge of her clit and then lower, never touching her where she wants it.

"Is that who you're wet for?"

She shakes her head.

"Don't be shy now. You want to be a smartass, now you have to pay for it. Who are you wet for?"

"You." She moans as I continue on the outside of her opening.

"Don't ever say around me that you were planning to be with another man. I can't take it, Syd." My voice carries my emotions too much even though I'm trying desperately to hide them.

Her hand reaches down and grabs my wrist. "Beckett, I was just trying to rile you up. I wouldn't—"

"I know. Stand up and strip." I step away from her, trying to get ahold of my reactions. I meant what I said; I know she was messing with me, but I can't disconnect the feelings it brought up in me.

She should be mine. She should be mine to please, mine to cuddle, mine to love. *Shit.* No, I can't go there.

This time, she follows directions as I lie down where she just vacated. I take a steadying breath and hope I don't fuck everything up. Once she has her dress off and I come to find out it's the only piece of clothing she had on tonight, I beckon her over.

"Sit on my face, baby."

"Beckett..."

"Don't make ask. Sit on my face so I can drink you up. Smother me so I can taste you all night on my tongue." I'm begging, and I don't even care. I need this woman like I need air. Like I need to *drive*, and that's scary as fuck. But I'll deal with the fallout if there is one.

She straddles my hips first, trapping my dick between my stomach and her wet pussy. As she slides against me, I have to close my eyes so I don't come.

"Open them, Beckett. See who's taking you to the edge." Her words are strong. There's no hesitation.

My eyes lock onto where we're connected, and I have to grit my teeth as I grip her hips. With little effort, I lift her up to my face and softly drop her down to my waiting mouth.

"Holy fuck," she whispers as I lick her ass to clit.

I leave nothing untouched. I'd gladly drown in her, and it's my goal to get her that fucking wet before we move onto anything else.

"This is going to be embarrassingly fast," she mutters as her hips start moving to the rhythm that she likes.

I nip her clit in response, and I feel her pussy clench up. She starts to pant as her hips move faster, and I maneuver my hand under her hip, sliding two fingers in right as she's about to orgasm.

She screams into the quiet room, back arched, giving me the most incredible view of her entire body mid-orgasm. But it's her face that has me too close to the edge. I gently bring her back down before flipping her underneath me and reaching over to grab a condom from the nightstand. It takes me seconds to put on before I move over her.

In her eyes I see so much. The lingering effect of her orgasm, sure, but it's more than that. I see hope, fear, and need that probably reflect back to her.

This feels like *more*, and it's scary as hell.

Chapter 17
SYDNEY

His gaze holds too much, and the tendrils of panic weave through me, hitting me straight in the chest.

"Stay with me," he murmurs like he sees all of me, even the parts I want to hide.

His palm grips my thigh, wrapping around it and shoving it up. My other leg wraps around his waist as he notches against my very wet pussy. I'll admit the man knows how to make me orgasm.

Our eyes stay locked as he pushes in slowly. I feel every inch, every ridge against me, and it's incredible. Like there's too much pleasure, too much sensation. Once he's settled, he tips his forehead to mine, and we take a minute to breathe each other in. My hand slides up his arm to his neck and tangles in his almost shoulder-length hair. His hips roll, just enough to give a little friction, making my eyes flutter closed.

"No, baby, open your eyes. Let me see you," he whispers.

It's frightening to have a man see so much of me because that's what he really means. He's not saying he wants to see my orgasm; no, he wants to see *me*. We may have been dancing around this the better part of two years, but now I can't seem to find the reasons why we ever denied ourselves.

"I-It's too much," I say on a broken whisper.

"I know, but we'll deal with it later. Not right now. Now, we feel." His hips thrust a little harder, making my grip in his hair tighten. He moans at the touch of pain, making me feral.

My hips canter up, sinking him impossibly deeper as we both groan at the feeling.

"This ... is going to be over too fast," he growls as his thrusts get harder.

"We can have round two. And three. And seven." I arch my back as he hits a spot that feels so good. "We're here for a couple of weeks."

He doesn't respond with words but with deep, punishing thrusts and by sliding his hand between us to pinch my clit. I try my damnedest to keep my eyes on him, but I fail when he swirls his fingers against my clit. My head tips back, and I feel his lips on my shoulder where it meets my neck.

"Fuck, I can feel you pulsing." He clamps his teeth on that spot, sending me flying.

He holds me so close it's like we're melding into one as he comes deep inside of me. He slumps against me, kissing the abused flesh he bit, but I couldn't care less. My mind is quiet. My body is relaxed. For once, I don't have anything else in my head. No travel plans, no resort upgrades, and no GM problems. Only Beckett and his comforting touch.

"You... That was... Holy hell, woman," he pants against my shoulder before rolling off of me and dragging me with him, keeping himself inside of me.

"I think you should be the one complimented."

"I'll take any praise you give me. Just be careful my head doesn't get too big."

I can *feel* him smiling against the crown of my head. Sighing, I play with his chest hair.

"No. You are not going to start thinking right now," he demands.

I chuckle. "Who says I was thinking anything?"

"That sigh. It's the one that says you're about to overthink the shit out of everything. Let's make a deal: no thinking past this holiday. Once we leave here, we can figure things out and overthink away, but not while we're here together."

I think on his words. Logically, I know it's a terrible plan. There is no way to simply figure things out between us, and we sure as hell should be discussing it before we both leave here, but right this second? I want to do what he offers. I want to live in this bubble while we can.

"Deal," I whisper.

***

I wake up groggy as hell. And hot.

"Jesus." I groan as I try to roll out from under Beckett's hold.

"No. Stay," he croaks.

"I'm sweating. You are a damn furnace, Beckett."

His arm loosens around me, and I finally get free. Walking to the balcony doors, I grab my robe before walking out for a second.

It stopped snowing last night. The fresh powder looks gorgeous on the property and the mountains. It's an idyllic setting. Maybe that's why Beckett and I connect so much here.

No, you connect because there's something between you two. It has nothing to do with where you are.

Stupid logical brain. It's easier to put stock in our location rather than the fact that we have a strong connection but can't find a way to make things happen outside of this sleepy town.

"I thought we made a deal." His arms wrap around me. "And you're freezing."

"Overthinking is my second job, I think." I try to lighten up the tension.

"Yeah, well, not for the next two weeks it isn't. I ordered breakfast already, so let's get you inside and warm."

I snap. I don't know if it's my overthinking or just being unsure of where we stand, but his thoughtfulness is too much for me right now. Contrary to what we agreed to last night, it's not so simple to shut it all off.

"Just stop," I mutter.

"What?"

"Stop. Stop being sweet. Stop looking out for me. Just stop being so damn nice to me. I don't deserve it." My eyes start to well up, and it pisses me off more. Angrily wiping at them, trying to hide them from Beckett, proves pointless.

"Okay. Inside, now," he grunts and lifts me over his shoulder, carrying me inside.

I smack his back. "Put me down. I don't even have underwear on!"

"Shoulda thought about that before you broke our deal." He drops me onto the couch then kneels before me.

"Beckett…"

"Nope. It's time to listen. You want to freak out? Great, do it with me. You want quiet time where you don't have to think? Awesome, I'll sit next to you and massage your feet. For the next two weeks, you're mine. You promised me no overthinking, just us while were here, and I'm holding you to it."

The earnestness in his eyes stabs at my heart. He's just so damn good. He shouldn't be wasting his time with me. With someone who barely has time to take these two weeks off. Who travels more than he does. Why set ourselves up for more disappointment?

"Baby, look at me." His soft words make me meet his eyes. "There is no pressure. There is no 'what's next' right now. It's just us, being together because we're damn good together. And we don't need to think past that. *You* don't need to think past that."

His words are imploring, and *God*, I want to ignore everything I'm feeling but…

"I don't know if I can. Hell, I don't know if I know how." It's as much of a confession as I can muster.

"Then let me help. Breakfast will be here any minute. After we eat, I'll be sure to take your mind off of everything except me." His smirk has nothing on the mischief in his eyes.

"You're awfully confident."

"Confident is my middle name. I'm an F1 driver, Sydney. It comes with the territory."

A burst of laughter comes from me at his cockiness. "Dear God, I think I like the humble side of you better."

"No, you don't. That side doesn't give you incredible orgasms." His palm slides up my leg to my inner thigh. His eyebrows wiggle as he gets closer to where he wants.

And then there's a knock at the door.

"Every fucking time, I swear," he mumbles. Tapping my thigh, he stands up. "Hold tight. I'll deliver after we eat. You'll need the energy."

I watch him walk to the door in nothing but joggers, his lean torso on display for me.

I don't know how he did it, but I'm out of my head. The panic I was feeling is pushed down deep, waiting for a time when I'm alone. But not now. He's right. We only have so much time and we are *damn* good together, so why not take advantage while we can? Who knows what the future holds, so why not jump in even if it crushes me when we leave? This is the pattern we're obviously good at.

Breakfast is a quick ordeal. I barely finish my last bite of pancakes before Beckett is lifting me up and wrapping my legs around his waist. The robe has afforded him ample opportunities to cop a feel, and it's no different now. His hands grip my ass hard, grinding me against his already hard dick as he makes his way to the bathroom.

The steam shower helps loosen the tension I'm still holding, and the orgasm Beckett casually gives me while washing me releases the last of it. He doesn't let me touch him, solely focused on me until we get out.

He's drying off, not paying attention to his cock standing at attention, but that doesn't mean I'm not. I grab a towel, tossing it in front of him, which causes his brows to furrow in question. Naked and dripping wet still, I kneel in front of him. Taking him in my hand, I look up at him as I stroke slowly.

"Sydney..."

Kissing his tip before I lick down his underside, I make sure to spend time on that ridge that feels incredible inside of me. His quads are clenched so tight it looks like they could cramp at any moment, but I continue. Sucking the tip into my mouth, I circle my tongue around it as I drag my hand up his leg and cup his balls.

"*Shit*," he curses as his fingers tangle in my hair.

Sliding deeper, I take him in as far as I can get him before I pull back. Breathing through my nose, I go again and try to get further. It takes me a few strokes, but I finally have him touching my throat. One more stroke, one more deep breath, and I slide down, taking him as deep as I can until I'm touching his pelvis with my nose.

"Fuck, fuck, fuck, fuck," he chants above me as his first tightens in my hair.

I bob a little as I roll his balls in my palm, squeezing them a little rougher when his hips start thrusting.

"Oh God. I'm going to come." He whimpers and the sounds makes me so wet and turned on that if I had a free hand, I'd surely be getting myself off right along with him.

Moaning with him in my mouth sends him over the edge. He rips himself out of my mouth, wrapping his hand around his cock as he jerks himself off the rest of the way, his cum hitting my chest and breasts with every stroke.

Never in my life has a man come on my body, but holy fuck is it the sexiest thing I've ever seen. His lack of control, his groans as he grips the edge of the sink hard to stay upright...

I don't even realize my hands are moving, trailing through his cum before moving down my body and circling my clit. I'm so turned on that I'm on a hair trigger and ready to join him with another orgasm.

Until he sees what I'm doing.

He drops to his knees in front of me, putting his hand on top of mine even as his cock is still twitching. "Tell me you're on birth control," he growls.

Nodding, I'm confused why he asks. We've always used condoms, so it hasn't been an issue.

But then he's scooping up his orgasm with his fingers before moving them back to where my hand is. This time, he doesn't stay at my clit. He moves lower, pushing inside of me two fingers covered in his cum, and I'm gone.

"Fuck, baby, you look so fucking good coming. So good with my cum inside of you." He licks up the side of my neck before kissing it, then my cheek. He holds me to him as I draw out my orgasm for as long as possible, silently screaming into the bathroom. He cups the back of my head, pumping his fingers inside of me. It feels like my orgasm is everlasting. Like the world will end before my body stops clenching.

I collapse against him, breathing heavy as he strokes my back.

"That was just supposed to be about you," I grumble into his chest.

"There's not a single scenario where I watch you get yourself off while I stand by. Don't get me wrong, that was the blow job to end all blow jobs, but the second you touched yourself, I was a goner. Seeing you get off does it for me, Sydney."

What he says isn't deep, isn't this huge declaration of love or anything, but it makes my heart pound just the same.

It's not like I've had a booming sex life before I met him, and during the year it's just my hand and my vibrators. But with this man? The sex isn't just going through the motions. There's a very real possibility it may change my life forever.

Chapter 18
BECKETT

It's Christmas day and I've been up for hours.

I haven't felt this excited since ... ever, I guess. I never had this feeling when I was a kid.

Fun wasn't in our family's vocabulary. Maybe that's why spending the past two Christmases with Sydney has made the anticipation, the excitement, so huge for me.

It's probably why I went a little overboard with a present this year. But for the first year, I knew she would be here, thanks to Luka and Daisy getting married so damn fast. It didn't hurt that I put a whisper of an idea into Luka's head about how nice the Vanstone is here. Daisy was easy as long as it was at a Vanstone—company hookup and all that.

"Why are you up so damn early?" Sydney's sleep-roughened voice sounds a few feet away.

"It's Christmas. I'm happy." Such a simple statement, but to me, it's something so new. I've spent my whole life, thirty-six years to be exact, working my ass off to become a Formula 1 driver. It's been singular focus for as long as I can remember. Sydney's changed all of that.

I want our Christmases together every single year. I want all of our days in between too, but she's not ready for that. And honestly, as much as I *am* ready for it, our schedules dictate things more than anything.

"I need coffee before I can be happy," she groans.

"Already ordered. Got the works for food, too, and they should be here in a couple of minutes."

"God yes. You're the fucking best." She rolls over and cuddles into my side, fitting so damn perfectly it's hard to remember this is all supposed to be temporary.

Her fingers play with my chest hair, a habit I've noticed she does more and more lately. I decide not to ruin the moment by talking, soaking up everything that is Sydney on this perfect snowy day.

Two days ago, I called down to the front desk and cancelled the rest of Sydney's stay and moved her in with me. There was no use in taking up another suite when there wasn't a chance in hell I was letting her sleep away from me. Since then, waking up to the hellcat that is Sydney has been more than I hoped for. Sure, I've woken her up with an orgasm or the beginnings of one, but she hasn't been shy about waking me up too. It's like neither of us can get enough of each other and are making up for the lack of physical contact over the last year. I'm sure as hell not complaining.

The ever-familiar knock on the door pulls me from my thoughts, and I carefully slide out from underneath Sydney. She sits up, the sheet pooling against her naked torso making it hard to leave even to get food. But I do because if she wants food, I'll provide it all.

After quickly pulling on some shorts, I get the food in and roll it into the bedroom then pour her a cup of coffee before I do anything else.

"You're making it very easy to get used to this."

"Good," I reply with zero hesitation.

She hides her face behind her coffee mug. I know she doesn't want to address the elephant in the room. Eventually, we'll need to talk about it, but today isn't that day. We made a deal.

Breakfast is uneventful, both of us realizing how hungry we are and demolishing everything I ordered. Once I put the cart outside the door, I come in and join Sydney on the couch. She's curled up under a blanket, looking at the Christmas tree that's been here since I checked in. I didn't even question it, but I knew she's the one who made sure there was one in here for me. Over the past couple of days, presents have slowly been added underneath. Both of us were trying to be inconspicuous even though it's obvious when something new lands there.

"Shall we open them?" She nods to the small stack.

I wordlessly grab them and distribute them to each of us. There are only five total, three for her and two for me, but it's more than I've ever received.

"You first." I gesture to her pile.

She gingerly picks the top one up and unwraps the poorly wrapped present. I could have paid someone to do it for me, but for some reason, I didn't want anyone to have a hand in something I got her.

"Oh, these are gorgeous," she whispers.

The dainty earrings are simple, but I saw them passing a jewelry store in Australia one day and immediately thought of her, so I had to get them. The little sunbursts with a glint of sparkle are symbolic in a new way for me. She's the sunshine when my mind starts to get dark. She keeps me focused and happy. It doesn't matter if we ever get together; her friendship keeps the light front and center for me, and they were the perfect find.

"Just saw them one day and thought you'd like them." I'm unsure and suddenly very embarrassed.

"They're perfect." She looks up at me. "I love them."

My shoulders slump with relief. The fear that she wouldn't like them was a worry I didn't even realize had.

"Here, open this one." She hands me a flat package.

I tear into the package, pulling out a coupon book of sorts. Flipping through it, my confusion only grows.

"It's a bunch of random things you can cash in on. Stays at a Vanstone, dinner, tickets to a hockey game, some stuff in Austin to go do…"

"This is amazing," I breathe. "And thoughtful."

She brushes it off. "It's nothing crazy."

"It's not nothing. I'm looking forward to using them all, especially the things in Austin. Thank you." Subconsciously, she just invited me to be with her more. By adding things in Austin, she's giving us more time together even if she doesn't realize it.

I wordlessly hand her a similarly flat package, and she tilts her head in confusion before she carefully opens it. She looks through the few papers in the envelope before gazing up at me.

"I'd like for you to be my guest at all of the U.S. races. If you can make them," I add quickly.

"This is more than just tickets to the races, huh?" she asks, still reading through the papers.

"You would be in the Legacy garage, watching with the engineers, with your very own set of headphones to listen to my radio."

Her eyes light up. "I get to hear you?"

"If you want to." My cheeks heat with embarrassment. Maybe this was a stupid idea. Maybe it's too much.

"Oh my God, I love it!" She jumps over to me in a hug I wish I could bottle up and keep for the lonely nights.

Once she lets go and gets situated again, she grabs a larger box wrapped in simple gold wrapping paper and black bow and hands it to me. She starts wringing her hands together. If she's nervous about if I'll like what she got me, she doesn't need to worry. Sydney could wrap up a pile of mud, and I would worship the ground she walks on.

I carefully unwrap it to reveal a white box. I get to work opening it. Bubble wrap unveils a familiar wood box, larger than anything we've gotten each other before.

"What did you do?" I ask as I open it to find a car—*my car*—in handblown glass.

"I didn't know if it was possible. I talked to them a lot about what they thought they could make, and they wanted to try a full F1 car. I must say they did a hell of a job." Her voice is excited and unsure.

I pull it out, amazed at the details. "This is incredible, Sydney." Turning it in all directions, I'm amazed at how realistic it is even though it's glass. It's one of the coolest things I've ever seen. The colors—hell, even the steering wheel—is a perfect replica.

"You like it?"

Startled, I look up at her. "I fucking love it."

Her soft smile could make clouds disappear. It's not her overly bright one.

No, this is the genuine one. The happy one.

I carefully place the glass Formula 1 car onto the table then quickly grab her last present. It's good to know our heads were in the same place, at least.

She slowly unwraps it, revealing another wooden box. Her eyes light up with mirth. "We seem to have a theme."

"We do." I hold my breath as she opens the box.

Gingerly, she pulls out the three separate pieces, putting them next to my car on the table. When they're all out, a mountain range mimics the one we have as our view every Christmas we've been together.

"Beckett..." she whispers.

"I don't know if it's as amazing as that car, but it felt fitting." Deflect, deflect, deflect because if I don't, my big mouth might open up and tell her I want to give this a real try. I'll push things too far, and the possibility of pushing her away is too high.

"I don't know what to say." Her quiet voice is unsure as she traces the edges of the mountain peaks with her finger. "I love it so much."

"Good. That's good," I mumble out, insecurity leeching into my every word.

I feel her hand on my thigh before she crawls into my lap, straddling me. Her hands cup my jaw, forcing me to make eye contact with her.

"This is the best gift I've ever gotten. I love everything so much." Pressing a kiss to my lips, she pulls back. "It's so fucking thoughtful," she whispers.

My hand moves to her waist, holding her in place. "Yeah?"

"Yeah, Beckett Davis." She smirks before her smile drops. "This has been the best Christmas."

"I can probably make it better." I tilt my hips up.

"Of that, I have no doubt." She kisses my lips, then my cheek and down to my neck, making me grip her waist harder.

It doesn't take us long to get naked and make it one for the books.

Chapter 19

BECKETT

Two weeks is all we got. Two weeks to fall for her. Two weeks to enjoy every minute in her world.

And now it's over. We move on like she didn't completely change my life.

But I have a plan. This thing between us doesn't end here; I won't let it. I just have to show her we can make this work even with our crazy schedules.

As I watch her board her plane, I make a vow to prove that we can be together, no matter what it takes. And in my head, I'm already planning the next time I can see her.

Chapter 20

January 31

Monaco/Austin

Thinking about you today. What's on your agenda?

Work. Drama hit one of my resorts, and I need to get it figured out ASAP before the GM tears the whole place apart.

Damn, sorry. If there's anything I can do, even if it's just someone to bitch to, I'm here. I don't have to be at headquarters until February 17, so I'm just training my days away.

Thanks. I'll be lucky to eat today, honestly. Gotta run!

I say this with all the respect in the world, but HOW IN THE FUCK did you manage to get lunch delivered to me?

Ah, you forget I have connections, baby. I'm not going to let you starve if I can help it.

Sydney 1:50 pm CDT (UTC-5)

Thank you so, so, so, so much. Thank you. This day went to shit, and Daisy's on her honeymoon, so I'm riding solo today. The food was absolutely perfect.

Beckett 8:52 pm CEST (UTC+2)

Anytime. If you need dinner, text me.

February 18

Mexico City/Costa Rica

Sydney 7:12 am CST (UTC-6)

I just watched the replay of the car unveiling! I wasn't feeling good last night and crashed before I saw it, sorry. It looks good. I think? I wouldn't know, but you looked good and sounded happy!

Beckett 2:14 pm BST (UTC+1)

You weren't feeling good? Are you okay?

Sydney 7:15 am CST (UTC-6)

Mostly. I have no clue, was just super tired and achy. Maybe the flu, but I'm hoping not because I don't have time to be sick.

Beckett 2:16 pm BST (UTC+1)

You should take it easy today. No one is in dire need of your time. Why don't you just call your boss/co-worker—whatever you call him—and say you're working from home today?

Sydney 7:17 am CST (UTC-6)

Because I'm not at home; I'm in Costa Rica. And because I'm fully capable of doing my job. Thanks for the vote of confidence, though.

Beckett 2:18 pm BST (UTC+1)

That's not what I mean, Sydney. I'm asking who's looking out for you. There's no question you're damn good at your job, but if you aren't feeling good, there's nothing to prove. Take care of yourself first.

Sydney 7:20 am CST (UTC-6)

Yep. Will do. Have fun training or practicing, or whatever it is you guys do.

MarcH 2

Bahrain/Austin

Sydney 10:03 am CDT (UTC-5)

Congrats on the win! Great way to start the season.

Beckett 6:05 pm AST (UTC+3)

Thanks. It was a tough one. Luka was too close for comfort. You're at home today?

Sydney 10:07 am CDT (UTC-5)

I thought he was going to overtake you on that last lap. I am for a change. Relaxing at home, watching the race live for once.

Sydney 6:08 pm AST (UTC+3)

He was not even close to overtaking me. Please, you know I wouldn't let Luka of all people show me up on the first race. Good. I'm glad you're relaxing for once.

Sydney 10:09 am CDT (UTC-5)

So territorial. Tell me, does the caveman stuff just heighten the bro love between you two? Or is it a form of foreplay? I'm just trying to understand the dynamic.

Sydney 6:10 pm AST (UTC+3)

Ha ha. He's like a pesky little brother. Trust me, the only foreplay I'm interested in is with you.

Sydney 10:12 am CDT (UTC-5)

I walked right into that one… Ditto.

Chapter 21
Sydney

Waking up in Miami, I lie in bed for an extra-long minute, trying to stretch my limbs and alleviate the stiffness. More and more lately, traveling has not been kind to my body, and the fatigue and stiffness in my hands and ankles are getting worse by the day.

I've talked to Pierce about slowing down a lot on the travel, which he was completely agreeable on. When he promoted me, the plan was never for me to travel as much as I still am, so this is forcing me to slow down to a pace Pierce always intended. It's annoying that I can't keep up, can't overachieve, and to some extent, micromanage. I know that's not what my job is anymore, and I know we have a very capable team, but it's hard to let go of the reins.

My reminder alarm goes off, and I know if I want to make it down to the garages in time to talk to Beckett before he has to practice, I need to get my ass up.

The hot water feels amazing on my bones, but the nerves start to ramp up. I'm not sure what to expect this weekend. Sure, I've watched the practices and the qualifiers, seen all the celebrities sitting in the garages with cameras on them, but I'm not a celebrity. I'm not sure if they'll just shove me in a corner and tell me to stay or what. Honestly, that's what I would do, so I won't even be upset if that happens. I'm just one more person to keep track of.

Making my way down to the garage, I pull at the above-the-knee shift dress I decided to wear. It's a T-shirt dress, casual yet dressy enough for the event. *I hope.*

Insecurity pulls at my chest. I may be in this world because of Pierce and working my ass off, but I'm still not used to it. I'm behind the scenes, making sure things run smoothly. I don't go to the events; Pierce is the face of the company, and I like it that way.

I hesitate before walking up to the poles that allow you to tap your VIP badge to gain access.

"Ma'am, can we assist you?" a gentleman off to the side asks.

"Oh, umm. I'm just trying to get to the Legacy garage." I hold up my lanyard with an awkward smile on my face.

"I can walk you there. Go ahead and tap the screen, and we'll head on over."

I do as directed, and before long, we're walking through the maze of tents and pop-up buildings that look more permanent than anything I've seen. Then we enter a sleek building with the Legacy logo on the top.

"They'll be able to set you up and get you situated in the garage from here."

"Thank you so much for your help." I nod as I walk up the two steps.

The door slides open, releasing a blast of cool air, which is welcome in this Miami heat.

"Welcome. Who are you here with?" a woman behind the desk off to the side asks.

"Oh, hi. Umm Beckett … ah, Beck. Beck Davis." *Duh, what other Beck is there?* I roll my eyes internally at myself.

"Sydney Johnson?"

"That's me."

"Perfect. Beck is already in the garage. He likes to be there early, but let me walk you over there and get you set up."

I nod at how complex and locked down everything is, but I guess it makes sense. You don't want a million people in the area and certainly not ones who haven't been approved. I've learned a lot about the sport since I met Beckett, and secrecy seems to be the name of the game here.

It's a short walk across the walkway, and we're entering the garage area from the back. Instantly, the noise takes over. It's not overly loud yet, but I know it's just a matter of time.

"Hey!" Beckett's voice immediately soothes my anxiety.

My shoulders drop, and a smile blooms on my face. "Hi."

He pulls me into a hug before stepping back.

He looks good. *Too good.* His race suit hangs at his waist, the tight long-sleeve shirt underneath showing every inch of his lean body, making me flash back to Idaho. His hair is perfectly styled, and the urge to run my hand through it to mess it up is almost too strong.

"I'm so glad you're here." His smile is perhaps the brightest I've ever seen on him. He looks at home here.

Last year, I didn't make a big enough effort to come and watch races in person because I was scared of what it could mean, but seeing him in his element now makes me regret that. This is Beckett Davis—*the* Beck Davis—in all his glory, and my God, it's a sight to behold.

"I'm happy to be here. I just want to make sure I'm not in the way," I add, not wanting to distract him in any way.

"You won't be in the way. It's just about to become really loud, so I want to get you situated with headphones."

Nodding, I follow him as he introduces me to his race engineer, Paul, and his trainer, Nate. I sit next to Nate as Beckett gets me headphones and places them over my ears reverently.

"Okay, Nate is staying with you. If you have questions or anything, or are bored, he's your go-to. He can get you anything or take you anywhere if you're over it."

"I won't get bored, Beckett." I roll my eyes.

"Well, it's an option. Or if you need a quiet space if work calls."

My heart clenches hard in my chest at his words. Work almost always calls; except, I've slowed way down lately. Beckett doesn't know that, though, and I'd like to keep it that way. He'll only worry, and at the moment, there's nothing to worry about. It's just overworking myself for too long, I'm sure of it.

"Thank you." I sit on the stool next to Nate, with a view of the entire garage and a bunch of screens that are like looking at *The Matrix.*

Beckett grabs my hand and squeezes it before heading to the front where his car is. Watching him get into the zone, gear up, and climb into the small space is wildly attractive. I've never been into athletes, but damn it if he's not the exception. His confidence shines through, and I can't wait to really watch him in action, not on TV and not when I was in shock about figuring out who he really is.

A voice sounds in my ears. "He talks about you a lot."

I startle and look over at Nate.

"We're on our own channel; no one can hear us."

"Umm, okay?"

"He's never brought someone to the garage, let alone a woman."

"This feels like maybe something he should be telling me, not you," I counter.

His smirk shows his boyish charm, somehow both the opposite of Beckett and the same. I would venture a guess that most people don't see that side of Beckett, though.

"And now I can see why he likes you."

"Why's that?"

"You're not letting me gossip about him behind his back, and you aren't eager for information. You also very elegantly put me in my place. You're protecting him, even if you don't want to own up to it."

His assessment is thorough for a two-minute conversation, but he's also not wrong.

"So, tell me, what do you do as his trainer?" Changing the subject and turning the focus onto him is the safe choice. And I need the safe choice right now. I don't want to analyze my feelings or talk about what could be if only we both didn't travel all the fucking time. Even with me slowing down on my travel, my schedule is still packed.

"So, he *does* talk about me." His eyes flutter as his hand comes up to his heart in exaggeration.

"Lovely. Another bromance? Luka wasn't enough?"

He scoffs. "Luka is child's play. He isn't with him twenty-four, seven like I am."

"So, you're his live-in boyfriend?" I tease.

He stares at me for a minute, either shocked I went there or appalled; I can't tell which.

"If he doesn't snatch you up, I call next," he murmurs into the headphones so low that I almost don't hear him.

But I do. I roll my lips inward to stop my laughter. No need to fuel his ego.

Turning my attention back to Beckett, I watch the mechanics direct him out of the garage, and then he's gone. As my gaze travels over all the people working, eyes meet mine before quickly shifting away, all of them telling me more about my presence here than any words would. I'm an anomaly, something strange in Beckett's world, and I suddenly feel out of place.

Nate points to a screen. "They'll have this one with all the colored dots on at all times. It's hard to follow if you don't know who you're looking for. And they'll have multiple screens with his view and other angles. We can see them all from here, the entire practice."

I nod, looking at all the screens. It's amazing how many viewpoints they have of one car, considering there are twenty of them on the track. Nate's right about the track screen; I don't know what I'm looking at, so all the dots circling the track don't mean much to me at the moment. What I do love is seeing things from Beckett's point of view. I subscribe to the whole F1 channel stream that allows you to watch this camera angle, but it's different when you can hear his radio the entire time. His voice is different, more serious and focused than I've ever heard.

Practice is roughly an hour. Nate shows me where the catering area is, and he and Beckett join me after their debrief.

The second practice of the day is much the same, and I don't get much time with Beckett, but I do get to know Nate more. I've learned he's Beckett's biggest support and has been with him almost as long as he's been racing. He's a great guy, and I'm glad Beckett has someone like him on his team, so he isn't so lonely on his road to success.

***

Race day is here, and Beckett is starting in pole position. I'm on the edge of my seat, gripping the table in front of me until my knuckles turn white.

"He'll be good," Nate murmurs into the speaker of his headphones.

I nod in reply. Talking won't be happening until this race is over. My heart is in my throat, and my breathing is halted as the lights move through the five series of red lights before the last one shuts off.

The cars zip off, and I *feel* the energy. Even from the garage, it's a different feeling than practice or qualifiers. Everyone is equal parts excited and nervous, sharp and ready to go at a moment's notice if a crash or a pit stop is needed. It's incredible to be this close.

I hold my breath for what feels like the entire race, all fifty-seven laps, and scream my lungs out as my man crosses the finish line first.

My man. Shit.

Nate is jumping up and down, and I quickly join him. His arms wrap me in a bear hug, picking me up as he jumps.

"Oh my God, he did it!" he screams into the microphone, and I wince at how loud he is.

"He did!" I chuckle. His emotions are coming out in full force, and I love seeing how much he supports Beckett. Nate's come to feel like an older brother I never had.

I tap his shoulder, pointing to the floor so he can put me down. Him squeezing my arms is making them hurt from the stiffness of inactivity. Being tense the entire race probably didn't help either.

Nate yanks my headphones off and leads me to the area where Beckett parks the car. The moment, the excitement, is infectious. It feels like everyone is vibrating. When Beckett gets out of his car then does his weigh-in, he sprints over to where the team is waiting for him. He jumps into them like he's going to go surfing in a mosh pit before they gently place him back on the ground. He bro-hugs Nate then turns to me with a huge smile on his face.

Cupping my jaw, he leans down and presses the softest kiss to my lips. Guess his image as the asshole driver on the grid is gone now. In a moment full of so much energy, it's like the world has stopped for a second with this kiss.

And then the cameras' flashing lights hit, and I step away. Moment over.

The rest of the day goes off without a hitch. I check my phone once when Daisy texts me, freaking out about all the media attention my and Beckett's kiss is getting, so I tell her I'm going dark and shut the damn thing off. I'll face what that kiss means eventually, but not right now.

Because right now, I'm going to take Beckett back to my room and show him what winners get.

Chapter 22

Beckett

I can't remember a time I felt this damn good.

Sure, winning Miami was great, but I've won races before. I've never won with Sydney in the garage, watching me. I've never had her waiting for me in the crowd.

I'm higher than cloud nine if that's even possible.

She drags me through the door of her hotel room, pausing just inside as I close the door. I slump against it, the relief of being done with the race and the exhaustion from the weekend hitting me all at once.

"Tell me what you need. I don't know how you decompress after a race," Sydney says softly, wringing her hands together.

"I need you, baby. That's it."

Her smile hits me like a sledgehammer. "You have me, Beckett. The question is *how* do you want me? Do you need to just crash in bed? Relax in the bath? Let out some adrenaline still floating around your system?"

"Well, a shower is definitely needed. Then maybe we order some food and lounge in bed? I really want to just hold you for a while." The exhaustion comes fast and hard after races. Even with Sydney being in the garage, my body is shutting down faster than I can keep up with.

"I can make that happen." She pulls my hand, leading me to the bathroom. She turns the shower on, shuffling things around on a shelf and acting a little frazzled.

"Hey." I pull her to me. "Do you want to join me?"

"I was going to put the room service order in," she whispers.

"Okay. Do that, then join me." I press a kiss to her too tempting lips. "Steak, all the sides please," I murmur against her before stepping back, leaving her dazed.

I quickly strip out of my jeans and team polo while I watch her refocus and pull out her phone to put the order in.

Once she's done, she looks up at me with so many questions written on her face. "They'll be about half an hour."

"Great. Now, get your ass in here." Turning around and rinsing out my hair, I count to five before the glass shower door opens and she steps inside.

Her soft touch trails up my stomach to my chest, before wrapping around my neck. I pull her close and let the water cascade over us both. The stress, the tension I've been holding since I got into my car a few hours ago, slowly starts to dissipate.

My mind wanders as we stand under the warm water. This woman has no clue how she's tilted my world on its axis. She has no clue that I'd do just about anything to call her mine. *Really mine*, not just friends who see each other occasionally and hook up. Because she's so much fucking more than that to me. She's *everything*.

And somehow, I have to convince her I'm worth battling the distance and the hectic schedules to be together.

Her hand cups my jaw as she looks up at me. "I am so fucking proud of you. I've never witnessed something so incredible as you winning that race today." I can barely hear her over the water spraying around us, but I do, and her words make my heart melt.

"It's just a car race, baby. I don't build entire resorts, run an entire company, and keep people happy every single day."

She scoffs. "Trust me, it's not glamourous at all."

Pressing my forehead to hers, I smile. "I'm going to need you to learn to take compliments because I plan to give you a shit-ton of them." I press a soft kiss to her nose, then her forehead, before making my way to her lips again. They're addicting, and if she's in the same room as me, you can bet I'm going to be kissing her every chance I can get.

"You're a charmer after a race, Mr. Davis."

"Only for you."

Her eyes shift between mine before she steps back. "I should get dressed for when they deliver the food. But, umm, take your time."

I watch as she damn near sprints from the shower, toweling off quickly, before going into the bedroom. Sighing, I lean against the tile and close my eyes.

I pushed it too far, too fast. I know she's skittish and that I have to ease into things, but I wish we could push all the formalities away and just be together. It's a delicate dance between pushing her just enough to move us forward while still holding back. I hate every second of it. It's been almost three years of waiting, and it's wearing on me more than I want to admit.

After quickly washing up, I step out of the shower and dry my hair with a towel before wrapping it around my waist. I vow to put all this uncertainty in the back of my mind for the rest of the night. I just won Miami; tonight is the night to enjoy the win and my woman, and get a look at what could be with us. To embrace the happiness and not think about all of the obstacles. Staying in the moment seems to be a theme with us.

After walking out to the living room, I spot Sydney wheeling the room service cart inside. After making my way to her, I drag it to the bedroom as she watches me with curiosity in her eyes.

"We're having dinner—well, late-night food, I guess—in bed. Pick a movie, show, or whatever, and come be lazy with me."

The soft smile on her face will be branded in my mind for years to come. This is what I want. After every race, every night, I want to come home and see her beautiful face. I want to hold her as we fall asleep, and wake up in the morning to see her grumpy face when she doesn't want to get up yet.

I leave the food cart by the side of the bed as I drop my towel and throw on some boxer briefs before climbing into bed. She follows shortly, climbing under the covers and propping herself up against the headboard. I dish out our food as she pulls up some reality TV show about people working on a luxury yacht.

"What are we watching?" Shoveling a bite of steak into my mouth, I tilt my head in question.

"Only the best drama ever. We can totally change it, but it's nice to get lost in the show and forget about the real world sometimes. It's my guilty pleasure. It's also super fun to see people with too much money acting crazy for someone else for a change." She smiles as she takes a bite of a french fry.

"I will watch whatever you want to watch, baby."

We watch a full episode as we finish our food. I quickly put the cart out in the hallway before rushing back and jumping under the covers.

"Did I miss anything?" I look at the television frantically.

"Nope. It just came back on. They're about to tell us who the new tenants are for this trip."

I sag against the headboard in relief, right as a giggle bubbles from Sydney's chest.

"What?"

"You're really into this." She gestures to the television.

"Seems your guilty pleasure has rubbed off on me. Now, shush. I want to see what the next bro does for a living." I tug her to me, wrapping my arm around her as she rests her head on my chest.

We watch another two episodes before Sydney starts to feel heavy on me. Gingerly, I grab for the remote, shut the show off, and try to slide down to get her more comfortable.

"Beckett?" she mumbles.

"Hey, I'm just getting you more comfortable for bed," I whisper.

She shimmies down the bed with me, moving back a little so we're face-to-face as we lie next to each other.

"I really enjoyed today. Watching you in your element, coming back here and just ... existing together was..." She sighs. "Perfect."

"It's been my favorite race and my favorite day in far longer than I can remember. Thank you for being here." Cupping her cheek, I press a barely-there kiss to her lips.

Before I can pull back, her hand moves up my arm to the back of my neck, holding me to her.

This kiss is different. It's not hurried or leading to something more. It's an intimacy we haven't had before. A closeness I desperately want in my life, but only with her.

The languid kisses seem to last forever. Minutes could have passed, hours, or days, and I wouldn't know the difference. I'm too lost in Sydney. Too lost in how damn *good* this feels.

Soft touches.

Fingertips trailing over skin.

Hearts beating faster.

The night feels vulnerable in a way we've never been, like we're wordlessly accepting this thing between us.

It doesn't mean things will change overnight. Lord knows we have too much shit to figure out. But for tonight, I'm going to bask in this happiness a little longer.

Chapter 23

MAY 26

Monaco/Austin

That was the worst fucking race I've had in a long time.

I'm sorry. I crashed halfway through and just woke up, so I didn't see all of it.

Are you feeling okay? Getting enough sleep?

I feel like I'm sleeping okay, but I'm so damn tired all the time. I don't know. I'm sure it's just a crazy work schedule catching up on me. Back to your race…

Absolutely not back to my race. How can I help? Do I need to call Pierce and make him let you work less? Take a vacation? You can come to any of my races as a break, although I don't know how relaxing that would be.

Sydney 12:17 pm CDT (UTC-5)

Beckett, I'm fine. I promise.

JULY 10

London/Cook Island

Sydney 9:21 am CKT (UTC-10)

Never before have I hated being in a tropical paradise.

Beckett 8:23 pm BST (UTC+1)

How come?

Sydney 9:24 am CKT (UTC-10)

I just want to go home. 90% of what I've been doing here could have been in an email or video conference. I'm tired, grumpy, annoyed, and over it all.

Beckett 8:25 pm BST (UTC+1)

Then go home. You took Pierce's private jet, right? Just tell the GM that you're out and to email you all that bullshit.

Sydney 9:26 am CKT (UTC-10)

I can't just peace out and ditch out on my job, Beckett. I came down here for a reason, and even if I think it's bullshit, I still need to see it through.

Beckett 8:27 pm BST (UTC+1)

Sydney … I'm worried about you. You've been tired and not feeling well more often than not. This is why I hate this fucking distance. I just want to take care of you, to force you to take care of yourself, and I can't because I'm stuck doing fucking training.

Sydney 9:29 am CKT (UTC-10)

We knew this was how it was going to go. It's sweet you're worrying about me, but I'm a big girl. I can handle it.

Beckett 8:30 pm BST (UTC+1)

You shouldn't have to handle it. Not on your own, at least.

AUGUST 29

Monaco/Austin

Sydney 2:41 pm CDT (UTC-5)

Good luck this weekend. You better kick Luka's ass.

Beckett 9:43 pm CEST (UTC+2)

Anything you say, baby. Honestly, though, in order to stay in the Driver's Championship race, I need a win this weekend.

Sydney 2:45 pm CDT (UTC-5)

Well, no pressure, but I'm watching everything this weekend since I'm home, so don't fuck it up. *wink*

Beckett 9:46 pm CEST (UTC+2)

Ah, shit, now I really need to kill it. Gotta impress you and make you think that driving a car really fast is peak hotness.

SYdney 2:47 pm CDT (UTC-5)

> I don't know… When you unzip your race suit and let it hang down from your waist, that might be peak hotness. But I've only seen that once in person, so what do I know.

Beckett 9:48 pm CEST (UTC+2)

> Good news, the U.S. race is only a month and a half away. I'll be sure to walk around like that the entire time you're in the garage.

Sydney 2:49 pm CDT (UTC-5)

> You sure know how to tease a woman.

SepTemBer 26

Monaco/Austin

Beckett 5:07 pm CEST (UTC+2)

> Are you sure I can't fly to you and spend some time there? I have most of the next month off; I can stay there and already be there for the Austin race.

Sydney 10:10 pm CDT (UTC-5)

> There's no guarantee that I'll even be here for most of that time. I already have one trip planned, so there's really no reason to come here and have no one to hang out with. It's not worth it.

Beckett 5:11 pm CEST (UTC+2)

> You are worth it, Sydney. If I only got one day with you, it would be worth whatever travel it takes to get there.

Sydney 10:12 pm CDT (UTC-5)

Beckett...

Beckett 5:13 pm CEST (UTC+2)

One day, you'll believe that. One day, we won't have this distance between us.

Chapter 24

BECKETT

I'm officially in Austin, and I've never been so nervous.

Not because of the race—I could drive this track in my sleep—but because things are ... up in the air with Sydney and me. There's not a ton I can do until the race is over, but I'm putting a plan together in the hopes that she can see the potential with us, maybe even want to take the leap into an actual relationship, not whatever it is we're currently doing.

I couldn't even classify what we are right now. I know I want her. I want to date her, be around her all the time, but we aren't on the same page. She pulls back when things get too close to commitment. It doesn't seem to be because she's scared of the actual commitment, although I could be way off base, but it's more that navigating it feels impossible. I've never been more annoyed with my job before. With both of our travel, we're mostly relegated to texting each other, and I fucking *hate* it. I need more.

It's why I'm pacing around the garage, trying to think of something—anything—to show Sydney I'm ready to go all in. Fuck the travel; fuck the distance. We'll figure it out. I'll fly to her after every single race if that's what needs to happen.

"I'm going to need you to chill out," Nate's voice calls from behind me.

I spin around and roll my eyes. "She should be here by now."

"And she will be, but pacing a hole into the floor won't actually help the situation."

"Nate, I love you, man, but go do something other than telling me what to do right now."

"Oh, touchy. I can go to the security check and wait for her if you're this worried about it," he offers instead of pushing back on my asshole comment.

I sigh. "Yes, please. Sorry I'm being a dick."

"I get it. You like her and have this weird pseudo-relationship with her, so your anxiety is going to stay high until she gets here." He doesn't wait for my response, not that I have a good one, before turning and heading toward the exit. His title may be trainer, but the man does so much more than that. He's a part-time therapist, part-time trainer, and full-time support system.

Twenty-seven minutes later—I wasn't counting or anything—Sydney walks through the back door of the garage like a blinding ray of sunlight. My anxiety releases all at once. All my tense muscles relax, and I breathe a sigh of relief right as Nate walks up behind her with a genuine smile on his face. He sees my reaction to her and is just happy he doesn't have to talk me down before practice starts. It wouldn't be the first time.

"Hi," she says with a shy smile on her face.

"Hi." I walk up to her and do what I've been holding in since Miami—I kiss her with all the built-up want, *need,* I've had for the last five months.

Her lips meet mine in a soft caress. I sink into her more, pulling her to me with an arm around her waist. Time means nothing in her arms, as it usually does. It isn't until Nate clears his throat that I step back, but not before pressing one more kiss to her forehead.

"Sorry. Media is here, and you have four minutes before practice starts." At least he sounds apologetic even if his face says otherwise.

Sydney takes a giant step back, taking the headphones that Nate offers her. I run my hand through my hair, agitated that I have to jump in my car right now. It's starting to lose its luster, and the more time I spend with Sydney outside of Idaho, the more I want it to be the norm. Driving just seems to be getting in the way of that. But it's also something I can't change right now, so it's time to get my head in the game and at least show off a little.

I drag my race suit up my body, shoving my arms into the sleeves before zipping it up and attaching the Velcro at my throat. I make sure my water tube isn't tangled before putting the flame retardant balaclava on. My race engineer rattles strategies we've gone over a million times in my ear as I walk over to my car. My steering wheel is off to the side on a shelf, along with my helmet. I grab the latter, put it on my head, and make sure everything is good before handing my steering wheel to Nate and climbing into the car.

I take one last look back at Sydney as a sort of good luck charm. Nate hands me the steering wheel and taps the top of my helmet twice before stepping back and giving me a thumbs-up. I get everything attached, test my radio, and lock in my wheel.

Then I'm off for the first practice of the day.

sydney

I don't think I'll ever get over Beckett racing.

Watching it on TV is one thing, and I get into it, but watching him win a race live is so exhilarating. To watch the sheer happiness on not only his face but the whole garage is infectious. One man has the power to affect every single person's mood here, and it's wild to have that kind of impact.

The only downside is that my body is rebelling against the long day. My joints hurt, and I'm exhausted. My hands hurt so bad from gripping the table for the better part of two hours.

I'll say Formula 1 is efficient. From the end of the race to the podium is only about ten minutes, and then Beckett has to do a debrief. I'm left to my own devices as Nate joins him for it.

Popping a couple of Tylenol, I look out onto the track where fans are still basking in the excitement of a Beck Davis win. A Legacy win. Chants and songs ring out periodically, making me smile.

Thirty minutes later, a gentle hand on my back startles me.

"Sorry." Beckett cringes. "You ready to go?"

I look around, seeing only the support staff putting things away, and no one else has left the other building across from the garage.

"Why do I get the feeling you just ditched out on your debrief?"

"Well, the thing about winning is it's something you can use to your advantage. There'll be plenty of time to dissect every minute of the race, and I already set up a time when we can hold a longer meeting to appease everyone." He winks. "Fear not, Miss CEO."

I roll my eyes. "Co-CEO."

"Point still stands. You ready?"

"Where are we going?" I stand slowly, trying to hide the grimace. My stiff muscles are screaming at me. I should have walked around more during the race, but I didn't want to miss a thing.

"It's a surprise, but I know for a fact you love this place." He grabs my hand and pulls me toward the walkway that leads to where the drivers park.

When he pulls up to Perla's, my heart warms. He must have talked to Daisy, because this is one of my favorite restaurants that I rarely get to eat at because there is never an occasion to. The last time I was here was with Pierce and Jane to celebrate my new title.

"Beckett..."

"If you're about to talk negative about anything, I'm going to plug my ears. You love this place; I've never been. I just won my race, so let's celebrate." He climbs out of his fancy car that I couldn't even put a name to before walking to open my door.

"What would have happened if you didn't win?" I take his hand as he helps me out.

"I would have been wallowing in pity and hoping that dinner at your favorite restaurant would help ease the pain." He mock pouts.

"You're ridiculous." I roll my eyes.

"Possibly. Now, let's go eat. I'm so fucking hungry." He leads me in.

The moment we walk in, it feels like there's a spotlight on us. Everyone's head turns, and the murmuring starts.

"I don't think I've ever been out to eat with you. Is it always like this?" I whisper while clutching his hand.

"Nah, but I did just win a race in the same city, so it's not shocking that racing has been a topic of conversation today. I promise to limit interactions if I can, though."

"It's okay. I'm just realizing I don't know what to expect going out with you. We usually just stay in." I've known Beckett going on four years, and I'm just now realizing how little we've done outside of Idaho and hotel rooms.

"Yep. That changes today." He leans down, pressing a kiss to my cheek before following the hostess to a secluded table in the back.

His words sound so simple, but they send a shockwave through my body. *That changes today.* It can't change today. We still travel too much, don't have actual time to see each other often enough to make a relationship work, and who the hell knows what's going on with my health at this point. I've gone to the doctor, and so far, nothing except I'm working too hard and under too much stress. Not exactly helpful.

But I'll let him have tonight because I can't bear to see him sad or upset because of me.

Dinner is delicious, but my appetite is nonexistent. I'm not sure if it's from the uncertainty surrounding Beckett and me, or if it's just another symptom in the long line I have to somehow figure out. If he notices, he doesn't say anything, either too distracted by the excitement of a win or just happy to be out to dinner with me regardless of what it actually looks like. And I don't have the heart to crush that.

As we walk out of Perla, a couple of people stop Beckett to get an autograph, but no one is pushy or rude. It's actually nice to see him in his element, how he cares about his fans and chats with them instead of brushing them to the side.

He's a good man.

He's the best and deserves more than I'm able to give him.

The thought strikes me so hard that I have to physically stop myself from tearing up.

Once we're back in his car he turns to face me. "My hotel or..."

I know the answer is his hotel. It keeps a level of separation we've always had.

"My house," I whisper instead.

Will I regret this in the morning? Most likely, but just one more night of feeling him with me, of him holding me and feeling like someone truly cares about me, won't make a difference.

Until you pull back and hurt him.

God, I hope I don't hurt him. Maybe we can figure things out. Maybe once my health shit gets figured out, I can sit down and really try to make things work between us. Make him and this thing between up a priority.

He's the only man I've wanted for years, and I can't picture anyone else in my life.

Clearly, my head is a fucking mess. It's even more reason to just enjoy tonight and push all the hard stuff to tomorrow. I'm obviously good at avoidance, so it shouldn't be too hard.

I give him directions to my house. His hand is on my thigh the entire time; his thumb brushes against the exposed skin, but he doesn't take it any further. Just a comforting touch.

By the time he parks in my driveway, I'm ready to crash, but I won't let him see the exhaustion.

Once we're inside, he doesn't even take in my house. Instead, he lifts me up bridal style and carries me to the bedroom I direct him to. He lays me down so gently it almost brings tears to my eyes.

"Thank you for being there all weekend," he whispers.

"Don't thank me for that."

"I'm pretty sure I won purely to impress you." He smirks as he unbuttons his shirt.

"You impress me with far less."

"Is it my dick? It's my dick that impresses you, isn't it?"

Laughter bursts from me. "We were having a moment and everything."

"You don't want to have a serious moment right now." He chuckles.

"And why's that?" I ask, but inside, I'm scared that he knows me so well. Having a serious moment means facing this thing between us head-on. I'm too chicken-shit to do that right now, and apparently, he knows that.

"Because you avoid the serious stuff if given the chance. I'm not saying it's a bad thing; I'm just saying we'll be digging into it all at some point, baby." He shucks his pants off.

My heart clenches hard in my chest. *I fear I'm already too far gone, and having the conversations is just a formality at this point.*

His hands slide up my thighs, dragging my dress up with them. Once I'm in only my bralette and panties, he lies down next to me, cupping my cheek.

"Can we just … *feel* tonight? No endgame, nothing fast-paced, just … being together?" he murmurs against my lips.

I nod. There's really no other response I can give this man. Our lives may be crazy and unpredictable, but he's shown time and time again that he wants me. He wants to be in my life and not just for a quick night here and there. Our commitment issues are firmly on my shoulders, and that's never been more apparent than right now.

For the rest of the night, he shows me exactly the kind of man he is and makes a strong case for me to figure my shit out.

Chapter 25

OCTOBER 28

Mexico City/Austin

Beckett 7:13 am CST (UTC-6)

Headed to the airport and back to Monaco. How are you doing? Feeling better?

Sydney 8:15 am CDT (UTC-5)

I'm okay. Just at the office trying to get some work done.

Beckett 7:16 am CST (UTC-6)

And how are you feeling?

Sydney 8:17 am CDT (UTC-5)

About the same.

Beckett 7:18 am CST (UTC-6)

Have you made an appointment? This seems like it's been going on too long to just be the result of being overworked.

Sydney 8:19 am CDT (UTC-5)

Yes, *Dad.* I've been going to the doctor to try and figure it out, but so far, no answers.

Beckett 7:20 am CST (UTC-6)

I'm not really into a Daddy kink, but if it makes you feel better, we could try it out.

Sydney 8:20 am CDT (UTC-5)

Ha ha. No, thanks.

Beckett 7:21 am CST (UTC-6)

Seriously, though, please keep me updated on what's going on. I'm worried about you.

Sydney 8:22 am CDT (UTC-5)

I'm fine, just annoyed there don't seem to be answers. You have enough to worry about without throwing me into the mix. Have a safe flight and text me when you land.

Beckett 7:23 am CST (UTC-6)

It doesn't work like that, and you know it. I'll always worry about you.

November 6

Monaco/Austin

Sydney 10:48 am CDT (UTC-5)

Just watched the Brazil race. Amazing win, Beckett!

Beckett 5:49 pm CEST (UTC+2)

Thanks. You okay? How come you didn't watch it earlier? (That's not me being self-important; you just usually watch it live or later that day.)

Sydney 10:51 am CDT (UTC-5)

Thanks for the clarification on that one. I had a rough day on Sunday and didn't do a whole lot. Then between work and doctor's appointments, I just didn't have time, sorry.

Beckett 5:51 pm CEST (UTC+2)

What are the doctors saying? Are you okay? I can fly out there. I don't have a race until Vegas.

Sydney 10:52 am CDT (UTC-5)

Take a deep breath, Beckett. I'm okay. It's just been a rough week. No answers. Lots of bloodwork and waiting on that mostly. If anything is wrong, I'll let you know. And don't fly out here. I have a shit-ton of work to make up for, and I'll be super busy until Vegas, basically.

Beckett 5:53 pm CEST (UTC+2)

I fucking hate this. Just let me come to you. I'll chill at your house. Or hell, I'll get a hotel. I don't care. Let me come take care of you.

Sydney 10:54 am CDT (UTC-5)

Beckett, I'm fine. There's no reason to be bored here when you have other shit to do.

Beckett 5:55 pm CEST (UTC+2)

Nothing about this is fine, and it pisses me off you won't let me come to you.

Sydney 10:54 am CDT (UTC-5)

Well, it's a good thing you won't be coming out here then because you'll just be more pissed sitting here doing nothing. If anything happens, you'll be the first to know. Go do your racecar driver stuff, and I promise I'll see you early in Vegas.

November 17

Las Vegas/Austin

Beckett 3:01 pm PDT (UTC-7)

Just landed and making my way to the hotel

Sydney 5:03 pm CDT (UTC-5)

I can't get the plane until tomorrow morning, but I should be there bright and early.

Beckett 3:04 pm PDT (UTC-7)

Then I can't wait for the wake-up call.

Sydney 5:05 pm CDT (UTC-5)

I'm excited to see you.

Beckett 3:06 pm PDT (UTC-7)

Same baby. It's been too long.

Chapter 26
Beckett

As my steering wheel clicks into place, my race engineer does a radio check. "Copy, loud and clear."

I don't feel my usual calm once I'm in the car. No, I feel antsy. *Worried.* Because of Sydney. A good luck kiss before I stepped into the car isn't enough. Hell, a week with her isn't enough.

I can't stop thinking about her. Her health, her subtly pushing me away... All of it runs through my head on repeat.

For three years, we've been running circles around each other. For three years, she's been the only woman I've wanted. And this year, she's actually given me the gift of *time.* She's been to more races than the last years combined. We've spent more time together—hell, we went on a date the other day—and I loved every single second of it. But I want more.

The mechanic in front of me signals me to pull into the pit lane and join the queue of cars. As we get lined up in our positions, I sit in second, anticipating the rush of the start. Luka and I are neck to neck in the standings, so I need every win, every point, in order to win the Drivers' Championship this year. After his win last year, it feels like I *have* to win. This season has been mine to lose, and I'm ready to claim the title.

However, Sydney is giving my concentration a run for its money.

I watch as the lights shift from red to the second red and will my mind to focus. The countdown continues, and as soon as the red lights shut off, I'm off.

It's a hard battle to the first corner, but I outdrive Luka and overtake him. He stays close on my tail through the chicane. The voice in my ear keeps me updated on how far back he is and if anything major is happening in the back half of the race. Luckily, the start of the race seems to have gone off without any incidents.

By the sixth lap, Luka and I have pulled away from the rest of the drivers enough to race our own race. It allows the stress of the initial start to roll off my shoulders and my mind to wander.

That's the thing about driving in Formula 1; we all know these tracks like the back of our hands. Even here, in Las Vegas, we've been virtually practicing the track all year, so nothing is a huge surprise. It lets your mind wander, especially with a significant lead. And to no one's shock, mine wanders to Sydney.

There's more going on; I can feel it in my gut. She's always tired, and she hasn't traveled outside of Austin in months. When we were together at her house, I could tell she wasn't one hundred percent. She moved a little slower, especially in the morning. Sydney may have thought she was doing a good job of hiding it all from me, but I picked up on every little twinge. Her face couldn't hide the small grimaces from me.

All I want to do is help. I know I can't. I'm not a doctor and I have no clue how to make things better, especially when she doesn't have any answers, but fuck, I feel so fucking helpless. It's my job to make her life better, to help her when she needs it, and I'm failing on so many levels. Yes, she hasn't exactly committed to this thing between us, but that doesn't change a damn thing for me.

It's no longer about wanting her in my life. I *need* her in it. Every morning I wake up, she's in my thoughts immediately. At night, she's the last thing I think about, and even then, she shows up in my dreams. Sydney is everything I want in my future, but we're just stuck in this limbo. I fear things won't change until one of us cuts back dramatically in our jobs, which is impossible right now. One of us needing to sacrifice their career to be together feels wrong too.

I take turn five, a hard right, and look toward my inside, seeing Luka trying to overtake me.

Not today, asshole.

There's too much turmoil in my head to let him pass me. This compulsion to dominate, to leave everyone in the dust today, is a personal vendetta against myself. A need to have control over *something*. Especially when the person I'd like to have more control with is currently hiding so much of herself from me.

I'm not oblivious; I know she's keeping herself locked up tight. What I can't figure out is why. The distance can't be the only thing. Hell, we both have the means to fly to each other every week if we wanted to. No, there's more to this, and no matter what I do, she won't open up to me.

So, taking out my frustrations on this race seems to be my only option.

"Box, box. We're on plan A at the moment, and you're looking great, Beck," the voice in my headset calls out.

On lap twenty-three, I pull into the pit and wait the almost two seconds before the guy with the jack moves out of the way, letting me pull out to the pit lane quickly. I watch my speed, and as soon as I'm clear, I haul ass back in the number one spot. Luka and I were ahead enough that our pit stops won't change the line-up—a luxury I'm glad for today since my head is such a mess. Nate would dick punch me if he knew where my attention was right now. I'm just glad he's on Sydney duty, so he isn't hyper-focused on me like usual.

Win or lose the race, tonight, I need to lay things out there for her.

By lap thirty-two, my thoughts turn to exactly what I want with the woman waiting in the garage for me. Obviously, I want an actual relationship. If I'm honest with myself, I've been acting like she's my girlfriend for a while now. I text her whenever something pops up. She's the first person I talk to when something exciting happens or when Nate decides to kick my ass training and I can barely move. The singular thing I'm missing is spending more time with her.

During the season, there are only a handful of weeks where we have races every week, so travel is a struggle. Otherwise, I can easily fly to her after races. Maybe that's what I need to commit to. She's struggling with things we have no control over right now, so if I step up, we could really make this work.

Should I look for a place in Austin?

Ideally, I'd rather stay with Sydney, but I'm not delusional enough to think she'd be all in at the same time I am.

"Tires are looking good, Beck. Keep an eye on them, but we should be good to the end," my engineer scares me.

"Yep, I'm watching them. What's my lead time look like?"

"Luka is currently six-point-nine seconds back with seven laps left."

Relief hits my shoulders, and if I could slump down, I would. Unfortunately, that's not possible in an F1 car, but knowing that I'm basically in the clear is nice. And I just have to hope nothing ridiculous happens.

Winning today means a decent cushion going into the final two races. Luka is still too close for comfort in points, but if I can win one of the last two, I'll be in the clear for the Championship.

With that stress off my shoulders, I spend the last five laps thinking about how I want the night to go with Sydney. Spilling all my hopes and dreams on her will inevitably push her away. I know her well enough by now to know that, but if I can be clear with her that I want to make a real go of this, it will give her a few weeks to sit on it.

God, I hope this isn't the wrong thing to do.

I can't even begin to think about what life would be like without her. Who knew a chance meeting at a remote Idaho resort would lead to something like this.

"Last lap, Beck. Keep it steady."

I ignore the message. Obviously, I'm going to keep it steady; it's my job, and with Luka too far behind to catch up, I'm not jeopardizing shit now.

As I cross the finish line, the only thing I want to do is hug Sydney. I feel like a dick. Our team has worked their ass off for every single win, and I don't even care right now. I want to ditch the celebrations, the podium, and just take my woman back to my room. Now that I've decided to lay my cards out for her, it's all I can think about.

But I can't ignore my job; I know that.

Pulling into the spot reserved for the race winner shifts my focus toward this win. Seeing the guys so excited is infectious. I body surf into the group, feeling pats all over my body before they put me down. I immediately look around for Nate and Sydney and spot them hanging off to the side. There's no easy way to get to them, and I'm expected to be in the cooldown room immediately after my weigh-in.

Nodding to Nate, a silent communication to stay close to Sydney, I turn to blow her a kiss before I get pulled back into the crowd.

Tonight. I'm ready to get this damn race over so I can go all in.

***

Anxiety courses through my body. After celebrations, food, and a shower, Sydney and I are lying in bed, cuddled together.

I comb my fingers through her hair as I try to come up with the words to articulate how I'm feeling.

"So, what needs to happen for you to win the Championship?" she interrupts my thoughts.

"I need to beat Luka on points for at least one of the remaining two races, preferably with a win. He has to win at least one race and outscore me on the other in order to win."

"That's good then, right? All you have to do is keep Luka in check?" she asks, fingers tracing circles on my stomach.

I laugh at her simple description. "Yep, super simple. He's tough, and he's not going to let me just have it. I expect him to give me one hell of a hard time."

"You're on a roll. You'll totally take it." Her conviction makes it all seem possible.

We lie there, soaking in each other. I'm not sure what's going through her head, but I know this is my chance. I need to take this step.

"I want this," I whisper, scared of the potential fallout. "As often as I can get it, I want this, Sydney."

"Beckett..."

"Pretending like seeing each other a handful of times a year is enough isn't working for me. I need more. I have the means to fly to wherever you are. There're only a few weeks throughout the year where I can't come to you after a race, but maybe we can work out you coming to me for those. I can get a place in Austin if that makes things easier," I ramble. I can't help it. Once I start, I can't stop, and now everything is coming out in one jumbled mess. "We can still do Idaho for Christmas every year. I'd honestly be sad if we ever stopped that tradition." I shake my head at my wayward thoughts. "I just... I want to make a real go of things with you, baby. We've spent so much time apart that I'm reaching a point where I can't do it anymore. I *hate* waking up without you. My bed doesn't feel right without you in it."

Her body tenses, and in this moment, I know she's going to run. Maybe not this second, but she's going to pull away. She's not ready.

"I'm not asking you for anything right now. I'm just telling you where I'm at and what I'm willing to do to make that happen. Take your time thinking about it; we can talk more about it all this Christmas." *Fuck, I hope she doesn't ditch me in Idaho.* I don't think my heart can take that. "I'm not trying to pressure you," I add, hoping it lessens the pressure she's inevitably feeling. I don't want to put her under stress—that's never my intention—but I know that's how she's taking it.

It was a risk to bare my soul tonight, but it felt like the words would burst from me at the wrong time if I didn't.

Her hand slowly starts to brush against my skin, and her muscles finally relax.

Pressing a kiss to the crown of her head, I vow to do anything in my power to make this woman mine. No matter how long it takes.

Chapter 27
SYDNEY

I've been a fucking mess since Vegas.

Between blood test results that have been inconclusive, no change in symptoms, and things with Beckett, I'm so unsure of myself—of my life.

Pierce has been incredible through it all. When I need to work from home, it's no issue. I've stopped traveling completely, and things haven't fallen apart. He was right all along; we have a great team under us, and micromanaging them wasn't helping anyone. I just wish it wasn't my body hating me that made me come to that realization.

As I cuddle under the blankets on my couch, Beckett is racing in Qatar. My heart is in my throat because Luka looks like he's a shoo-in to win today, and that puts more pressure on Beckett for the last race.

I also haven't stopped thinking about that night in Vegas. I'm not a fool; I knew that was where we were headed all along, but for whatever reason, I thought we had more time to stabilize our lives a little. It still feels so distant. His travel is still all over the place, and who the hell knows what's going on with my body, but the quest to find answers is proving to be time-consuming. I don't know how to make this work. I don't know how to give him what he wants.

Maybe I am scared.

Beckett is every woman's dream come true. He's smart, attentive, so damn good to me I can't even begin to wrap my head around it, and yet I feel like I'm not enough. I barely make time for myself, so how can I bring a man into my world? How can I give him the time and the effort he deserves? I told myself I'd figure out my shit, and yet here I am months later, with no progress.

Honestly, I don't know if I can. My heart breaks at the realization that maybe

I just have to accept that I can't be enough for Beckett. Maybe I have to accept that I'm not cut out to be a girlfriend.

Tears fill my eyes as I watch the final lap. Beckett can't catch up to Luka, which means all the pressure is on the final race. In some convoluted way, I feel like I've cursed the race. My lack of commitment to him has made things harder for him. My hesitation means he has to work all that much harder in the last race.

Fatigue hits me hard. I fall asleep with tears trailing down my cheeks, and I never hear my phone ringing. I don't get the messages, the pleads to call him back, until the next day when I feel like I'm a lost cause. When the guilt that things will just be too hard for us settles deep into my soul.

***

Two days later, I'm bustling into the office almost late for a conference call with our resort in Turkey.

I'm not proud to say I've been mostly ignoring Beckett, only responding with the bare minimum. I can't wrap my head around what being with him means and how the hell we even have a relationship with our busy lives. He threw all these crazy ideas around, like getting a place here, but I'd be pulling him away from his life in order to be with me, and I *hate* the thought of that.

"Everything's set up in the conference room!" Daisy yells as I rush past her.

I wave my hand up, letting her know I heard her, and round the corner too quickly, catching my foot on the edge of the wall.

I go down hard.

The pain doesn't register at first. Just the embarrassment that I tripped while being in a hurry. Daisy comes to my aid at record speed, kneeling down and frantically looking at my limbs for injury.

"I'm good," I grunt. "Can you go let the GM know I'm running five minutes late? Then you can help me up."

She stares at me like I've lost my mind, but I'm already focused on the job. She does as I ask, and I don't register the fact that I can't really move my body right now until she comes back.

"I'm a little freaked out that you're still lying here," she says with worry in her eyes.

"Yeah, me too," I whisper. I move my hands; they're fine. Next, my feet. A twinge radiates up my leg, and I whimper. "My foot."

Daisy moves to my left foot, softly pressing into it to help narrow down where the problem is. I jolt when she hits my ankle, tears rushing to my eyes as I shift myself to sit up against the wall.

"Okay, here's what's going to happen." She pulls out her phone, taking charge. I'm immensely thankful for her and her ability to step in whenever I need her. "I'm going to call Pierce and let him know what's going on. Then, I'm going to cancel your conference call, send them all cliff notes, and request all the things you need to be sent by email. Then, we're going to the hospital."

"It's not that bad, Daisy." I flex my foot and cry out at the pain. *Shit, this is not what I need right now.*

"It is that bad, you stubborn mule." She isn't even looking at me, too busy being Wonder Woman and handling all my shit for me.

The feeling of inadequacy I've been wrestling with for days rears its ugly head. I can't even do my job to the full extent. Fat, ugly tears fall from my eyes as I realize just how little I can handle right now.

"Oh, Syd. It's okay. No tears. I've got it handled." Her voice is a little panicked and a lot placating, and it just makes me cry harder.

A failure on all levels. That's the predominant feeling.

Once she handles things, she gingerly helps me up, and we hobble out to her car. Thank God the elevator is close to both where I fell and her car. As we make our way to the hospital, my tears finally dry.

"How do you do it?" I ask in a gravelly voice.

"Do what?" She looks over at me with a furrowed brow.

"How do you handle everything so well? How do you have a relationship—hell, a marriage—with Luka and still make things work?" If there's anyone who understands my struggles, it's Daisy. I still don't know how she and Luka committed to things so easily.

"Umm, I don't? I have support and help, and you pay me nicely so I can afford to fly out to see him whenever I want to, although he's more than capable of flying me out too. But you allow me to work from anywhere most of the time. That's the best part of our job; we're not relegated to an office, and on the rare occasions we actually need to go to a resort, it isn't for any extended amount of time."

She hits a bump, and I hiss in pain.

"But how is it just so easy for you? How do you handle the times you're not together?"

"Can I be super blunt right now while I have you incapacitated and you can't do bodily harm?"

"When have I done bodily harm to you?" I ask in mock outrage.

"Never, but I'm about to be mean, so you never know." She shrugs.

"Just lay it on me."

"If you want it—want *him*—bad enough, you make it happen. It will never *not* be scary. It will almost always be hard, but it's worth the fight. It's worth the travel and the distance. Being with Luka is the best thing that's ever happened to me, and I'll take every minute I can get with him."

"But what if it doesn't work out and we went through this hell for nothing?"

"How did you become co-CEO of Vanstone Properties?" she asks out of left field.

"Umm, I made sacrifices and did whatever I needed to do to be the best assistant Pierce has ever had. And I continued to work hard as I rose up through the ranks."

"So, why can you do that for a job but not a man you're in love with?"

"I'm not in love with him," I immediately counter. *I'm not, am I?*

Daisy snorts. "Sure, Syd. Whatever helps you sleep at night. I'm just saying, if you're so willing to bust your ass for a job, why is it any different to do the same for Beckett? You're happier with him, less stressed, and less of a workaholic. You've delegated more in this last year than you ever had, and the company is all the better for it. Don't let fear stop you from living the kind of life you want to live. Don't let the what-ifs and the distance be an excuse to not be happy. You both have the means to not allow distance to derail you. Hell, from what Luka's told me, the man is ready to move to Austin for you. So, what are you so afraid of?"

Daisy, ladies and gentlemen. Somehow, my bubbly and sometimes ditsy friend and assistant is the wise one between us now.

"I'm afraid I'm not enough. He's so damn good, Dais. How do I keep up with that?" I murmur.

"I love you so much, but you are so damn irritating right now. You are more than enough. You are the best person I know. You will literally drop everything for someone who needs help. You're on your way to the hospital right now, but you made sure things were handled at your job first because you didn't want to waste people's time. You put everyone ahead of you. When is it your turn? Beckett sees it; that's why he's so gone for you. I won't pretend to know what's going on with the two of you, but letting him decide what and *who* he wants is probably a good approach. At the end of the day, if you both want a relationship with each other, then what's stopping you?"

Great question and one I don't have an answer for. Well, all of my answers now seem flimsy.

Daisy pulls up to the emergency department entrance.

"Stay put. I'll be right back." She issues the order in a no-nonsense tone.

"Yes, ma'am."

Within a minute, she's back with a wheelchair, and the pain I pushed away while we were talking about my love life—or lack thereof—roars back to life.

We struggle to shift me to the wheelchair, but once we finally do, we get settled inside and they call me back within minutes. Before I can process what's happening, they have X-rays taken and a fresh round of blood work.

They refer me to a specialist after the results come back and boot my foot. Luckily, it appears to be a small fracture that I won't need anything other than a boot for a couple weeks for.

Daisy gets me settled at home several hours later and tells me she'll handle all the things. I fall asleep quickly, thanks to the pain meds I was given, and the pattern repeats for another day. Sleep takes my mind off the pain and Beckett.

The next night, I shut my phone off and fall into a dreamless sleep.

I don't wake up until mid-afternoon the next day to a pounding on my door.

Chapter 28
BECKETT

Worry like no other courses through my bones.

I haven't heard from Sydney in almost two full days, and even after our shaky time in Las Vegas, we still talk every day.

I jog over to the Empress Racing area to find the one man who may have a clue what's going on.

Heads turn as I check the garage, but no one has the balls to kick me out. Thank God because I think I would seriously hurt someone if they stopped me from finding Luka right now.

I finally find him in the little lounge in the building behind the garage, pacing.

"Does Daisy know what's going on with Sydney? Did something happen?" I rush out.

"Woah, man, slow down. Why can't you just call Sydney?"

"What a wonderful fucking idea, Luka. What a revelation and definitely not something I've been trying since yesterday."

"Wow, okay. Chill out, man."

I don't think. Rational Beckett is nowhere to be found, as evidenced by my next actions.

Shoving Luka up against the wall, I get in his face. "Now is not the time to tell me to chill. There's something wrong. There has to be, and her fucking phone is off." I push off of him, running my hand through my hair as I start to pace now. "I'm sorry. Fuck, I'm sorry, Luka."

"No apology needed. Let me call Daisy and see if she knows what's up."

"Thank you." A gush of air releases from my lungs just from him helping me.

"Hey, Beckett just came and found me. He can't get a hold of Sydney. Is she okay?"

His one-sided phone call brings all my nerves to the surface. I'm scared that this is her cutting me off for good. That she doesn't want me the way I want her.

"Oh shit, is she okay?"

My heart drops at his words. Pulling my phone out of my pocket, I text the owner of Legacy Racing.

"Okay, I'll let him know. Thank you. Yeah. Yeah. Okay, I will. Love you."

I barely listen to the end of his conversation.

"She fractured her ankle."

My head pops up from the text I was sending. "What? Is she okay?"

"She's in a boot with some good pain meds for a couple of days. Daisy said she's been sleeping most of the day."

My mind races. I don't know how to help her from all the way across the world.

"She also said some of her bloodwork came back abnormal and she has to go see a specialist in a couple of days."

"What kind of specialist?" I grill him.

He holds up his hands from of his chest. "That's all I know, man. We shouldn't have even told you that because it's medical information, you dick. If she wants you to know, she should be the one to tell you."

I tilt my head back and yell at the ceiling. "Fuck!"

I think about my options. I've already set one in motion; now, I just have to find the most efficient way to get there.

"Does Daisy have contacts for private planes?"

"Umm, probably." He looks like I just gave him whiplash.

My phone rings, but I hit decline.

"Beck, what are you doing, man? She's got people looking after her. Don't do anything impulsive."

A humorless laugh leaves me. "Can you have Daisy text me some contacts for places please?" I'm already committed at this point; nothing will change my mind. I shoot off a text with a brief explanation before turning back to Luka.

"Congrats on another Championship, man. I'll be sad to miss it."

He jolts back like I just slapped him. "Fuck no," he whispers. "I can't let you do this, Beck."

"You don't really have a choice. Enjoy it, and I'll kick your ass next year, okay?"

"Beckett—"

"I can't let her do this alone, Luka. If it was Daisy, what would you do? Is this job worth more than your wife?"

He scoffs. "Never."

"That's why I need to go to her." I step up to him and give him a bro hug. "Don't lose the fucking race, okay?"

"Never." He smirks.

***

A seventeen-hour flight, one angry phone call from the owner of Legacy, and too many doom scenario thoughts to keep track of, and I'm finally standing at Sydney's door.

I knock and wait.

Nothing.

Knocking again, I try to draw up every ounce of patience I can.

Still nothing.

Finally, I pound on the door, seconds away from a full-blown panic attack.

"Hold on!" Sydney yells from inside the house, and my heart calms.

It takes her a few minutes to open the door, but when she does, she looks more exhausted than I've ever seen her.

"Sydney," I breathe out.

"Oh my God, Beckett. Why are you here? I mean, why aren't you at qualifiers?" Her voice is frantic.

I step forward, pulling her to me in a tight hug. "You scared the shit out of me."

Her little fists pound at my back. "What the fuck are you doing here?"

"You didn't answer your phone. I panicked and made Luka call Daisy. She gave me the bare minimum and helped me secure a jet here."

"I swear, when I can walk again, the three of you are getting my full wrath. What the fuck are you thinking? You're just not racing? Giving up the Championship? Are you even allowed to do that?" Her voice gets shriller with each question.

Instead of answering her, I sweep her into my arms and kick the door shut once I'm inside. I walk her to her bedroom, gently placing her down where she's clearly been sleeping.

"Beckett Davis! Answer me!"

I strip down to my boxers and crawl into bed with her, adjusting her booted foot before pulling her to me.

"I swear to G—"

"You had me so fucking worried. When Luka called Daisy, nothing else mattered except getting here. How's your ankle?"

"How's the... What the actual hell, Beckett?"

"Do you need anything? Ice, pain meds?"

"I need to know why you aren't fucking racing!" she yells.

"Because you are more important than the Championship. You are more important than anything. You're hurt, and I need to be here to support you."

"I am absolutely not more important than the Championship!" She's outraged, but it only makes me smile wider.

"How about you let me decide what's more important to me."

"This is crazy," she whispers.

"Luka said the same thing." I chuckle.

"This isn't funny, Beckett!"

"No, it's not. You fractured your ankle and apparently need to see a specialist?"

"Jesus, Daisy." She pinches the bridge of her nose.

"To be fair, I was about to punch Luka out if he didn't get me answers."

She gasps, pulling back to look at my face. "You were not."

"I absolutely was. We don't go a day without talking, so when I couldn't get through to you, I panicked."

"Panicked" seems like the tamest way to put what actually happened.

I stay quiet, letting her process the fact that I just blew off my job and ran here because I physically had to. I know it's a lot for her, so I'll give her time. Now that she's in my arms, I can finally breathe again.

"I have an appointment with a rheumatologist tomorrow," she says softly.

"What does that mean?"

"It means that I shouldn't have fractured my ankle so easily. Combined with all the other symptoms I've been having, it seems like a possible musculoskeletal or autoimmune problem, both of which they can diagnose."

A lot runs through my head, but the one thing I'm glad for is that she'll get answers.

"How's your ankle feeling?"

"Better. The boot has helped, and they gave me a handful of heavy pain meds that let me sleep for a couple of days."

"Good. That's good, baby," I murmur. My heart rate is finally something close to normal, and I can feel myself crashing hard.

"We're talking about all of this in great depth when we wake up," Sydney whispers.

"Whatever you want."

***

My body naturally woke up me early. I'm still on Abu Dahbi time, and my internal clock is all sorts of messed up.

I know the media coverage of the race is currently happening, and I'm doing everything in my power to avoid anything race related. Not because I'm regretting my decision but because it's bittersweet watching a race I should be in, that I should win. What I did yesterday is unheard of. It'll be the talk of every news source, and the last thing I want is to make Sydney feel guilty about my decision. For me, there was no decision. If I can't be there for her, then what's the point of having this fancy job? Of having all this money? I'd quit tomorrow if it means I get to be with her forever.

"How long have you been up?" Sydney's soft voice says from the hallway.

I whip around to face her. "A while. Jet lag." I shrug.

She holds my gaze for a minute before her shoulders slump. "We need to talk about a lot of things, but I need to get ready for my appointment."

"Let me get dressed, and you can give me directions." I'm already moving to the bedroom when her hand on my chest stops me.

"You don't need to come. I'm good going by myself."

Disbelief hits my chest. She really still believes that I'm going to just let her handle the hard shit on her own. That I'm not going to be here for everything I possibly can be, even with a hectic racing schedule.

If I still have a job after this season.

Nope, can't even think about that right now.

"Not happening, baby. I'm taking you, bringing a notepad, and taking a shit-ton of notes. We're going to figure this shit out together. You can't get rid of me now."

She visibly swallows. "I'm really overwhelmed," she whispers.

My whole body softens at her confession. I don't think she's ever been this vulnerable with me, and I won't take it for granted.

"I know, but we'll take this one step at a time, okay? Let's go to your appointment, see what comes from it, and then we can go from there. No pressure; we don't need to find answers for everything today. I just want to make sure you're okay."

A tear falls down her cheek.

I reach out without thinking, wiping it away with my thumb. "We'll figure this out, okay?" I murmur.

"Which part? My health or us?" She hiccups.

"Both, but your health first. I'm not going anywhere." I cup her jaw.

Her eyes close as she takes a deep breath. "Okay, let's get ready to go."

The drive only takes fifteen minutes. As we pull into the parking garage, my nerves start up.

What if it's something really bad? What if there's no treatment, no cure?

Nope, I've had enough doomsday thoughts to last a few years on the flight over here. I'm staying positive for Sydney.

Once all the paperwork is complete and all the basic vitals are taken, we're left waiting in a sterile room. Sydney's leg bounces in a frantic rhythm, but I know nothing I do will calm her down; only answers to what's plagued her for the last year will help.

A knock on the door followed by its opening announces the doctor.

"Good morning. I'm Doctor Lucy Kane. You must be Sydney. How are you doing today?" Her question is directed at Sydney, and I'm glad for it.

"I'm okay."

"I'll take okay. And you are?" She turns to me.

"Beckett. I'm Sydney's..." I trail off, realizing I just did the most faux pax thing ever.

"Boyfriend," Sydney adds.

My heart thumps heavy in my chest at her words, but it's not something I can focus on right this second.

The doctor takes a seat on the rolling stool, scooting closer to Sydney while she places her notes on the counter. "So, I'm just going to jump right in. I've taken a look at your records from the hospital and what your primary care sent over as well. How long have your symptoms been going on for?"

"A little under a year. It's mostly fatigue and joint pain in my hands and ankles."

"And are you feeling any muscle weakness?"

"Not really. It's mostly my joints that hurt regularly."

My heart hurts hearing how much she's been going through. I thought it was just fatigue, working too hard and needing to slow down. I'm realizing there may be something really wrong.

"Okay. Well, I'd like to do a physical exam today. We're lucky in the sense that the hospital did extensive bloodwork, so it's already given me an idea of what this could be, but I want to make sure I'm on the right track before I lead you astray and get your hopes up."

Sydney nods, almost in a daze. Dr. Kane leaves so Sydney can change into one of the scratchy hospital gown things before I'm mentally ready to hear what this could all mean.

Tapping my fingers on my knee, I keep my eyes averted as the doctor looks over every joint, and tests Sydney's muscle strength and reflexes.

"Okay. I'm going to let you get changed back into your clothes, and then we can discuss a diagnosis and possible treatments."

"You know what's going on?" My head whips up as I ask.

"I do," she says softly. "I'm just going to grab some booklets while she gets changed."

Sydney changes quickly then sits next to me. I can feel her nervous energy, and I don't know how to calm her down. I feel like I'm just as nervous to hear about what's going on.

"I'm scared," she whispers and threads our hands together.

"Whatever it is, we'll handle it. I'll be here every step of the way."

She rests her head on my shoulder as we wait for Dr. Kane to come back.

"All right." Dr. Kane opens the door. Her eyes soften when she spots us. "Y'all are adorable. I can see the stress radiating off of you both, but I don't want you to worry."

Sydney sits up straight, trying to put her hand back in her lap, but I don't let her. I need to support as much as she does, I think.

"Based on everything I've looked over and looking at the joints that are bothering you the most, you have rheumatoid arthritis."

"Arthritis," Sydney says in confusion. "I thought that was mostly in older people."

"Regular arthritis, sure, but RA is an autoimmune disease. It basically attacks your healthy joints because it thinks it's an infection."

"Are there treatments, Dr. Kane?" Sydney asks.

"Lucy, please. And there absolutely are. It's going to be a little bit of trial and error to see what works the best for you, but because we're figuring this out so early, we'll be able to monitor it and treat it as it develops. My aim is to lessen its progression and keep it stable. There is no cure, but we can lessen the effect on your everyday life."

We both nod in a daze. This feels huge, bigger than I think either of us thought.

"I know it's a lot to take in, but my phone and office are always open if you ever have questions. My aim is to be available to you whenever something pops into your head. An autoimmune disease can feel scary, and I want you to know you have a doctor who will pick up the phone or call you back quickly when your brain starts to overthink."

Sydney laughs, and it breaks all the tension in the room.

"I can't tell you how much I appreciate that."

"I get it. The mind can wander to the worst-case scenario, and I don't ever want you to think you have to just suffer through that. Mentally or physically."

I clear my throat. "So, it's an autoimmune disease. What does that look like long term?"

Sydney squeezes my hand. I look over at her quickly, and all I see is gratefulness in her eyes.

"Long term, it's mostly about management. This won't ever go away, but there are different levels of treatment we can move through as symptoms get worse. Anything from topical creams to surgery is an option, surgery being on the table when your joints aren't responding to any other treatment and it's affecting your life on a daily basis. The good news is that you'll be able to live a happy and healthy life with this, as long as it's managed." She hands Sydney the booklets she brought and talks about possible treatments to start immediately. "So, I want to get you started on methotrexate to really slow the progression and save the joints right from the word 'go.' I'll also get you some topical pain cream for when the joint pain flares up. I want to have a follow-up in three months, but please don't hesitate to call me if something feels off or is bothering you. The name of the game is staying on top of things. Do either of you have any questions?" She looks between us both.

"Not at the moment. It's just a lot to take in," Sydney says.

"Totally understandable. Read over the booklets, look up all the things, but please reach out with any questions. Nothing is too big or too small."

"I really appreciate it," Sydney says.

I'll admit, even with the sheer amount of information we just got, everything feels doable thanks to Dr. Kane. She's approachable, available, and listens. I'm not sure how Sydney found her, but I'm grateful nonetheless.

"I'll have the nurse send in those prescriptions to your preferred pharmacy, and we'll get your follow-up on the schedule." Dr. Kane turns to look at me. "Make sure she isn't working too hard. I get the feeling she's a workaholic." She winks.

Laughter bursts from me. "You definitely have her pegged."

"I'm right here," Sydney deadpans. She cracks a smile, and we laugh alongside her.

Once we're in the car, we both slump down.

"How do you feel?" I ask.

"Relieved. Freaked out. Confused."

"Understandable. Dr. Kane seems amazing, though."

"So amazing. I've never had a doctor actually spend time with me and then offer such an availability like she did." She sighs.

I don't want to push her after such an emotionally taxing appointment, so I stay silent as I put the car in reverse.

"We have a lot to talk about, but I... My head is a jumbled mess."

"I'm here whenever you're ready. There's no pressure, baby. There never is." The truth of my words sinks into my chest. I've been waiting for this woman for the better part of four years. Nothing will change that now. She's stuck with me even if she doesn't realize it yet.

"Thank you," she whispers.

She gives me directions to the pharmacy, and we pick up her medication. It feels domestic, and I realize with a start that I haven't even thought about the race currently happening. Once we finally make our way home, I tuck her in and sit on the bed next to her. Pulling up the race on my phone, I watch as Luka wins the Driver's Championship with a hearty lead.

Instead of regret and sadness, I feel nothing but rightness. Looking over at the woman who means more to me than I ever thought possible, I realize I'd give up everything to be by her side if that's what it takes. But the thing that rings though my head is that she would never let that happen. I'm already preparing for Sydney's wrath over me ditching the last race of the year to be here. She may be on the fence about us, or confused about how we make us work with all the distance, but she'd never let me give up something I love just to be with her.

I think I understand more of her struggle with us, her hesitation. She wants to make sure neither of us sacrifice what's important to us in order to be in a relationship with each other. The careers we've both busted our asses for are just as important as being together is. And for the first time, I realize what love really is.

Because that's what this is.

I'm in love with Sydney Johnson.

Chapter 29
Sydney

The snow falls as I sip my coffee, the soft snowflakes comforting in a way I never expected.

It's been a week since my appointment with Dr. Kane—Lucy—and collectively, the two of us thought keeping my annual Idaho trip would be good for me, help me come to terms with what my diagnosis means and give me some good rest.

Beckett hasn't left my side.

It's been ... eye-opening. We've... Okay, *I've* been avoiding talking about things with us, what our relationship is, and how I dropped the B word at the doctor's office. How he lost the Driver's Championship because of me. And he's just been letting me. It's a testament to him allowing me to come to terms with all the things that are happening in my life.

Big changes are on the horizon, and now I need to pull up my big-girl pants and talk to Beckett about it all.

"Think we'll have a white Christmas this year?" his soft voice sounds from behind me.

"I think there'll be snow on the ground, but who knows about snow falling on the actual day." I take another sip as his arms wrap around my middle.

"This will forever be one of my favorite places in the world," he murmurs into my hair.

I chuckle. "Idaho is your favorite place?"

"Oh yeah. It's the place where I met you. Where this crazy life brought us together more than once. What's not to love?"

I sigh, leaning back into his body. "We need to have some conversations."

"We do, but I'm not in a hurry. Whenever you're ready to talk about everything, I'll be here."

Gah, this man. After years of doubts, of thinking things could never work between us, he's showing me just how wrong I am.

"I'm sorry it's taken me so long to see what's right in front of me."

"Syd—"

"You've always shown me you're willing to put in the effort. I think I was just … scared."

His arms squeeze around me.

"And then you gave up the final race because of me, and as much as I still hate that you did it, I also can't deny I love the support. Your willingness to make me, make us, a priority is … mind-blowing."

"Can we sit down?" he asks softly.

I nod, following him to the couch, where we sit and face each other.

"I think I was a goner for you when you shot your gin and tonic in one go. You gave me shit for butting in where I wasn't wanted, and I was done for."

I laugh at his version of events.

"Do you know how pissed I was I didn't get your contact information? I looked for you everywhere. Looked up the most useless facts on the rare chance it would magically lead me to you. Nate had to take my phone during training because I would compulsively look up things."

"You did not." I gasp.

"Oh, I did. It wasn't my finest hour." He chuckles.

"I suspect I've wanted more for a while," I say.

"Oh yeah?" He lights up. This Beckett makes all the bad days go away. His smile is one of my favorite things.

"Oh yeah. My reaction to the whole Vivian situation should have been a huge clue, but I kept using our distance as an excuse to not commit."

"You weren't wrong, though. Getting to know each other took longer than it would have had we been able to see each other frequently."

I nod at his assessment. He's letting me off the hook, and it's sweet, but I want to lay all the cards on the table, and that means taking responsibility for holding us back.

"Fair, but I made a conscious effort to keep our interactions to mostly texts. I held back because I didn't think I could have a career that was time-consuming as well as a boyfriend who traveled as often as I did. It was too much for me to try and handle, as much as it pains me to admit that. It was never about our chemistry."

"I know," he says with a smirk.

"Shut up." I laugh. "Just because you're good in bed doesn't mean anything."

"Oh, it means everything, baby." He winks before chuckling.

"Jesus. I need to figure out a way to knock you down a peg. Your head is way too big."

"Downside to earning my living from driving a fast car?" he asks with a twinkle in his eyes.

"One hundred percent. How does Nate put up with you?" I roll my eyes with a smile on my face.

God, I've missed this banter. It feels like my health has stopped me from living life how I usually do this year, and it feels so damn good to be getting back to my normal.

"Well, I pay him, so he has to." He shrugs.

"Poor Nate." I shake my head.

"Don't poor Nate him! He's half the reason my head is this big."

"Then I need to chat with him." My smirk slowly fades as I continue. "This year has been so hard. The fatigue has knocked me on my ass. The pain in my ankles and hands has been ... awful. Pierce has been incredible at figuring out a way to restructure things so I don't travel. But I didn't want to tell you how bad it was, how shitty I was feeling more often than not. I think, on some level, I knew you would play hero and want to come help. That you wouldn't focus on what you needed to in order to win."

"And you were right. I called the owner of Legacy immediately after Luka talked to Daisy and didn't give him a choice. If I wasn't who I was, with my track record and popularity, I'd already be blacklisted. Plus, saying I had a family emergency doesn't give them a lot to hold against me."

"See, I fucking hate that you did that," I whisper as tears come to my eyes.

"I don't. I'd quit tomorrow if it meant being here for you. I don't need the money, Sydney. I need *you*."

"But at what cost?"

"Baby, it's at no cost. You are worth more than any contract. *You* are what matters." He cups my cheek, making sure I really hear him.

"You worked so hard for that contract." I start crying more. "And you just threw it all away because I was clumsy."

"It wasn't because you were clumsy, though. There was something major happening to your body, and as unfortunate as it was to break your foot, it led to an actual answer. An answer that I was there for, so I was able to learn how to help you. I wouldn't change that for anything."

The tears don't stop. I can't understand how he would just give up everything he's worked so hard for just for me—a woman who has a disease she will never be rid of.

"Hey," he says softly, pulling him to me. "I'm not trying to make you feel sad or guilty."

"I know, but I feel like such a mess." I try to wipe away my tears, but they just keep coming.

"I mean, you are, but you're my mess."

I smack him playfully as he laughs.

"I'm serious, though, baby. I've already talked to the owner and smoothed things over. He's not completely heartless, and they still won the Constructors' championship. He just told me to come back hungrier next year, and I plan to."

"What did you tell him happened exactly?"

His cheeks turn an adorable shade of pink I've only seen a couple of times before. "I told him my girlfriend was hurt and in the hospital. That it was an emergency, and I had to miss the race."

"What did you tell him after the fact? How did you smooth it over?" I tuck the girlfriend card in my back pocket for a second.

"I, umm, may have said something about my future wife getting a life-changing diagnosis and that I was here to support you." His whole neck is tinged red now, and my heart beats rapidly in my chest.

"You said that?" I squeak.

"I did. There's still no pressure, though. I just needed him to understand it was an actual family emergency."

Family. Such a simple concept, yet something I've never really had. Except now that I think about it, I've had Jane, Pierce, and Daisy in my life for years. They're all there for me regardless of if I accepted it or not.

"I'm such a bitch," I whisper.

"Umm, no you aren't. What the hell?" Beckett's confused. Understandable, because I'm having three different conversations in my head no one else could keep track of.

"I've been pushing everyone close to me away because I thought I need to solely focus on my job. If I was successful in my career, then everything else would eventually happen, but I never let it, so caught up in micromanaging everyone in my job that I didn't step back until I was forced to."

It's a huge revelation, one Pierce has been trying to get me to understand for years, but I never quite grasped it.

"No one is perfect in life, Sydney. It's a journey filled with mistakes, stumbles, and in the end, you just hope you lived it to its fullest."

"Do you feel like you're living it to the fullest?" I ask.

"I think I've pretended to for a long time. And then I met you, and I realized life is so much more than what's on the racetrack. I've looked forward to the season being over for the past couple of years so I could come here and be with you. Driving is a privilege, yes, but *you* are a necessity in my life."

I'm astonished.

"Do you feel like you're living yours to the fullest?" he asks softly.

I really think about it. With my job and getting the opportunity to travel all over the world, I used to think that was the peak way to live life. But this RA diagnosis has made me do some real self-reflection. Now, I'm less sure if I was actually living at all.

"No," I whimper. "But I want to."

"Oh, baby." He pulls me to him as my emotions wreak havoc on me.

We sit cuddled together, seemingly both lost in thought.

In his arms, I make a vow to make myself a priority. To do what I want to do in my life and focus less on what I'm supposed to be doing. Just like Beckett, I'm not hurting for money, and I know Pierce will work with me to figure out a sustainable schedule.

It's not just myself I want to make a priority, though; it's this man who dropped everything the second he heard something happened to me. The man who's waited patiently for me to realize he's been it the whole time.

Leaning back, I look into his eyes. "I think I want to take a hard look at my schedule and see what's doable this next year. I'd also like to come to as many races as I can if my body will let me."

"Then after Christmas, we'll sit down and make that happen," he says with zero hesitation.

It's a strange feeling, finally letting him in fully. I never realized how keeping him carefully balanced on the edge of friendship and a yearly fuck buddy was taking a toll on me. Now, all I feel is the relief that he forced his way into a more prominent role, like he's taken the weight of the stress off my shoulders and is carefully handling it while I figure out this new normal.

This is how a relationship should be.

Now, I just need to figure out how to do the same for him. He deserves an equal partner, one who goes above and beyond to make him smile and does the little things to make him happy.

Chapter 30
Beckett

I t's a white Christmas after all. Not that it's uncommon this close to the Tetons, but it's idyllic nonetheless.

I had a hard time coming up with something to get Sydney this year. There are only so many options with blown glass, and I've been planning this one for over six months. There's a real possibility that it's stupid, but it felt sentimental to me. I also couldn't wrap it, so it'll be delivered to her whenever she goes back home.

"Merry Christmas, Beckett," Sydney's soft voice sounds from behind me, making me smile.

This Christmas feels different, *more*, because of what Sydney is still coming to terms with from her diagnosis. It's less hurried, and for once, it doesn't feel like when we leave here the clock will strike midnight and we'll be in this strange limbo with each other.

"Merry Christmas, baby. I made coffee. You want some before we see if Santa came?" I ask with a grin.

"I would love a cup." She sits down, snuggling under the blanket. She looks … content for the first time since I've known her. I know the journey won't stay this simple, but for now, for this trip? I'm thankful that she feels safe and comfortable.

I doctor up her coffee the way I know she likes and sit next to her with my own cup.

"Can I just say I'm a shitty … whatever we're calling each other because I slacked on a Christmas present this year? I'm sorry." She winces.

"You mean that between feeling like shit most of the year, flying out to see me drive a car in circles, and keep up with your job, you didn't have time to plan a present for me?" The sarcasm is thick.

"Still. I might have been avoiding it and not planning to be here this year." She buries her head in her arms, but there's no shame. I knew she was struggling with what exactly we were to each other. She wasn't ready to commit; I'm not clueless to that fact.

"I think I would have dragged you here if you tried to ditch me this year." I raise an eyebrow. "This is our tradition. No matter what's happening with us, this is something I don't ever want to stop doing." Our Christmas tradition feels like home. I can't imagine spending Christmas any other way anymore.

"Why are you so … understanding? It's not like I've given you a reason to be this supportive of me. Don't get me wrong"—she puts her hand up to stop me from talking—"I appreciate it more than I could ever say, but I've been so distant and conflicted."

"Still haven't figured it out yet, huh?" I smile at her. I don't want to scare her, but she's adorable in her obliviousness.

"Ugh, I don't know!" She throws her hands up.

"Hey," I say softly, pulling her to me. "I'm not trying to frustrate you. You, Sydney Johnson, are it for me. If it takes you years to recognize that, I'll be here. If you decide tomorrow you're all in, then I'll bust my ass to make sure you don't regret it."

"Beckett Davis." She takes a deep breath and pulls away to look at me. "I'm scared shitless. About us, about what this diagnosis means for my everyday life, and about how to be the kind of partner you deserve in life. But I don't want to keep playing this coy game anymore, pretending we aren't together because of our schedule or traveling. I know it won't be easy to figure out how to really *be* together, but I'm in. That's my Christmas gift to you this year."

My smile hurts my cheeks; that's how big it is. She's looking down, picking at her cuticle, waves of uncertainty coming off of her.

I'm fucking ecstatic.

"This is the best Christmas I've ever had," I whisper before cupping her jaw and forcing her to look at me. "I don't want any presents; I just want you."

Her eyes shift between mine as a wide smile stretches across her face.

"I'm sorry I've been a mess. We wasted years for what?" she murmurs.

"Never be sorry. Everything happened the way it needed to. And now we're here, in Idaho, with the snow falling, and everything is … perfect," I breathe out.

"You know, the paddock would shit a brick if they heard you talking like this." She smirks.

"You're the only one who gets this side of me." It's the truth. Nate gets all angles, but no one would mistake me for anything other than driven to the breaking point, a one-track mind with little tolerance for platitudes. Everything is different with Sydney.

"Is it wrong that I kind of love that? Makes me feel all kinds of special." I can physically feel her losing the tension in her shoulders, the seriousness of the conversation we needed to have slowly draining away to the familiar.

"After Miami, when I kissed you before I got in the car, the debrief after was so focused on us that we had to postpone the meeting until people 'learned to be mature about shit that's none of their business'—my engineer's words, not mine." I chuckle.

"We're just going to have to make a habit of it, so you kick ass every single race then." The twinkle in her eye sends my heart blazing.

She's really all in; I can feel it in my bones.

"Can I give you your present now?" I ask.

"It better not be crazy extravagant," she says pointedly.

Shrugging seems like a better response than the truth. I'm sure she'll have words for me when she opens it.

I shift her to the side so I can stand up and retrieve the small box under the ever-present Christmas tree. I'm nervous as I walk back to the couch. Maybe she'll hate this and not want it in her house.

Sucking up my insecurities, I hand her the box and sit next to her.

She gingerly unwraps it and opens the envelope sitting on top.

"A spa day?" she asks, looking over to me.

"It's been a hard year, and I doubt you've had a spa day in years, probably since Jane got you one for Christmas. So, I'm forcing you to get pampered while we're here."

"That's super thoughtful." Her voice catches as she wipes below her eye.

The sight makes my heart clench in my chest. I know they're happy tears, so I attempt to not react how I normally would seeing her cry.

She sets the envelope off to the side and pulls out the next one. This one has a postcard inside, telling her what the gift actually is. Her eyes widen as she looks from me to the postcard. "Beckett..."

"If you don't like it, I can have it shipped to my place instead," I say quickly, hoping to make her feel okay about hating it.

"If you take this from me, I will dick punch you." Her soft voice doesn't match her words, and I bark out a laugh. "It's Miami, isn't it? The first race I was in the garage for."

The fact that she knows exactly what she's looking at is one of the reasons I'm so in love with her. It's the Miami circuit made entirely out of blown glass turned into a work of art. You'd only know what it is if you're in the racing world.

"It is. Since the whole track is handblown glass, it's pretty big and extra fragile, so the company said it would be easier to ship it directly to you. They're holding it until I give them an address."

She throws the box and postcard to the side before swinging her leg over my lap. With her straddling me, I'm helpless to resist. I've been extra cautious with her since her doctor's appointment, but how am I supposed to tell her no?

"Baby, I don't want to hurt you." I don't want to push her too far and have her body rebel against her. We're still figuring out how rheumatoid arthritis works, and I don't want to be the reason she's in bed all day tomorrow.

"If I promise to tell you if anything hurts, will you shut up and fuck me? Because I swear if you treat me like I'm made of glass any longer, I'm going to explode." It's bordering on a whine, and I can't deny her.

"You better be honest with me. I'll spank your ass so hard if you're not," I growl as I grip her ass and haul her up me as I stand up.

"Don't tempt me with a good time."

"I'm serious, Sydney." I stop in my tracks and pull back so she can see how serious I am. "I won't hurt you; I can't. It'll kill me, so I need you to be honest with me."

Her face softens as she leans forward and presses a kiss to my lips. "I promise. We can take it slow and find a new normal."

"Thank you." I kiss her back and head to the bedroom.

Carefully setting her down on the bed, I waste no time stripping out of my T-shirt and joggers. I leave my boxer briefs on because I need a fucking barrier with this woman before my dick takes over and ruts her into the damn mattress.

"Strip for me, baby." I slide my hand down my stomach and squeeze my cock head to the point of pain. I'm going to need more control than I have tonight in order to make sure she knows damn well what I can do to her body.

The good news is that stripping out of my oversized T-shirt she threw on and a pair of boy shorts takes no time at all, and before I can get myself under control, she's lying gloriously naked beneath me.

Kneeling next to her, I trace the subtle show of her ribs. Something that hasn't been visible since I've known her tells me the toll this disease has taken on her body this year.

"The new meds have helped with my appetite," she murmurs.

"Good." I continue my path, just on the bottom edge of her breast to her nipple, causing it to bead up for me.

God, I'm already salivating.

Her back arches as she grips my wrist to keep my hand on her.

No worries there, baby. I couldn't keep my hands off of you if there was a fucking avalanche headed our way.

Leaning forward, I press soft kisses to her jaw, then lips. We get carried away in the kiss, but my hand keeps moving, circling her nipple before moving to her other breast. She whimpers against my lips. I move my hand down her stomach, not wasting any more time. My fingertips circle her entire pussy, not hitting her clit yet, but close enough for her to get worked up for my touch.

"How're you feeling baby?" I lean back, checking in.

"So fucking good." She moans.

"Good." I move to kiss her neck.

I swipe my finger through her entrance, collecting her wetness and circling it around her clit. Her body bows off the bed, but I use my chest to gently push her back down.

"Take it easy, baby. Can't have you hurting," I say into her collarbone.

"Are you going to micromanage my every move?" She groans, and I push my finger inside of her.

"You bet your ass I am. You know I'll make you feel good, but I'm not letting you take charge and go balls to the wall. There's no need for that. I'll get you your orgasms while you lie there like a queen, not lifting a fucking finger." I nip at her neck as she cups the back of my head and sighs.

"You drive a hard bargain, Beckeeett," she drawls out as I tap that sweet spot inside of her before circling her clit again.

"You are so fucking sexy." I groan before tracing her nipple with my tongue.

I shift to lie down next to her, hooking my leg around hers that's closest to me, splaying her wide open for me. I slide two fingers through her arousal, getting them nice and wet before plunging them into her.

Her hips try to move to the cadence of my fingers thrusting. My hips are moving of their own accord, humping her leg to try to get some relief. Tossing my head back, I blow out a steady stream of breath to try to get my shit together, but it's useless.

"Check-in, Syd," I grate out. "How you feeling?" My teeth are clenched so tight I'm shocked I can get the words out.

Chapter 31
SYDNEY

I'm so close to coming that when the words register in my head, exasperation takes over. "If you make me come right now, I'll be great." Sarcasm is thick in my voice.

He looks down at me and stops moving his fingers, drawing a frustrated growl out of me. His stupid, sexy smirk takes over, and I'm screwed. He can play with me, edge me all fucking day, and I'm powerless to resist him.

"How. Are. You. Feeling?" He punctuates each word with a circle of his fingers on my G-spot, and my eyes roll back in my head.

Honestly, I couldn't even tell you how my joints and body are feeling. I can only feel where he touches me and the pressure low in my belly telling me I'm about to combust.

"Good!" I strain the word as my pussy clenches around his fingers. "Perfect. So damn good." I whimper as I come.

I can feel him smile against my neck. "I swear if I could do this and watch you come every hour of every day, I would. Fuuuck, you're killing me." He groans and pumps his hips against my leg.

I'm panting—words are not going to happen for a minute—but I can give him a gentle nudge in the direction I want. Reaching down between us, I cup him through his boxer briefs, and I feel him shudder against my body.

"Baby, I can't," he whispers.

I ignore him while I catch my breath. My fingers slide underneath the band and meet his hard, hot cock. I wrap my hand around him, giving him a firm stroke before words come to me.

"I need you. I don't know what you had planned, but scrap it. Please. Just fuck me now." My breathy words lack the convection I was going for, but it doesn't matter. Beckett gets the picture, just like he always does.

His teeth meet my shoulder where my neck starts, and I feel them gently bite down as he shifts his hips away from me, shoving down his underwear with the hand not on me. His overgrown hair calls me; my fingers thread through it and grip the strands tightly as he shifts on top of me.

He hovers over me, face-to-face, with so much depth in his eyes.

I see his soul. And the part of mine that will irrevocably be his from here on out.

Holy shit, I think I love him.

As the thought hits me like a lightning bolt, he shoves my thighs up further and lines himself up, sliding inside of me at a slow, measured pace. I'm already primed for another orgasm. Judging by the clench of his jaw, he's feeling it too.

Once he's fully seated, he presses his forehead to mine, closes his eyes, and breathes in deep. "I'm sorry to say this is going to be quick," he mutters.

I choke out a laugh at his unexpected observation. "There's always round two. And six. We've got a couple of weeks."

"You're ambitious."

"Well, we have two weeks of 'just us' time. I don't know about you, but I plan to utilize it to its fullest."

He rolls his hips, giving me just that hint of friction I need. "You're not the one in charge, baby. I thought we covered that."

"Ugh, just move, then we can negotiate later," I whine.

"How're you feeling?" he asks softly.

The change in his voice has my heart pounding. "I'm feeling really good." The words are getting stuck in my throat from the emotion of it all. I'm not just physically feeling good; I'm emotionally and mentally feeling good. All thanks to Beckett.

A chaste kiss followed by the slow thrust of his hips makes everything feel *bigger*. It's like I can feel every glide inside of me, every ridge, and every spot he hits, magnified to a level that has tears coming to my eyes. It's too much yet not enough all at the same time.

My grip in his hair stays steady as my other hand grabs his bicep. My legs wrap around his hips. The need to get closer is overwhelming.

"Baby, I want you to get there, but I'm so fucking close I don't know if I can hold off." His hand wraps around my shoulder, anchoring me to him more, if that's possible, as his thrusts get more powerful.

I tilt my hips so the base of him hits my clit with every push. My mouth opens as my orgasm is triggered so fucking fast it should be criminal. My lack of sound is made up for by Beckett. His moans against my lips, his stuttering hips, have me clenching around him so tight that he couldn't pull out if he tried.

We stay frozen in this moment in time, neither of us willing to give up an inch of space.

I only move when my muscles start to tire from holding him to me so tightly.

"Shit. Are you okay?" He loosens his hold.

I collapse back onto the bed in sheer bliss. "I'm fucking phenomenal. I'm just not used to using my puny arm muscles for that long."

"They're cute puny muscles, though." He gently pulls out and heads to the bathroom.

I shamelessly watch his ass as he goes, amazed that I'm lucky enough to call him mine.

He comes back with a warm washrag, wiping away the evidence of the most powerful sex I've ever had. An illogical sadness presents itself at the fact that it's just gone and I can't revel in it longer. It's a weird thought, but I'd venture to say my mind isn't completely recovered from the orgasms yet.

When he crawls into the bed next to me, life feels right. With Beckett by my side, I think I can work through anything that comes my way.

"You sure you're okay?" he asks as he pulls me to his chest.

"I promise I am. I'll be interested to see how I feel when I wake up, but the medication seems to be helping a lot. If I'm super sore in the morning, I have that cream I can put on too."

"I'm not going to lie; it stresses me out to not know how your body is going to react to things. I don't like the uncertainty. And if we do something and you hurt in the morning or an hour later, it's going to crush me. I fucking hate seeing you in any kind of pain or discomfort." His hand strokes my arm as he says it.

"The not knowing is by far the worst part. I feel like I'm less stressed about it now because I have a solid answer as to what's causing it all. But having to be cautious with things I've never thought about before extra sucks."

"We'll figure it out together." He presses a kiss to my temple.

The security I feel in his arms and the support in his words give me a comfort I never knew I wanted in life. Combined with our sexual adventures, my eyes start to droop, and sleep takes over.

***

Waking up to the sound of the hotel door closing has me shooting up in bed. Beckett strolls in through the door then stops in his tracks at my alarmed look.

"Just me. I ordered food." His soft smile instantly puts me at ease.

"Sorry, I don't know why I panicked," I admit.

If I'm honest with myself, it's because I still expect him to say I'm not worth all this trouble. I mean, what man would stick around when you know this disease is for life? It's something that won't ever be cured—something I've yet to come to terms with.

He wheels the cart into the bedroom before sitting on the edge next to me. "Hey, I'm not going anywhere. I know that'll take a while to sink in, but I'll keep reminding you if it helps."

God, his understanding is too much sometimes. Beckett doesn't get annoyed or short with me; he just accepts that my hyper-independence is going to take some time to unlearn.

"It helps," I say.

"Good. Well, I got a little of everything: breakfast, lunch, and snacks." He stands to take the lids off.

I moan as I see the spread, not realizing how hungry I am.

He chuckles, putting it all on the bed with a bed tray he produces out of nowhere. "I'm in the mood for some Christmas movies. What do you say we binge some and eat our weight in deliciousness for the rest of the day?"

"Sounds like heaven." I sigh, content for the first time in too long.

Chapter 32

Beckett

Two weeks went too fast.

I made sure Sydney was relaxed, pampered, and loved, but now it's time to go back to work.

I'm not ready. The only good thing is that we're flying to Texas together to drop off Sydney, before I need to make my way to Monaco to do some hard-core training since I've ditched out on it while I've been with Sydney.

"So, I need to look at my schedule, but at the very least, I should be able to be at your first race." She curls up against me in the Vanstone private plane. I'd venture a guess that she has better connections than I do.

"Two months is too long," I complain.

"I know, but all I'll be is a distraction when you need to buckle down and get ready for the season," she argues.

"What if I want the distraction?" My fingers comb through her hair.

"Still no. You're not very level-headed when it comes to me. Just ask Nate."

"Nate can suck my dick," I say automatically.

Her burst of laughter is a balm to my soul.

"I believe that's my job, but if you'd rather spend some quality time with Nate, I suppose that can be arranged."

Tickling her side, making her squeal, I veto her suggestion. "Hell no. The only lips I want anywhere near my cock are yours."

"Good to know."

"Seriously, though, once the season starts, I think it'll be easier to get into a rhythm."

I'm already looking at places in Austin. Monaco won't be my home base this season, but she doesn't know that yet. I don't want to freak her out. It took two weeks for her to finally relax, and I'm not jeopardizing that for anything.

"We still need to talk about that." She sighs.

"Well, my thought is race weekends are Thursday through Sunday. As long as I'm there Thursday morning, I have Monday through Wednesday every week to be wherever you are."

"You can't do that every single week! What are you going to do, red-eye every single Wednesday there's a race?"

"Exactly. Thursdays are just press and meetings with team to plan. And if you want to come to any race, you can just tag along with me," I not-so-subtly hint.

"We're really doing this?" she asks.

"Yeah, baby, we really are. Even if you don't come to any races this year, I'm still all in."

"I'll come to races." I can feel her eye roll even though I can't see it.

"I'm just saying, I'll still see you every chance I get."

"This feels very one-sided."

"Well, my shit is easier to plan. I pretty much have a set schedule; you don't." I shrug.

"You're annoyingly flexible with all of this." Her shoulders shake against me with her laughter.

"It's taken us four years to get to this point. I'm not letting some bullshit like my job get in the way of it."

"Yeah, why let the thing you've worked your ass off for your entire life get in the way of some crazy woman who made you wait four years to commit. Totally doesn't sound reasonable at all."

"You're feisty today." I chuckle.

"And you're so damn nonchalant about all this." She sits up and throws her hands up.

"Baby." I cup her cheeks in my hands. "I would rather fly all over the world to spend a few days with you than only see you a few times this year. We're doing this thing, right?"

"Yes," she whispers.

"Then that means doing it right. I *need* to see you on a regular basis. I will actually combust if I don't. If you want me to win the Drivers' Championship this year, then don't question my methods." I arch an eyebrow.

"Well, now you're playing dirty."

"You're damn right I am. I want more time with you, Sydney, and I'm going to make it happen no matter what," I say earnestly.

"Okay, then I want to come to as many races as I can."

"Done. Tell me which ones you're coming to, and I'll have your access ready to go. You'll stay with me and be in the garage for everything."

"No choice in it, huh?" She smirks.

"Sorry, baby. I race better when I know you're in the garage."

"So fucking dirty." She laughs.

"I'm not apologizing. I'm taking all the time you give me and running with it."

"I think I like that."

"Good." I lean forward and press a kiss to her lips.

"So, while we're flying to Austin, I'll put all the races in my calendar and see if I can swing the March races. Daisy can shift things around if I need her to, but the good thing about being so fatigued this past year is that we've adjusted to doing a lot of work remotely, so it shouldn't be a huge issue to continue that. I'll also talk to Pierce about it and make sure he's okay with everything," she rambles, and it's the most adorable thing ever. She's planning, something she hasn't done since we've met, and it feels like such a huge step in our relationship.

"Whatever you need me to do, let me know. I can talk to Pierce if he's giving you a hard time," I offer.

"Pierce is easy; I'm not worried about him." She scoffs.

"Does he know about your diagnosis yet?"

Her eyes turn down. "Not yet."

"And Daisy?"

"Also not yet."

"Sydney..."

"I know. I'll have a meeting with both of them when I get home and tell them everything. It all happened so fast; I needed time to wrap my head around it."

"Do you feel better about it now? Or are you still stressed about everything?"

"Mostly better. The medication is already working wonders on the fatigue and soreness in the morning, but I still have that what-if going through my mind. What if the meds stop working? What if this gets progressively worse faster than what the doctor says? What if it affects my joints so terribly that I can barely walk?"

My heart hurts hearing this, although I think I would be feeling the same. It's hard to not have concrete answers.

"Then we figure that out if it comes. You have a great doctor, who's at the top of her field. I have confidence that she'll do everything in her power to stop that from happening."

"I know you're right, but my mind wanders when I have too much quiet time." Her voice is so small I want to do everything in my power to boost her up and support her when she needs it most—and when she thinks she doesn't need it.

"When that happens, call me. I don't care what time it is; call me, and we'll talk until you feel better."

She slides her fingers into my hand and intertwines our fingers. "You have no idea how much that means to me."

"We're in this together, which means you don't have to worry and stress about this stuff by yourself. Even if we aren't together physically, I'm here for you. Always."

"I l— Thank you." Her initial words have my heart pounding in my chest.

Was she going to say she loves me? God, I wish she would. I've been in love with her for over a year.

But I hold my tongue. I know I need to wait for her to voice it first. There's no way in hell I want to push her. This upcoming year is about figuring out her new normal, and I won't be the person to put her needs and wants on the backburner. All I want to do is live my life with her. I don't care what that looks like as long as I'm by her side.

For the rest of the flight, we fill up her calendar and talk about which races are my favorites. She discreetly adds an asterisk to all of my favorites, but I see her do it. She may be hesitant about a lot of things involving the two of us, but her actions are speaking far louder than her words right now, and I'm running with them at full speed.

***

Walking up to my apartment in Monaco feels wrong. Spending the last almost three weeks with Sydney has spoiled me, and now I'm grumpy as hell that I'm walking into an empty apartment. Shutting the door behind me, I slump against it, trying to restrain myself from sprinting back to the airport and saying "fuck it."

"About time you showed up." Nate's voice scares the shit out of me.

"What the fuck, man?!"

"Umm, I'm always here. Why do you think I asked you what time you're landing? I thought it was obvious I would just meet you here." He tilts his head in question before taking a bite out of an apple I didn't see him holding.

"Jesus, you could have cleared your throat or something." My hand is still on my rapidly beating heart, willing it to slow down.

"You're jumpy." He rolls his eyes.

"Maybe I should take your key away," I grumble, heading toward my bedroom to drop off my suitcase.

"Then who would kick your ass out of bed so you can work out for five hours?" he yells.

"Contrary to popular belief, I am an adult capable of doing shit by myself!" I yell back.

"Head all fucked up because of Miss Johnson?" He smirks as he follows me.

Sighing, I drop to my bed and put my head in my hand. "I fucking hate leaving her, especially now. I may not see her for almost two months, and that's not something I can deal with," I tell him honestly.

"Okay, let's figure it out, then. It's not like you have to stay here to train, and I'm not really needed anywhere but next to you." He shrugs.

"I looked at rentals in Austin." Holding my breath, I wait to see if it's too much for him. I wouldn't blame him if it was. My plans negate anything he had planned if he agrees to come with me.

"Texas? For the next few weeks? Sunshine?" His excitement pours out of him.

"At least until we need to be in London for the car unveiling and training there. It would give me an extra month with her and only a couple of weeks until Bahrain." The more I talk this out, the more I wonder why I even came back here.

"I'll find us a flight." He pulls out his phone, and I'm grateful for such a great friend. He doesn't try to talk me out of it; he just makes it happen.

Pulling out my phone, I hit the call button and hope that my neediness doesn't blow up in my face.

"You make it home okay?" she answers as soon as she picks it up.

"I did. How are you doing?"

She sighs. "Good. Tired. Missing you."

I don't think I could be smiling any harder. "I may have a solution for that last bit."

"Oh yeah? Phone sex already?"

I choke on my laughter at her dry humor.

"No, but I'd never say no to phone sex," I say as I get my shit together. I unzip my suitcase, empty the cold weather gear from Idaho, and change it for clothes for warmer climates.

"I could negotiate."

"How about negotiating a new living arrangement?"

"What do you mean?" she asks.

"What if I spend the next month in Texas?" I hold my breath.

"Seriously?"

I can't tell if she's excited or not.

"If you're amenable."

"I mean, I still have to work most of the time, but I would love for you to be here until you have to work."

"Yeah?"

"Heck yes! I seem to sleep better with you in my bed anyway."

"About that... I'd be bringing Nate because I still need to train. I was looking at a rental."

"You guys can stay here. It's not like I have a small house. The guest bedrooms are on the opposite ends of the house from my room. You can totally say no, though," she adds quickly.

Nate walks in at that moment.

"Hold on," I tell Sydney and put my phone down on my leg, blocking the sound. "How do you feel about staying with Sydney? She's got a nice-ass house, and there's plenty of room."

"I mean if she's okay with it, I'm down."

"You find flights?"

"Done and booked. We leave in four hours."

"Awesome. I'll pack, then we can head to your place." I nod then pick up my phone again.

"You're leaving today?" she asks without preamble.

"Well, yeah. Why wait?"

"Umm, I don't know... Maybe so you aren't stuck on an airplane for, like, twenty-four hours straight? You just got off of a flight." Exasperation is heavy in her voice.

"I don't care about that. I care about getting more time with you. I'll fly overnight, get there in the morning, and get to spend the next month with you. I told you I'd fly across the world to spend more time with you. Now, let me do it."

"Okay," she whispers.

"I'll keep you updated on the flight information."

"You're crazy." She chuckles. "I can't believe you're just flying here after flying to Monaco."

"Possibly, but it's worth it. I'll see you in the morning, baby."

"I'll make sure the coffee's ready."

I can't wait to have her in my arms again.

Chapter 33
Sydney

The past few days have been both hectic and calming. Having Beckett here more long term is something I didn't realize I needed, but I can't imagine spending a month away from him now. We were fools to think we could handle it. *I* was a fool.

The tides changed in Idaho last Christmas. We both committed to making this work and, to that end, making sacrifices to physically be together. It doesn't seem so hard to make happen now, though; it feels as natural as breathing.

A bonus I didn't see coming is Nate. Our budding friendship has turned into a full-blown one. He's like the brother I never had, constantly ribbing me while also being protective. He knows about my RA and has been looking into it, getting in touch with some medical professionals he knows to see what the newest, best treatment is. He told me it's always good to know the options and have them in my back pocket if I ever need them.

Work's been fairly quiet too. Pierce, Daisy, and I had a long, emotional talk over dinner about what my diagnosis means in the long term. We've already started shifting the way we do things, moving all the travel to our regional managers. Pierce and I now only look at the big-picture things. Everyone reports to us, but we don't touch the day-to-day workings. It's something Pierce was mostly doing anyway, but now he's let me join the fray—something he tells me weekly is what he intended all along.

In a matter of weeks, I've gone from not feeling like I have this tight support system to one that is more than I could ever dream of. People who would drop anything for me with one word. It's the best kind of overwhelming, and I've cried more from the emotional release of it all than I ever thought possible.

The door swings open, pulling me from my thoughts as Beckett strolls in.

"Get dressed, baby. We're going out." His excitement is contagious.

"Where are we going?" I maneuver myself out of the corner of my sectional and stand up to head to the bedroom.

"On a date."

I stop in my tracks. "A date?"

"Yup. We've only been on one, and I barely consider that a date because it was to celebrate my win. It had dual purpose, so it doesn't count."

"And where are we going on this date?"

He closes the door behind him as I strip off my T-shirt.

"It's a surprise." He smirks.

"That doesn't help me figure out what to wear."

"Wear something you feel comfortable in; we're not going anywhere fancy."

I smile over at him. He's always so thoughtful. He doesn't give me adulation; he gives me an actual response. Beckett lets my brain be quiet, takes over the work, and just lets me come along for the ride.

"I can make that happen." I grab a pair of my extra stretchy jeans and a loose button-up. My favorite boots cap it all off before I spin in a circle for him.

"Gorgeous," he murmurs.

"Yeah right." Scoffing, I roll my eyes and head to the living room. The brush-off is mainly to hide my blush.

He pulls my arm, forcing me to stop. "If I tell you you're gorgeous, don't brush it off. You, Sydney Johnson, are the most beautiful woman I've ever had the pleasure of knowing. Let me compliment you; it's going to happen a lot."

"Yes, sir."

He arches an eyebrow at me with his signature smirk.

"No. I'm not calling you sir in bed." I chuckle.

"Well damn, way to shut that down entirely too fast."

I can't help it; a giggle takes over my whole body.

"I would pay an obscene amount of money to make you laugh like that every single day," he says in awe.

"You might be the only one who can make me laugh like this," I say through my laughter.

"You two are looking adorable," Nate says from the hallway.

"It's date night." Beckett says it so proudly that my heart pounds in my chest.

"Well, you two have fun now, and have her back by midnight." He directs his words at Beckett, and my laughter continues.

"Jesus. The two of you need to stop hanging out." Beckett scrubs his face with his hand.

I pull him to the door. "See you later, Nate!"

We rush to my car, him opening my door like the gentleman he is before getting in the driver's side.

"I give you both shit, but I'm glad you two get along." He looks over at me like I'm something truly special.

"He's a good guy. I want to go on a matchmaking hunt for him, but Lord knows I only have, like, two friends." I smile over at Beckett.

"He's gotta settle down a little before that happens, I think. He's still very much in his 'wild and crazy' stage of life. He may be one hundred percent professional on the job, but the man knows how to let loose."

"He'll get there."

We drive in comfortable silence for a while before he turns into a parking lot. Confusion sets in when I don't see a building until he drives around the corner, and butted up against a wooded area is a huge screen with more parking.

"Did you find a drive-in movie theatre?" I ask in awe.

"I did."

"And why are we the only car here?"

"Because I rented the whole place out."

I stare at him and all his ridiculousness. "Extreme much?"

He shrugs. "I wanted a peaceful date, and this guaranteed it."

"It's certainly peaceful. The only questions is what movie are we watching?"

"You'll see." He parks, then gets out of the car and pops the trunk. He comes back a minute later with a basket filled to the brim with food and drink.

"Beckett, this is so thoughtful," I whisper, trying to not let my emotions take over.

"You deserve thoughtful; I'm just sorry it hasn't happened until now."

He starts pulling out all of my favorites: a salad from my favorite Greek restaurant, a bag of Doritos, Nashville hot chicken that's my new obsession, and my favorite dessert of all time—a chocolate mousse from this little Italian place a couple of blocks from my house.

"How in the world did you hide this all from me?" I open the bag of Doritos and shove a whole chip into my mouth. Our comfort level with each other has only grown since he's been in Austin.

"You really don't realize how busy work keeps you, do you?" He chuckles, sticking his hand in the bag and grabbing a handful of chips.

"It's been a light week for me too."

"No wonder Pierce is begging you to slow down, jeez."

I look over at him, chip held an inch from my face. "Do I really spend a ton of time working? I've lightened up my load so much that it feels like I'm slacking, and I don't feel like I have a great handle on what's too much anymore. Clearly." I gesture between us.

"I mean, I'm not your boss and I don't have a normal job, but the fact that Pierce and Jane, and Daisy, are getting onto you more and more leads me to believe you might be."

"Pierce called me yesterday and got onto me about my hours," I say shamefully. "Said my health was more important since we've built a company that can run without either of us on a daily basis. I just don't know—" I sigh. "I don't know how the fuck to slow down. Outside of my body forcing me to slow down, I don't know how to just leave a lot of things alone."

"Well, that's why you have me, and with me crashing at your house for the next month, you have to listen to me."

"I have to, huh? Doesn't sound like something I'd do." I smirk and pick up the salad.

"I have my ways to get you to see the light." He winks before picking up his phone and typing in something quickly.

The lights flicker around the area, and the stuttering of the movie reel starts up on the giant screen.

"I would love to see you try, Beckett Davis." I shove a huge bite of salad into my mouth to hide my smile. This man could get me to do anything—happily—but letting him know that isn't nearly as fun.

The familiar opening credits of *The Princess Diaries* show on screen. The iconic drive through the streets of San Fransisco followed by the nostalgia of early 2000s pop music make my emotions run the gambit.

"How the hell did you know?" I whisper, trying desperately to keep myself in check over a movie I've watched a million times.

"I listen, baby. To everything. No matter how big or small, I listen to everything you say." The conviction in his voice, his words, make my decision and commitment to him clearer than ever.

"You're going to sit through one of my all-time favorite movies, which also happens to be a teen rom-com, willingly?"

"I think you know I'd do a hell of a lot more if it means being next to you."

"I do." I put the salad on the dashboard and lean over to kiss him.

His hand threads through my hair, lingering a moment longer before pulling back. "Now, show me why this movie is so great."

Two hours later, he pulls me out of the car to dance to the credits.

"If you tell Nate I actually liked the movie, I'll withhold your orgasms for a week."

Gasping, I pull back. "You wouldn't. My orgasms are your favorite thing ever."

"Damn it, you're right," he says in an exaggerated tone, making me giggle. "Just don't tell him; then, we both can be happy."

"Deal. Me and Mia Thermopolis won't tell a soul." I mime zipping my lips but can't keep the smile off my face.

His smile is peaceful, and my heart pounds in my chest at how I was a part of putting it there.

"How are you feeling?" he asks as he gently spins me around the empty parking lot.

"So fucking good. Better than I have in a year." The new medication combined with Beckett staying with me for an extended amount of time have been good for me. I feel healthier, happier.

The credits are long done by the time we finish dancing under the stars. This is a moment, a date, that I will forever call a favorite memory.

"All right, let's head on home. I have more planned."

"Beckett Davis, there is nothing that would make this night more perfect," I scold him as he leads me to the passenger side.

"Well, I'm going to damn well try, so just enjoy the ride, baby."

I watch the city blur past us as he drives us home, and I can't remember a time where I've ever been this happy. This in love.

I never want it to end.

Chapter 34

BECKETT

As I drive us back to Sydney's house, my mind is blissfully blank. The usual stressors that creep in are nowhere to be found.

Now, I'm only thinking about her in my arms as we danced around a parking lot and how it was better than winning a race. Better than getting my contract. The simple normalcy of a drive-in movie date is anything but normal. It felt magical, like *this* is where I'm supposed to be in my life. *This* is what's important.

Pulling into her garage, I'm grateful that Nate went off to do his own thing tonight. He wordlessly knew I wanted the place to ourselves, even if we are separated by the entire living area.

Scooping Sydney out of the passenger seat, I carry her to the bathroom that I bribed Nate to set up before he left. Her gasp of surprise makes owing him a favor later for the entire setup worth it.

Battery-run candles are on every surface—I didn't want to burn the place down—with a variety of flower petals lining the bottom of the bathtub that's just waiting for me to add water. Chocolate-covered strawberries and her favorite wine sit on the counter.

"Beckett..." I can hear the emotion, the tears, in her voice.

It's not that I want to make her cry; it's that I don't think she's ever felt like she *could* cry, always having to be the badass boss, the loyal assistant who handles everything. Emotions never played a role. Now, she's battling a disease that's attacking her body, and the need to slow down—something she doesn't know how to do—is more necessary than ever. My goal, always, is to make slowing down easy for her. To make her *want* to slow down because it means spending more time with me. I've never been surer than I have been the last couple of months that she's who I'm meant to spend my life with. Now, I just need to show her what that life actually looks like.

"Just … let me take care of you," I tell her softly as I set her down on the counter.

Sliding my hands up her sides, I move them to the center and start unbuttoning her shirt slowly. Our eyes stay locked as I work my way down until the last button comes loose. I lean in, pressing a soft kiss to the corner of her mouth, then her cheek and down to her jaw. Sliding her shirt off of her shoulders, I never stop the trail of kisses.

Her eyes flutter shut as her hands move to my shoulders. My fingertips move to her bra straps, slowly sliding them off her shoulders as I keep my lips on her skin. She tilts her head to the side to give me more room, and I take it greedily.

"Why"—she moans—"am I the only one"—*kiss*—"losing clothes?"

"Because," I breathe into her neck. "I'm in charge."

Her strangled groan as I unhook her bra, dropping it to the floor and moving my kisses south, has me rock hard. I'm supposed to be taking it easy, cuddling and taking care of her, but I can't stop. Not with the way she reacts to my touch.

My hands land on her hips and scoot her forward, right to the edge of the vanity, as I move to kiss her lips again. My under-six-foot frame proves to be a benefit as my hips meet hers.

She rips her lips off of mine, cupping my jaw in her hands. "Take your clothes off please."

Instead, I take a deep breath, smelling the hint of her arousal, and step back. Reaching over, I turn the water on and start filling up the tub.

"Beckett," Sydney whines.

"I promise, baby, I'll take care of you. Just let me do it my way." I kiss her once more before reaching behind my neck and pulling off my T-shirt.

Her eyes light up as she watches me, making me feel like I'm a real king on this Earth.

Popping the button on my jeans has her chest moving in quick pants. But she doesn't move to take the lead. The sound of my zipper, each tooth coming free as I slowly pull downward, is the only other sound in the room besides the water flowing into the tub.

Sydney shifts on her hips, broadcasting her need.

"Feeling needy, baby?"

"God yes," she moans.

I waste little time kicking off my shoes and socks before shoving my jeans down. Now, only in my boxer briefs, I step back up to my woman, popping the button on her jeans.

"Grab onto my shoulders," I whisper into her ear as I try to rein in my dick, but it's getting more and more challenging with the sounds that come out of her mouth. She does as told, and I lift her up with one arm as the other shifts her jeans over her ass. It's an awkward battle, but we're both so lost in lust that it doesn't even faze us.

Eventually, I get her jeans off, along with her boots and socks. She's panting in my ear, her hands roaming my shoulders and chest making it difficult to leave her, but I've got to stick to my plan.

Stepping back, I grab the small bottle behind her and move to the tub. Shutting off the water, I dump in a small amount of oil, and the scent of orange blossoms fills the room. It's a picture-perfect sight, only missing Sydney covered in water and flower petals.

"Come here." I beckon her over.

She slowly slides off the vanity, stripping off her panties as she walks toward me.

"Naughty play, baby," I chide.

"Just trying to help out," she says innocently.

Helping her step in, I watch as she sinks down to her shoulders. I can see the physical release of tension rolling off of her, and I make sure to remember every single detail of her lying here, covered in a multitude of colors, happy and relaxed.

Palming my cock, I hope I can hold my shit together long enough for her to hold onto this peace.

Blowing out a steady breath, I strip out of my underwear and step up to the side of the tub. "Scoot forward, baby," I tell her softly.

Her eyes flicker open, and a blinding smile stretches across her face. The water shifts as she moves forward, making room for me to climb in. Once I'm seated, I pull her to me, sliding my hands to her stomach to hold her close.

"I love this," she murmurs.

I love you, I think, but I don't want to break the moment. I don't want to pressure her, so instead, I go with a simpler but no less true response. "Me too, baby. Me too."

My thumb strokes the tender skin of her stomach as her head lolls back against my shoulder. I know she feels how hard I am against her—it would be impossible not to—but she doesn't assume sex is where I'm going with this. She's sinking into the moment, being present with me as I pour all of my feelings into being with her right here, right now. I want to show her that I love her, that I'm in this for the long haul, so she doesn't question it when the words finally come. I want her to feel it long before she hears it.

Her hand slides over my leg, down the outside of my thigh that's pressed against her, at the same time as she turns her head and kisses the air. I grin before leaning forward to press a kiss to her lips as her hand continues to roam. The kiss stays chaste for all of two seconds before her tongue sneaks out and licks my bottom lips.

"Sydney..."

"Beckett, please," she begs against my lips, and I can't deny her. One hand cups her cheek, pulling her lips to mine, while the other slides down between her legs.

I start slow, my fingers swirling against her clit at the same leisurely pace I'm kissing her. Her hips move to get more friction, but I don't give it to her. I let my mind wander into nothingness, only feeling.

The feel of her slick arousal on my fingers every time I dip them lower.

The feel of her soft lips against mine, her tongue dueling mine with no real end goal.

The feel of her hips grinding against my cock, making my movements stumble every so often.

The feeling of knowing this is where I'm meant to be.

Minutes pass; hell, an hour could have passed, and I wouldn't be able to tell. My pace quickens as my need to be inside of her starts to take over. Her clit pulses against my fingertips as she gasps into the kiss.

"Let me feel you, baby," I whisper.

Sliding my fingers down, I push two inside of her as the heel of my hand presses hard on her clit. It sets her off in a second, and feeling her pulse and squeezing me almost sends me over the edge. Quickly removing my fingers, I grab her hips and clumsily spin her around in the tub. Her legs land on either side of my hips as my cock lines up perfectly with her still pulsing pussy. I grip her hips and slide her slowly onto me. I have to bite my lip hard to not come immediately at the feel of her surrounding me.

"Jesus." She gasps as I fill her to the hilt.

We both stay still as she adjusts, and within a minute, her hips are moving of their own accord.

"This is going to be over too fast if you keep that up," I say through clenched teeth.

"That's what round two is for." She moans as she hits a particular spot.

"Am I just a fuck machine for you to use?" I try to joke, but the intensity of it all is making it hard.

"You are pretty good at it." She sucks in a breath. "I thought I'd take advantage."

"Take everything you want, baby." My grip tightens on her hips as mine thrust up to give her more.

"Careful giving me that kind of power." She smirks as her head tips back.

"You already have it, Syd. You have all the power, all of me... Anything you want." I strain to hold on.

I open my eyes, and I can physically see her orgasm break. Her limbs start to shake, her breathing is shallow, and then everything stops for a split second—a suspended moment in time where her pussy locks onto my cock, and then this tidal wave of feeling hits hard.

Her stomach muscles clench and her arms grip my shoulders tight as her hips canter with her spasms. I'm helpless against it all. My balls tighten as the tingle races down my spine, and I let go. I pulse in rhythm with her orgasm, and as we both come down, she collapses against my chest.

"What the hell was that?" she asks breathlessly against my skin.

The only thing I can think to tell her is, "Serendipity."

Chapter 35
SYDNEY

It's race weekend, the first of the season, and I haven't seen Beckett in three weeks.

It's been harder without him than I thought. The almost two months we were with each other nonstop quickly became my comfort zone, and leaving it sucked more than I want to admit. It's not like we haven't talked every day since he and Nate left for London to train, but it's not the same.

I miss him so damn much, but today that drought ends. I'm sitting in his little room next to the Legacy garage in Bahrain while he does a quick meeting with his engineers. Nate had to practically drag him away from me so he wasn't late.

I smile, remembering the warm welcome I received when I got here. I had a couple of meetings I couldn't miss and wasn't able to get here when Beckett did, so Nate picked me up from the airport and drove me straight to the track to wait for the first practice.

When I stepped into the garage, it was like the universe narrowed down to just two people, me and Beckett. No one else was there or mattered, and the speed at which he ran to me was almost comical. Picking me up, he swung me around and kissed all over my face before putting me down.

"Never again. We are never going that long again," he said, pressing his *forehead to mine.*

"So glad you could join us for the first race," a slightly accented and well-spoken man says from behind me.

I spin around and come face-to-face with Legacy's team principal, Felix Karlsson. I know of him and have obviously seen him around the garage, but

I've never spoken with him.

"Oh, um, thanks for letting me be here. It's such a different experience to be in the garage than in the stands." I give him what I hope is a gracious smile, considering the one he's giving me is just shy of condescending.

"Of course. We love Vanstone Properties."

Vanstone. He purposefully mentioned my job, which leads me to believe he doesn't like me here as anything other than an extension of Vanstone.

"Well, Vanstone loves Legacy." My curt smile does nothing to hide my disdain for his tactics.

It's a man's world, and I've navigated it longer than he's been team principal, so his attempt at intimidating me isn't going to rattle me. However, I don't want anything like this to affect Beckett.

"Yes, well, I hope we can remain friends through this season. I would hate for one of our favorite sponsors to have to be relegated to the VIP section instead of the garage." He smirks.

I look at him with an assessing eye and decide to go for it; he needs to know I'm not like these other women who hang around and cause distraction because they just want to fuck the drivers. I'm here for as long as Beckett races.

"Felix... May I call you Felix?" I arch an eyebrow at him before he nods in answer. "Great. Listen, Felix, I hear your message loud and clear, but don't confuse me for some pushover you can use big words with to make compliant. I've been in this business longer than you've been in charge here, and I have as many strings if not more that I can pull to make your life a little difficult. I am here to support my boyfriend, my partner. I'm not going anywhere. If at any point I feel that I'm distracting him, I will happily remove myself if that's what I feel is best. But don't mistake me for someone you can give orders to. I want what's best for Beckett. We're on the same team. It would be best if you remember that." My smile is my professional one, the one I give when the men think that I'm just a pretty face for the company and not damn near running the whole thing.

He stares at me for a beat before his smile broadens. "I can see why he's so taken with you. Welcome to the team, Sydney. I apologize for my ... tactics, but you understand the need to keep these men focused. Especially with him missing Abu Dahbi last year."

"I do." I nod, still not convinced everything is suddenly fine between us.

He holds out his hand, and I tentatively shake it. His firm grip changes to pulling me toward the door and hovering his hand behind my back. "Let's go see how that man of yours is doing." It's like he just gave me whiplash, but I'm grateful he's looking out for Beckett, I suppose.

We walk down the stairs and across the street to the garage to find everyone rushing around. I forgot just how engrossing the energy in the garage is, even for a practice session.

Nate beelines it for me but abruptly stops when he sees Felix next to me. I try really hard to hide my smile, but it peeks through.

"You enjoy having the power," Felix says next to me.

I look up at him in question.

"People underestimate you, and you love running circles around them to show just how much power you hold over them."

I think about it and discover he's not wrong. For so long, it's felt like a fight. This new position was supposed to give Pierce and me some freedom, and it felt like it just gave me more work because I constantly had to prove my worth to people. It became a game, how quickly I could show this or that person that I'm the one in charge. Felix is right; the power when people back down is intoxicating, but it's not something I need. I don't constantly need more to feel complete. Giving away some of this ultimate power within the company is what Pierce and I have been slowly doing, by giving our regional managers more of it and more responsibilities along with it.

It's been freeing to not feel the need to prove my worth, my power, as Felix says.

"I do, but I've come to not need it so much for the past year. I'm happy to oversee the bigger projects at Vanstone and travel to wherever Beckett is racing."

He gives me a side glance.

"But I do enjoy proving to men mostly"—I give him an apologetic smile—"that I know my shit." I smirk.

"That, you do. If you ever want a tour of our headquarters, don't hesitate to call me." He hands me a business card before veering off to the other side of the garage.

"Well hello, baby."

The familiar voice sends a warm feeling throughout my entire body.

"Hey." I realize Felix walked me right to Beckett's car. Perhaps he isn't a total pretentious jerk after all. "You ready?"

"So ready." His excitement is childlike. There's still the seriousness underneath it, but getting to drive fast cars for a living is still something he gets giddy about.

He pulls me up to him by my waist and kisses me like it'll be the last time.

"See you soon, baby." He smiles, then takes the helmet that Nate hands him and takes a couple of steps back.

Nate leads me back to my usual area, where I put on the headphones and watch the first practice.

***

I'm settling into my stool, butterflies taking over my body, as everyone rushes around the garage to get ready for race number one on the F1 circuit.

The energy is heightened and the nerves are on everyone's faces, but there's also a renewed hope. A new season means new possibilities. Beckett and I have only really had the nights together, but it's more than having no time, so I'll take it.

I watch as he maneuvers through all the people and heads straight to me.

"I need a good luck kiss," he says urgently like I didn't give him a lot more than that before we headed over here this morning.

As I look at him, I see the tension and nerves. He has a lot to prove this season, and I know it's stressing him out, though he won't tell me. He wants to keep it all bottled up and not put more stress on me. The one downside I can't treat with medication for this stupid disease is Beckett treating me with kid gloves sometimes.

"Hey." I grab his cheeks and pull him to me. "You are Beckett Davis, not Beck Davis. You are *my* Beckett, and you're going to go out there and race your best race, and you're going to win the whole damn thing. Race one, the Driver's Championship, all of it. This is your year," I tell him with conviction I hope he feels.

"I'm going to go win, baby," he says softly before pressing a kiss that holds all of his emotions to my lips.

My foot taps as I watch all the television monitors, the notebook and pen I've now got a habit of bringing left discarded on the table top. Nate finally settles in next to me once Beckett is in the car, and he looks like he's going to throw up.

"He'll be fine," I murmur.

"Yep," he clips.

"Nate." I wait until he looks at me. "He can do this. He's the best racer on the grid right now, and he's going to prove that."

"He's the best." He nods like a bobblehead.

I hear the countdown in my headphones, and then I watch for the next two hours with my heart in my stomach. Every turn, every close call, every straightaway, I watch as Beckett takes a commanding lead and never lets up. As the final lap comes around, Nate grabs my hand. Both of us are squeezing so tight that the circulation is probably cut off in both of our hands. I don't feel pain, though.

As Beckett rounds the last corner, he's clear to the flags. The checkered flag waves as he crosses the finish line. I jump up and down with Nate in celebration.

I hear Beckett over his radio, screaming and hollering, but once the excitement calms down and his engineers and Felix have congratulated him, he calmly says, "This is the year, baby. We're winning the whole damn thing."

I don't think my smile has ever been so big. Hearing him repeat what I told him and knowing he believes it is everything.

This year is turning out to be my favorite yet.

Chapter 36
SYDNEY

I can't believe it's already May. I blinked, and half the year is gone.

I'm sitting in my office, going over some financials for our resort in Turkey, when a knock sounds on my office door.

"Come in!" I call out.

Daisy walks in with Pierce behind her.

"To what do I owe this special occasion?" I stand up and give Pierce a hug. It's been weeks since I've seen him, and we usually see each other once a week at a minimum.

"Do I need an excuse to see my favorite co-worker?" It's still weird to hear him call me his co-worker, surreal that I've worked up to such a high level within the company.

"Usually, yes. Or Jane told you to do something."

"Well damn."

"It's good to see you, regardless of the reason. Sit." I smile at him.

He and Daisy sit in the chairs in front of my desk, and I wait them out.

"How are you feeling?" Daisy breaks the ice first, like she usually does. The woman hates silence.

"Good. The methotrexate they put me on is doing wonders. I started on the pills, and the side effects were ... not a good time..." I cringe, not wanting to remember the nausea that had me down for the count for a couple of days before I couldn't take it. "But I switched to injections, and it's been night and day difference."

"That's great to hear," Pierce says.

I realize I haven't been doing a great job of keeping them updated between my duties on the job and traveling to most of Beckett's races.

"Sorry I haven't been keeping you guys in the loop."

"No need to apologize. I'm glad you've been busy with things besides work," he says.

"That's actually why we're here," Daisy pipes up, and Pierce shoots her a "chill out" look.

"Oh?"

"Things are basically running themselves here, as we intended," Pierce says. "And I had a thought."

Him dragging this on has me worried.

"I want to buy a team."

It's like a bomb blew up in my office. No one makes a sound; everyone is holding their breath as I try to piece together what he just said.

"A team."

"An F1 team," he says cheerily.

"You don't even like sports." It's the first thing that pops into my head.

"True, but you do. Well, you like F1 well enough, obviously."

"Ooookaaay," I draw out.

"I want to be the financial backer to the team that you, and possibly Beckett, run."

"What the fuck?" I whisper, more confused by the minute.

"I'm basically retired. I have more money than I care about, or than Jane cares about, and I want a new venture." He shrugs like this is an everyday ask.

"You're talking billions of dollars." Does he not know how much teams cost?

"Yep."

"And you knew about this?" I ask Daisy.

"She's the one I've been talking logistics to because she has Luka," Pierce adds helpfully.

"You're basically retired too. We've shifted things so much between the two of you that neither of you are working even part-time hours. Well, you are, but that's because you're just finding more shit to do." She points at me.

"Thanks." I roll my eyes.

"I'm just saying." She shrugs.

"I— Break this down like I'm ten." Am I having an aneurism? Is that a side effect? I don't understand what's happening here.

"I'm going to buy an F1 team that you, Beckett, Daisy—and if Luka wants to stop racing, he'll join in too—will run. That's assuming Beckett is done racing after his contract is up next year. Things would move fast, but I already have the ball in the court with the FIA president. Beckett could always drive for us if he doesn't want to retire yet." He rubs his chin in thought.

"You've lost your goddamned mind! I can't run a team! I don't know shit about the sport!"

"Oh please. I'm married to a driver, and you know ten times more than I do. How much logistics have you researched in the last year?" Daisy asks, and I can feel my cheeks heat. "Exactly. I bet you already have a little spreadsheet of where Legacy could improve, that you've dug into the financials that are easily available."

I look over at Pierce, but his goofy smile just irks me more.

"It's fucking annoying how well the two of you know me."

"How much more efficient could you make their spending just from what you know?" Pierce asks.

"Seventeen percent," I grumble.

"That's a shit-ton when you're talking about a billion-dollar company," Pierce oh-so-helpfully points out.

"You can't just make a team. F1 doesn't work like that. You have to go through a voting process, other teams have to have input..."

"We're not making one; we're buying one."

"Who the fuck has a team for sale?!" I throw my hands up in exasperation. "How do the two of you even remotely think this is a good idea?!" Even as I say it, my mind is spinning with the possibilities.

"Well, technically, no one has a team for sale, but everything can be bought." Pierce's smugness from days of old peeks through.

"Jesus, I forget sometimes where you came from. You're all nice and caring now; it's so far removed from who you were in London."

"It does still come in handy occasionally." Pierce looks at his nails like he's bored of this conversation.

"You still didn't answer me. Who are you potentially buying with this asinine idea?"

"Oh, don't act like you aren't already thinking of changes to make and how things work." Pierce rolls his eyes. "We're looking at Empress Racing." *Whom Luka drives for.*

My eyes shoot over to Daisy, who's smiling like the cat that ate the canary. "Does Luka know?"

"No, because nothing is final. I can't tell him shit; he'll just blab to the whole damn garage." She rolls her eyes, but I see something else as she tries to play it off. She won't be telling him because of something else going on. Shit, are they okay? I haven't talked to her about her personal life in too long. I need to be better about that.

"If— and this is a big if," I say pointedly at Pierce, "I agree to this ... wild idea, it's not exactly less stress and less work. With my RA, I don't want to push shit more; I like the easier schedule," I admit.

"Way ahead of you, Syd." Pierce claps. "You'd be the CEO, President, whatever you want your title to be, but it would run just like it does here. Your team principal would run the show, and you would just oversee and work on whatever you want to."

"This is insane," I whisper as my eyes dart between the two of them.

"But you're thinking about it." Pierce smiles.

Sighing, I cave. "Yes. You are both so annoying. Yes, I'm thinking about it, but you would literally be buying *me* an F1 team. You know that, right?"

"Well, yeah. I'd make a boatload of money off of it still, but you'd make the bulk of it, and it would be yours under the Vanstone umbrella."

"What all needs to happen?" I ask, and I see the second I say it, Pierce knows he has me.

Daisy is rolling her lips inward to make her smile less obvious, but it's pointless.

"I've been in talks with the owner of Empress. They seem keen on a deal because, outside of Luka, they haven't had a great track record of late. It's losing them a ton of money, and they want to be done with it."

My eyes drift to my desk, to the notepad I've been bringing with me to races, and I think about Empress's standing. Their second driver, a rookie, is in the back of the pack consistently; he and Luka both have contracts ending this season, and neither have a new seat on the grid. Their car improvements haven't been great, and no one can figure out why they've had such a drastic drop from last season.

"When can I talk to Beckett about this?" My eyes drift back up to Pierce's.

"I'm confident you know him well enough to use your own discretion. The deal was contingent on you saying yes, so now that you have—"

"I haven't."

"Now that you have," he continues. "I'm having the lawyer draw up a contract as soon as I leave here. The FIA president is excited to see a fresh brand in the sport, one that can bring the added bonus of resorts to tie to the races, so it's now a matter of legal bullshit and signing the paperwork. Then, your work begins on overhauling the team."

"Jesus." I run my temples. "I didn't even say yes, Pierce."

"Yes, you did, Syd. But if saying the actual word means something to you, go for it." He crosses his arms and leans back in his chair.

I look at Daisy, who just looks too excited for this whole scenario.

"I want it noted on the invisible record kept between the three of us, that you, Pierce Vanstone, owe me a very large birthday present for this shit."

"I'm buying you an entire team. Chill, woman." Pierce rolls his eyes.

I arch my eyebrow and wait him out. He's too easy. Between Jane and I, he caves every single time now.

"Fine. Talk to Jane and figure out what you want. I'll make it happen."

I smile then take a deep breath. "Yes."

***

Three weeks later, the sale of Empress Racing's paperwork is sitting on my desk, waiting for me to sign.

Holy shit, I'm about to own an F1 team.

Chapter 37
BECKETT

The most grueling three weeks of the season are upon us, and for once, I'm excited for them instead of dreading them. The June/July stretch of the Spanish, Austrian, and British Grand Prix's are always a turning point in the season. It's where drivers pull ahead and where they lose out on contracts for next year as well.

Sydney will be with me the entire time, three weeks straight without her leaving my side except when I race, and I'm so fucking ready for it.

She's been working a lot more recently, and I'm not thrilled. I thought she was supposed to be slowing down, not taking more on, but she's been quiet about what she's been up to. It makes me worry. Sure, the medication she's currently on has helped her function greatly, but that doesn't mean things can't change in a second.

I'm coming back to our room after a quick meeting with my chief engineer, then ordering some room service and having my way with my woman.

I open the door of our suite and see Sydney working away on the desk in the corner.

"I thought it was a no-work weekend," I tell her, not mad she's working but concerned about her workload.

She turns her head, and I see it in her eyes before she says anything. Whatever she's about to say is going to blow my mind.

"Hi. Umm, it was supposed to be, but that drastically changed when some stuff went through. Some contracts, if you will."

"Contracts. For resorts? I thought Pierce wasn't buying any more places."

"Places? No, he's done with that. This is a new venture."

"And he's making you work more for his little project?" I can't hide the annoyance in my voice. He knows about her RA; we text periodically about it to make sure both ends of Sydney's life are taking care of her.

"You might want to sit down for this."

I grab a dining room chair, slam it next to her harder than I mean to, and spin her legs to face me. "Don't beat around the bush, baby. I'm already about to punch Pierce out."

"You're cute when you're all protective like this."

"Sydney, now is not the time."

"I know." She smiles. "What I'm about to tell you does not leave this room. Not even to Nate."

"Done."

"Vanstone Properties bought Empress Racing, and at the end of the season, I'll be taking over as the president of the company."

A bomb went off; I can even hear the whooshing sound in my ears.

I can't wrap my head around the words she just spoke, but she just lets me take my time. She doesn't say anything, doesn't reiterate what she just said.

It takes me—hell, I don't even know—a while to let it all sink in.

"You're the new president of Empress Racing." A statement I say robotically.

"I am. Well, technically not yet, but in December, I'll officially take over."

"Holy shit."

"I know."

"Where the hell did this come from?"

"God, I don't even know. Pierce waltzed into my office a couple of months ago with the crazy idea, and for some reason, I agreed."

"How much work will this add to your plate?"

She smiles— the one I love so much, the one that says she's as far gone for me as I am for her. "Initially, probably a lot because I'm a control freak, but the goal is to just oversee like I do for Vanstone Properties."

"And what about Vanstone?" I ask.

"Pierce is insane and won't let me jump ship. I'll keep my title, pay, and benefits. Empress will be in addition to, but Vanstone runs itself now. I'll only have to attend shareholder meetings and our yearly corporate meeting, as long as nothing detonates. We've delegated everything."

"Holy shit."

"I know." She nods. "Want to hear the best part?"

"I don't know if my head can handle any more."

"Well, I'm telling you anyway. Whatever you decide at the end of your contract, I'd like you to join us at Empress. Whether that means you drive for us or you retire and help me run the joint—my personal preference—I want you to be a part of Empress as we move forward and grow it."

"Holy shit." I realize I'm a broken record, but I don't have the words to tell her what's going on in my head.

"It's a lot to take in, I know. The stuff that was just sent over to me is all of the financials. I'm mainly interested in the employees right now, but it means while you're practicing and having meetings and press, I'll be working on this."

"This is crazy."

"It's absolutely crazy," she says with a laugh.

"Why did you even say yes to this? This world is ... hectic and back-stabby—"

"I don't think that's a word."

"It is when you're talking about F1. The politics of it all are awful. I don't want you anywhere near that. I need you relaxed and calm, not stressed out all the time." I'm panicking now; I can feel it. My breath is getting shorter.

"Hey." She puts her hand on my forearm. "I know you don't know a ton of what I've had to do to get to this point in my life, how much I've had to handle within Vanstone, but I'm not scared of F1. I'm not scared of the politics or the prejudice I'll undoubtedly get because I'm a woman. Just ask Felix; he'll tell you I can handle myself. And Beckett?" She waits until my eyes lift to hers. "I need a new challenge. While I love the more leisurely pace, I can't keep it up forever. I'm so fucking bored. It's just not me. And I promise, once I get things where I want them, I'll slow down. We can go to Idaho every single Christmas, we can spend breaks wherever you want to go, but during the season, I figure out how to make Empress not only sustainable but thrive."

"You are so fucking sexy right now," I whisper.

She's a force to be reckoned with. I realize I've never actually seen her in action. I've only seen her in Idaho or on the circuit with me. She became the co-CEO of Vanstone Properties for a reason, and it's one hell of a thing to witness in action.

"God, I've wanted to tell you for so damn long, but I wanted to wait until things were more certain," she continues like I didn't say anything.

"Sydney."

"There's so much to do, but I'm so fucking excited about it."

"Sydney."

"I know it's a lot to take in, but—"

"Baby, shh." I smile before leaning forward and pressing a kiss to her lips.

Our foreheads tip together as we pull back.

"I'm so fucking happy for you," I whisper.

"Thank you. I'm nervous. It's a lot of work, but after spending so much time at races with you, I've come to love this stupid little sport."

"Racing fast cars in a weird-shaped loop for fifty-plus laps is pretty stupid," I murmur.

"So repetitive. Full of egotistical men who make too much money." She smirks.

"Way too much." I press a kiss to her lips.

"I really want you with me." She sobers as she pulls back.

"I will be right by your side. We'll just wait closer to December to see in what capacity."

"I love you," she whispers then jolts back.

"I love you so fucking much," I rush out.

Before I register what happened, she's on top of me, and we almost tip the chair backward. I steady her on my lap as I kiss her with every ounce of love I feel for her.

***

Three weeks, three races, and three wins.

I've never been happier or so excited for my future.

Sydney, true to her word, has worked mostly when I've been racing. She's moved herself to the little debrief room in the back of the garage that we use when we're pissed off or fucked up and crashed the car. She told me it was because she didn't want anyone accusing her of using insider knowledge once she takes over.

What's been really interesting is her relationship with Felix. If I didn't know better, I swear he knows about her takeover. He's taken her under his wing and showed her more of the administrative ropes. Hell, maybe he does know, but he's damn good at keeping a secret. It really wouldn't surprise me.

We're back at my house after a win at Silverstone, showering, changing, and waiting for catering to get here. I wanted to throw a party for our friends after the grueling three-week grind, to let loose and celebrate my win.

Sydney made us shower separately so we didn't get "distracted"—her word, not mine—so I'm waiting for her on my bed with just my boxer briefs on, hoping she breaks.

The water shuts off, and when she opens door, steam billowing around her, I just think about how fucking lucky I am to call her mine. I don't know what I did in this or a past life to bring this woman into my orbit, but I refuse to take any of it for granted.

"It's still a no, Beckett." She smirks as she walks by me, totally naked, dragging her fingertips across my chest.

"You're a cruel woman, baby," I sulk.

"You, my dearest sweet, sweet man, don't have a fast bone in your body when it comes to sex. Everyone is coming over in a half an hour, and I know that's not long enough to do what you want to."

"You know me so well." I pull her to me, hugging her with my head on her stomach. "Thank you for being here for all three races. I know travel sucks and is hard on your body." I snag one of her hands off my shoulders and massage her wrist.

She groans with relief. "I'll be honest; I feel obligated to come to every race now because you've been on the podium for every race. I feel like if I don't come, you'll lose and I'll never hear the end of it."

I can feel her giggling, so I nip at her stomach.

"I don't care about the reason; I'm just grateful to have you with me. I like knowing you're just in the garage if anything happens. That if I need you, I can talk to you through my radio." I switch to massaging her other wrist.

"I love you." She sighs. "But I really do need to go get ready, or someone's going to get an eyeful."

I growl at the thought of anyone except me seeing this body. "Fine. But later, you're mine."

"Always."

Chapter 38
SYDNEY

I'm nervous, which is so ridiculous. I know everyone coming—some are my friends—and yet this feels so ... domesticated.

Standing in the middle of Beckett's closet, feeling a bit lost, I laugh at the sheer luxury of everything in this semi-detached house. When I lived here back when Vanstone was headquartered here, I was in a shitty flat and barely even slept there. The craziest part is that this is his *other* home; he has an even nicer place in Monaco.

"What are you laughing about in here?" He strolls in, snagging a Legacy-branded T-shirt off a hanger, and puts it on.

"How ridiculous this house is when you spend maybe a month total here a year."

"You know one of the things I love most about you?" He asks, completely disregarding my words. "The fact that you make more money than I do and act like you're still struggling and are shocked by all the luxury surrounding you." His arms wrap around me as I laugh harder.

"I've never thought about it that way. I've always joked that I'm the imposter in this world because I never grew up in it; I just got lucky with Pierce. I mean, my house in Austin is nice, but it's one of the first, and only, for that matter, things I went a little overboard on."

Now that I think about it, I am an oddball. I have the wardrobe to reflect my standing within Vanstone Properties, but the rest of my life doesn't really back up my salary.

"You didn't get lucky, baby. You worked your ass off, proved yourself, and excelled. Like you do with all things. That's why Empress will not only succeed but thrive."

I smack his shoulder. "You're not supposed to be making me emotional right now. We have people coming over."

"Someone has to boost your ego," he mumbles.

"I think you have enough ego for the both of us." I chuckle as I grab a loose pair of linen pants and a tight tank top then put them on as he finishes dressing.

"Hey," he says softly as he gently grabs my elbow, pulling me toward him. "I'm serious. You're an incredible woman. Even if we weren't together, I would admire the hell out of you."

My eyes fill with tears, and I don't even attempt to stop the flow. "Thank you," I croak out. I bury myself in his chest as he rubs my back while I regain control over my emotions.

"All right, no more tears, baby. It's a happy day. We're going to celebrate, eat copious amounts of food, and talk shit about people on the grid."

"Well, that's just a dickhead move," I counter.

"See, you're already thinking like a president of a team, trying to stay diplomatic."

"Sure, diplomatic. We'll go with that." I grin up at him before pressing a kiss to his lips and stepping back.

"Daisy and Luka are on their way, and then the rest of the crew should be here in the next hour," he says, sliding his watch onto his wrist.

My eyes move down his body, taking in his casual outfit of jeans and a T-shirt. He somehow makes it look like a million bucks, and I not-so-subtly lean to the side to check out his ass.

"Did you just..." He twists his head around to look at his back. "Do I have something on me?"

"Nope, just a damn fine ass." I sigh wistfully.

"Go, woman. Get out of this tiny closet before I maul you." His head tips back to look at the ceiling like it's such a hardship to keep his hands to himself.

I giggle my way out of the closet, down the stairs, and head to the kitchen to grab a water bottle. No sooner do I down half the bottle does the doorbell ring.

"Hi," I say cheerfully as I usher the caterer in. Not having to cook when I'm utterly exhausted is definitely a perk of that salary we were talking about earlier.

"Is it okay if I leave the door unlocked so I can grab a couple of loads of food?" she asks.

"Oh, absolutely. Let me help you."

"I've got it, baby," Beckett says, walking into the kitchen. A kiss to the cheek and a squeeze to my shoulder are his way of wordlessly telling me to take it easy.

Taking a seat at the kitchen island, I watch as the man who was supposed to be a Christmas fling proves he was always meant to be mine. I can't believe I pushed back against him for so long when I could have had this—this love and support—for years.

"I know that look," Beckett whispers in my ear.

"What look?"

"The look that says you're thinking about our past and how long it took us to get here."

"Okay, mind reader." I huff out a laugh.

"No matter the what-ifs or the could-have-beens, our paths always would have collided. If it took a little longer to get here, then this was how it was supposed to be. I don't care how many years we took, as long as I get to keep you."

"Get a room," Nate catcalls as he enters the kitchen.

"Way to ruin the moment, dickhead."

"Hey, I thought we were being nice and not shit talking." I point at Beckett.

"I never agreed to that," he says pointedly. "He deserves it. And it isn't talking shit; it's insulting him. Big difference."

I roll my eyes at my ridiculous boyfriend. "And you." I point to Nate. "Knock first or call out when you enter the front door. Jesus, this isn't a fucking hostel. You never did this shit in Austin."

"Sorry, my dearest Syd," Nate says sweetly before turning to Beckett as he cringes. "I'm not apologizing to you, though, asshole."

"Can we stop the insults?" I whine. "We're supposed to be celebrating and being *nice* to each other."

"I never agreed to be nice to Nate."

"Yeah, I'd never agree to that." Nate nods.

"I need a drink." I sigh.

"Wine?" Beckett asks, already moving to the counter.

"Can you drink, on the medication?" Nate asks then winces. "I shouldn't have asked that. I'm sorry, that's personal."

"It's all good." I wave him off.

He's seen me relegated to the couch because of joint stiffness; he's one of the few who can actually ask questions without them feeling intrusive.

"I can have small amounts without much effect. I haven't really gone crazy except a glass of wine here and there, so I limit myself to a glass."

He nods as Beckett sets the glass of rosé in front of me.

"So, who all is crashing this place?" Nate asks, moving to a more comfortable subject.

"Luka and Daisy, Eli and Cruz from the pit crew, Nina from analytics, and I think that's it." Beckett ticks off people on his fingers.

"And Susie!" I add. Felix's assistant has become a good friend to me, and I'm trying damn hard to poach her from Legacy, but we'll see if it happens. Felix treats his staff well and is king on the circuit for a reason. Although, he has been helping me on the sly when I have questions.

"Oh! Eli has such a crush on her." Nate rubs his hands together.

I roll my eyes at the high-school-like gossip that comes from these grown-ass men on a regular basis.

"Knock, knock!" Daisy's voice calls from the front door.

"In the kitchen!" Beckett counters.

Daisy and Luka step into the open space, and the tension between the two of them is practically visible. I glance at Beckett at the same time he arches an eyebrow at me. We both shake our heads, unsure about what's going on between the two of them.

They make the rounds; the men shoot the shit as Daisy settles in next to me.

"How's it going Boss Bitch?"

"We're not calling me that." I roll my eyes.

"We need something that will scare all the drivers and put fear into all the

Empress employees."

"What in the world, Mistress of Doom?" I murmur into my wine.

"Huh, I kind of like that," she says contemplatively.

"You've lost the plot. I don't want anyone scared of me." I chuckle.

"Well, that's no fun. Might whip some people into shape," she mumbles.

I barely hide my wince. Looks like there's trouble in paradise, and I'm not sure if I even want to know. If she hasn't told me up to this point, then I'm not going to pry. She'll come to me when she wants to. If she wants to.

"Hello, Beck and Lover!" Cruz peeks his head into the door.

"I have a name!" I yell back.

"Hello, Beck and the always gorgeous Sydney!" he says in the same tone.

"Watch it," Beckett growls, making me laugh. If there's one thing this group has figured out, it's how easily they can rile up Beckett.

Eli enters more subdued behind Cruz, and they all hug like they hadn't just spent the last four days together.

Before long, Susie and Nina show up, and we all dig into Mediterranean food that was dropped off.

I sit and watch as this makeshift friend group chats about everything from the food to who tripped over a wench at the race. The only thing missing for me is Pierce and Jane, but they have a family to take care of, so it's not so easy for them to just fly off—

"Well, hey there, children," Pierce's voice cuts my thoughts off, and my jaw drops.

I turn to face Beckett, who is smiling so big I don't have to wonder who made this happen.

"Oh my God!" I jump up and give Jane a huge hug first before moving to Pierce. "How in the world did you both keep this from me?"

"Beck said he wanted to have a party and wanted you to have all the people you care about here. We didn't hesitate."

"Where are my babies?" I ask, wondering where their kids, who are the closest thing I have to nieces, are.

"Bea and Andy." Jane smiles. "When you get back to Austin, we can go do something with them."

"Deal."

Beckett walks up behind me, pulling me by my middle flush against him. "Happy?"

"Deliriously so. Well played, Beckett, well played." I smile over my shoulder, and he kisses my temple.

The rest of the evening is spent with my favorite people, talking about everything and nothing. It's perfect. For the first time, I don't feel like an employee or a boss. I feel like a friend to all of these people enjoying the evening with us, and it's all thanks to Beckett being in my life.

It's hours before everyone leaves, but once they do, Beckett pulls me into his arms, swaying to the low music in the background.

"How you pulled this off, I'll never know, but thank you," I murmur.

"You know this whole group came tonight because of you, right? Pierce and Jane didn't even bat an eye to fly out here."

"Lies." I scoff.

"Sydney Johnson, people love you. They are so happy to have your friendship, and you don't even see it."

"Maybe..." I whisper.

"We're all so lucky to have you in our life, and I think it's time that we show you what that friendship means to us all."

"That's really sweet. And it's really overwhelming, but in a good way. I'm glad we could get everyone together. We could maybe make it a tradition. End of the season or during break, have everyone over."

"I love that and can make it happen."

"You, Beckett Davis, are too good to me. Thank you for everything."

"Never thank me, baby." He presses a kiss to my lips as we dance around the living room.

My thoughts are full of excitement for our future together, of the life we'll hopefully create together.

Chapter 39
BECKETT

The Austin race might be my favorite race now, not because the track is amazing or because I perform well on it. No, it's because I don't have to travel for a month and a half before this one. Our break goes from Singapore at the end of September to Austin at the end of October. I get extra time with Sydney, and it's like a boost to the system, giving me energy to finish out the season strong.

The sale of Empress was announced in Singapore, which means that for the rest of the season, Sydney will be over in their garage, not mine. I may have pouted like a petulant child for a long while, but I understand the reasoning. Can't look like she's getting insider information with it already looking a little iffy.

What's been the most interesting is how this season has played out. I've been on the podium for every single race, winning a good chunk of them too. My points are adding up quickly, and as long as I stay consistent, it's going to be a good year.

Luka, on the other hand, cannot say the same. Something is going on with him. I can't tell if it's his car not performing or Luka having a hard time this year outside of racing. Either way, he's in danger of getting bumped off of Empress next season. It's putting Sydney in a hard position, because even though we're all friends, she can't take that into consideration when forming the team next season. Today, he's starting at the back of the grid in twentieth, and it's not doing him any favors.

"You ready for this?" Sydney sidles up next to me in the closet, both of us facing the mirror.

"I am; are you? You're looking tired, baby." Concern thrums through my body.

"I am fucking exhausted." She laughs.

"Do you need to take a breather and stay home?"

"Beckett, I can't just stay at home. I'm the new face of Empress. I have to be there."

"You're the president; you can do whatever the hell you want," I tell her, outraged.

"Thank you, really, for being this concerned, but I'm fine. I'm just not used to race weekends where I have to actually work the entire time. I can't just lounge around the garage with Nate." She smirks.

"Syd, this isn't a joke. If you need a break, take one." My voice softens as I turn to face her.

"I know. I will. But all we have left is the race. I can sit my way through that and then come home as soon as trophies are handed out. I promise I won't stay longer than I need to."

I stare at her, looking for any clue that she's not okay and can't handle that load, but she looks confident and strong. She may be tired, but she's not hurting, and that's the most important thing.

"Okay. Well, I'm off. I love you, and don't work too hard," I murmur as I close the distance between us.

"I will probably work too hard, but I won't push it. I love you too. Kick ass, and don't let me down." She smirks.

It's been our ongoing joke all season; she told me to win the whole damn thing, and I've taken it to heart.

"Always."

"Be safe, Beckett." She kisses me after she whispers it.

"I'll be running to you when I cross the finish line," I promise. No matter what place I finish, I always run to her first.

***

Lap forty-three. I lead by more than nine seconds. I had my final pit stop six laps ago, and now I just need to keep the lead.

"Speed is looking good, Beck. Tire degradation is looking fair," my engineer says on my radio.

"Still plan A on pits?" I reply.

"Correct."

"Copy."

The line goes quiet, and I focus on watching the corners to keep my tires in better shape. Within seconds, my steering wheel flashes a red flag and my radio clicks on.

"Safety car, Beck. Safety car's coming out."

"What happened? Are they okay?" I slow my pace and prepare to head to the pit lane if needed.

My heart always drops to my stomach when a safety car comes out. It means there's enough damage to a car that they need everyone to slow so they can clean up. That can mean a variety of things, and you always hope for the lesser.

"Unclear. They've got fire extinguishers coming."

"Who?" You never want a bad crash, no matter who it is.

"Luka."

My heart drops further, if that's possible. As I follow the safety car around turn thirteen, I see the flames first. I don't know if he's out of the car yet, but physically restraining myself from stopping my car and jumping out to help is harder than I could have ever imagined.

"Is he okay?" I ask again urgently as I pass the wreckage.

It's a good thing we have halos now because this crash would have been worse without it. His car is flipped upside down, and I can't make heads or tails of anything.

"They're calling for an ambulance."

The safety car follows the track, and we get word that they're suspending the race until the track is clear. It's insane to think that's the verbiage they use when we're talking about an actual person who is likely hurt.

"Beckett." Sydney's voice in my ear calms me a little.

"Is he okay?" I persist.

"They're pulling him out right now. He flipped, hit his head hard from what we can see, but he hasn't been coherent enough to get anything else. And then the car engulfed in flames."

"Fuck!" I scream into my car.

I see the pit lane entrance, and I'm both elated and dreading it. Once we get my car into the garage, I get out and head back to the little cooldown room to collect myself.

Sydney bursts in seconds after I shut the door. Her eyes are red-rimmed as we hug each other close.

"What the fuck happened?" I ask.

"He jerked his steering wheel, hit the barrier hard, and flipped it down the track. From the onboard video, that's all we can see. There was nothing around him," she whispers.

"We need to get back out there." I clear my throat.

"I know. Just one more." She squeezes me tighter before we leave the room, her heading back to Empress as I turn the opposite way and make my way back to the garage.

Nate meets me, solemnly nodding to me as we wait for any update.

It's like the entire grid—hell, the whole track—is holding their breath. We watch as the crew cuts open what they can of the halo and eventually pull Luka out. He's immediately put on a stretcher and driven away in an ambulance.

Felix walks over to me and puts a hand on my shoulder. "No news on how bad it is. Track should be clear in fifteen minutes. FIA is saying we finish the race."

"What fucking assholes," I mutter.

"Agreed. But this is still a job, however fucked up it is right now. You going to be able to go out there and drive?" He's not asking for the benefit of Legacy; he's asking as a friend.

"Yeah. I can do it." Even as I say it, I know it'll probably be one of the harder races I've ever driven. But winning it for Luka seems like a good enough driving force right now.

Fifteen minutes later, we're all in our cars and lined up in the pit lane. The safety car leads us out for a lap before dropping off to the pit lane as we resume the race. Twelve laps to go. Twelve laps with men who want to win for Luka just as badly as I do.

The rest of the drive is fairly uneventful. I have to fend off the hotshot at Amaro, Alejandro, who's been my only consistent competition this year, but I get the job done. I cross the finish line; the black-and-white-checkered flag waves above me, and I wave to the crowd as I do my cooldown lap. But I don't feel happy. There's no joy in this win, only worry about one of my best friends.

The trophy ceremony is lackluster. No one wants to celebrate when one of our own is in the hospital.

I meet Nate and Sydney by the exit that will take us to where I parked Sydney's car, and we head to the hospital. Daisy texted Sydney and told us where she was, so we rush to join her side and offer her the support she needs.

"They said"—she sniffles—"that he has one hundred percent burns on his hands. It moves up under his sleeves, so his forearms too. And his ... his face has some too. They said it's not as bad as his hands because of the balaclava. He also has a concussion." The tears fall faster as she tells us the extent of the injuries.

"Oh, Dais, I'm so sorry." Sydney hugs her close.

"The safety gear worked," Nate says softly. "Those flames were over the whole car, and his suit protected him."

"The doctor said more, but I can't remember," Daisy says softly, her head resting on Sydney's shoulder.

"Hey, it's okay," I tell her in what I hope is a soothing tone. "Have you been to see him?"

"Not yet. They have him in the ICU because of the possible infection, and they're running scans on ... everything, I guess."

"Okay, we'll stay here with you the whole time," I tell her.

"No, no. That's not good for anyone. I can call you whenever he's up for visitors."

We decline her offer and stay well into the next morning. Daisy is the only one allowed to see him right now, but we stay, learning more about what Luka's future potentially looks like.

"Guys, I'm okay. He's okay. Go home. I promise to call you the second I get more information," Daisy says as we're eating lunch in the private room we've been hanging in.

Sydney nods to me, so I tap Nate's shoulder to let him know we're leaving. She bends down to hug Daisy tight, whispering words of encouragement and support, I'm sure.

Once we're all loaded back in the car, I sag against the seat. "I knew he was struggling with something, but I didn't try and help. I didn't push him when he shrugged me off."

"Beckett, there is no blame on anyone. Accidents happen, and if there was something going on with him that jeopardized his focus, maybe getting in a car that goes over a hundred and fifty miles per hour wasn't the best move," Sydney says.

"That's shitty," Nate murmurs.

"It is, but that's part of racing. Knowing when your head is in it and when it's not is paramount to safety. I'm not blaming Luka—what happened was awful—but if something was going on with him, he needed to be aware it wasn't safe for him to be out there."

"Spoken like a true owner," I say.

"There was no one around him. I can't help but draw conclusions, however much of an asshole that makes me," she says sadly.

"Hey, everyone in this sport just wants it to be the safest we can make it. You're right about the mindset, and I honestly hope you're wrong about Luka."

"I do too," she whispers.

Back at home, Nate heads to his side of the house while Sydney and I change into pajamas.

In bed, she curls up tight against me. "I don't like seeing things like that," she murmurs.

"I don't either. People always say it's part of racing, but it shouldn't be. It's scary."

"When I saw him hit the barrier, logically, I knew it was Luka, but my heart couldn't reconcile the fact that it wasn't you. I thought I was going to pass out. I was so scared."

I consider her words. It's always scary to consider, but as I think about something like that possibly happening to me, leaving Sydney to deal with whatever happened, it shakes something in me.

"I'm retiring at the end of the season," I say to the quiet room. No hesitation, just a keen clarity after a day like today.

She jolts up, eyebrows sky high as she gapes at me. "What?"

"I can't..." I sigh. "I can't put you through something like that. I don't want to take the risk; I don't want to play on a razor's edge. I don't *need* the racing anymore."

I'm not even sure if I'm making sense. For so long, my life has been about being the best Formula 1 driver in the world. Winning Drivers' Championships, trophies, and recognition was my sole focus. Now, I don't need any of that; I just need Sydney.

"I don't know what to say. I support you in whatever you decide—you know that—but this feels like a knee-jerk reaction to Luka."

"Luka was a tipping point, but I've been tossing it around more and more lately. I've had the best season I've ever had. Even if I lose the Drivers' Championship, it won't make it any less successful for me. I want to lessen our travel, although you taking over Empress puts that into question. I want to do spontaneous things with you. I just want to do life with you, without driving taking over nine months of my year."

Her eyes shift between mine, looking for something. She must find it because she cups my cheeks and presses a kiss to my lips. "I don't plan to travel a lot with Empress. I'll stay at headquarters or remotely for most of the year."

"So, does that mean we're running off into the sunset together?" I smile up at her.

"It means we might want to turn our living arrangements into something more permanent."

"Tell me where to sign, baby." I stretch up to kiss her.

Chapter 40

BECKETT

Abu Dahbi. The last race of the season. One race to win it all. One race to go out on top.

Alejandro is within striking range, and it all comes down today.

Sydney is over at Empress. The fallout of Luka's crash has been far reaching, and their reserve driver has taken over his seat, essentially displacing Empress's chances to win the Constructors' championship unless he pulls out all the stops. Tension on the team has been high, and I know Sydney is ready for this race to be over so she can jump in and be the hard-ass boss she needs to be for them.

Me? I'm ready for the race to be over so I can spend every single day with the woman I love. I'm ready to travel less, maybe buy a place in Idaho, and spend a couple of months there in the winter. Sky's the limit—as soon as this race is over.

"You ready?" Nate claps my back.

"I am."

"You're too calm," he says skeptically.

No one except Sydney and Felix know I'm retiring. And if all goes to plan, I'll announce it during interviews after the race.

"I feel good. I just need to race my race, and we'll see where the cards land." I almost feel bad for not bringing Nate into the fold, but he's a talker and it wouldn't stay quiet if I told him.

"You've got this." He hands me my helmet—the last time he'll ever do so—as I double-check my gear and get suited up.

The choreographed dance of triple checks, radio checks, and clearing the space around me always feels like controlled chaos. We do our practice lap, pulling the cars into position on the track before getting out and doing the grid walk, gladhanding, and the anthem. Finally back in my car, I take a deep breath, trying to take in every second of my last drive.

The formation lap heats my blood, the adrenaline pumping, as the rest of the grid follows behind me. Once we're at a stop again, I slow my breathing, stretch my hands, and watch the red lights count down.

Then I'm flying.

Alejandro is still on my ass for my first pit stop. He's not letting me lead without a fight.

He passes me on lap twenty-three, and my anger flares at my decision to go wide instead of on the inside at the turn. It allows him to pass me easily.

"Still sticking to plan A, Beck," my radio sounds.

"Can we beat him on plan A?"

"Sticking to our pits and pushing hard, at the pace you're pulling... You'll be good."

On lap thirty-seven, my radio clicks. "Box, box. Box, box."

As I pull into the pit lane, my team changes my tires and tops off my fuel in record time.

"Alejandro is in the lead. You'll need to push your tires hard, but you have the pace to take the lead."

I don't respond; instead, I tune all my focus onto beating Alejandro.

By lap fifty, I've tried several times to pass him, but he keeps outmaneuvering me. I yell into my radio, cursing the Spaniard.

Eight laps to pull ahead.

Eight laps to take the lead.

And I'm not sure I can do it.

"Beckett," Sydney's voice sounds in my ear.

"Sydney," I breathe.

"Listen to me. Turn five is your best chance. Bide your time and overtake. Don't rush."

"Okay."

"Beckett?"

"Yeah, baby?"

"Go win the damn thing."

I smile. "Will do."

With Sydney's voice in my ear, I calm down, keeping a close distance until turn five. Alejandro gets cocky, taking the corner a little too wide, and I sneak in. As we come out of the turn, I pull ahead and take the lead.

"Yes! Keep it up. Keep it steady, Beckett!" Felix comes onto the radio.

Six laps.

"He's two tenths back," one of my engineers says.

Five laps.

"Four tenths—"

"If I want the gaps, I'll tell you," I cut him off. Unless I'm at risk of being overtaken, I want to stay in the zone. Race my race and bring it home.

Three laps.

I can feel the energy elevating in the stands like it's a physical presence pushing me that much harder.

Last lap.

I look in my mirrors and see my distance has only increased from Alejandro. As I round the last corner, the last straight is in front of me.

Cheers sound in my ears as I see the checkered flag.

Crossing the line feels surreal. No words come to me until I hear Sydney's voice.

"Oh my God, Beckett!" I can hear the tears in her voice, and I holler into the open air.

"We did it! Thank you all for everything you've done for us to bring this home," I tell the team through the radio.

"So proud of you, Beck. A textbook race, and I can't think of anyone more deserving," Felix says in my ear.

"Thank you," I choke out.

The cooldown lap is like a dream. I wave to the stands as the cheers breach my earpieces. I pull up to the number one spot below the podium and waste no time climbing out. I don't even unhook my helmet, just run to the group of engineers and mechanics and jump on top of them. Hands pat over my entire body, the excitement palpable.

Getting back to my feet takes a minute, as does my weigh-in, but once it's done, I take my helmet off and search out Sydney. She's off on the edge of the large group of Legacy employees, hands clasped together in front of her mouth, tears rolling down her cheeks.

Hugging her to me, I take a minute to let it all sink in.

"We did it, baby," I say into her ear.

"No, *you* did it. You fucking did it!" She chuckles like she can't quite believe this is real.

"I love you."

"I love you too. And I'm so damn proud of you." She kisses me, and I turn it a little more PG-13 before she pulls back.

Water gets handed to me, and I head to the area where the finishers are being interviewed. Third place talks, then Alejandro, who gives a gracious congratulations to me and the hard-fought battle.

Then, it's my turn.

Chapter 41
Sydney

The tears won't stop.

What's more than proud? I have no clue, but that's how I feel right now. Beckett has worked so hard for this, and to see all of his dreams come true is one of the best things I've ever gotten to witness.

When they were down to ten laps, I could see he was struggling to pass Alejandro, and I couldn't stay in the Empress garage and let it happen. Was it unconventional to just get on the radio? Sure, but I was going to do everything in my power to help him achieve his dreams.

As I watch the interviews, nerves hit me hard. This is a big moment, some would argue bigger than actually winning the whole damn thing.

"Beck Davis, congratulations. This feels like it's been a long time coming. How do you feel?"

"Thank you," he says into the mic, waving to the crowd as they cheer. "It's been a journey to get here, and I'm so grateful to everyone who helped make it happen. Truly, it's been a team win."

"It looked like Alejandro might have had it until you kicked it into another gear. Can you tell us what happened?"

"The voice of a much wiser and more level-headed woman came onto my radio. She kicked my ass into gear— Sorry." He cringes, remembering he's on live television. "Settled me down and allowed me to think of it like any other race."

"Is that the lovely Sydney Johnson?"

"It is." His smile could be a light source for half the globe.

My cheeks hurt with a matching one, I'm sure. I've never been a part of something this big. Opening a resort is cool and all, but seeing the exact moment someone's life goal comes to fruition is otherworldly.

"It's been quite the journey to get here. You almost went without a contract a couple of years back. What's next?"

I hold my breath.

"I'm so glad you asked. I'm retiring. This was my last race, and if I might say, what a way to go out." Beckett smiles.

Shocked gasps fill the area. Spectators and everyone surrounding me are visually shocked.

"Oh, uh... Well, congratulations on the amazing career," the interviewer stumbles as Beckett hands his mic off.

Now, he has to go wait in the cooldown room with the second and third place finishers before the trophy celebrations.

Less than ten minutes later, the men are lined up on their podiums. Anthems are played, trophies are handed out, and champagne is being sprayed.

The smile hasn't left my face since he crossed the finish line. This intoxicating feeling of being the best or even being associated with the best is addicting, and I finally understand why Pierce thought giving me Empress would be a good move. It makes me hungrier to get here, to make moves and get drivers who want it just as badly as I do. I'll have a secret weapon in my repertoire, at least. Beckett will be holding the title of Technical Consultant at Empress as of January 1.

Felix taps my elbow and tilts his head to the garage. I follow him to the building behind, which is set up like a mini headquarters, and join him in his office.

"Thank you," Felix says, catching me off guard.

"For what?"

"Knowing what he needed. He had me worried, and then I see you booking it into our garage and grabbing Nate's headphones." He chuckles.

I cringe. "Probably not a good look for the new president of Empress." It's not like I thought my actions through. I was worried about him, wanted to give him the push, and didn't even think about the optics.

"Fuck image. You'll forever be known as the ballsy woman who took charge and loved him enough to do whatever you could to help him. You're going to be a fierce competitor." He tips his head to me.

"I can't wait to give you a run for your money." I smirk.

He's become a close friend over the last year, teaching me the ins and outs of managing a Formula 1 team and how to handle the cutthroat politics.

"Yeah, yeah, just remember you like me when race day is over."

"Always." I smile over to him.

He's a great guy, and I'm lucky he took me under his wing.

"Sorry to interrupt the love fest," Beckett says from the doorway.

"No, you're not." Felix smirks.

"I'm going to miss your smart-ass," Beckett says as Felix stands and walks over to him.

They hug tightly, a show of respect and brotherhood in a season that was a hard fight.

"Proud of you, Beck. You did a phenomenal job."

Both men clear their throats before pulling back. Beckett turns to me and holds out his hand. I take it greedily, waving to Felix over my shoulder.

"I've never wanted to ditch a podium like I did today," he rushes out, leading us down the stairs and to his own little room. Once we're both inside, he slams the door and clicks the lock before gently pushing me against the door. He rains kisses all over my face, neck, and chest.

"Aren't I supposed to be the one rewarding you?" I murmur, sliding my fingers into his hair.

"Nope. This was a team win. You and me. I couldn't do it without you."

"Yes, you could have." I scoff.

Beckett pulls back and makes sure I'm looking into his eyes. "I couldn't have. I was panicking, trying too hard to pass. I wouldn't have won. The second I heard your voice, it was like tunnel vision. Everything slowed down, and I just repeated everything you said as I got to turn five."

"And then you won," I say softly.

"And then I won. How's it feel being the girlfriend of a champion?" He grins, pulling my dress to the side and kissing my collarbone.

"It feels like I'm the one about to get lucky."

"Damn straight you are." Pulling my dress up, he hooks his hand under my ass and bolsters me up against the door. "This is going to be quick, but I'll make it up to you."

My head tips back, hitting the door, as he shoves his racing suit down just far enough on his hips for his cock to be free.

"Do you wear your suit like that because you know it turns me on?" I ask.

"Fuck yes, I do." His finger moves my panties to the side before brushing against my clit. "And it worked like a fucking charm. You're so wet for me, baby."

I throw my arm over my mouth and moan as he circles my clit a couple of times before pushing a finger inside of me.

"So ready," he whispers in awe.

His finger moves back to my clit as the blunt head of his dick notches at my entrance.

"Oh my God." My breathy groan is louder than I want, but my mind isn't on who can hear us.

"Check-in, baby. How are you feeling?"

"Good. So good. Joints good, muscles good." I run through our usual checklist before we do anything strenuous now.

"Good." He grunts as he shoves in to the hilt, making me whimper.

He sets a hard and fast pace, both of us too high on adrenaline to care how fast things go.

I grip his shoulders hard, needing more. My head thrashes side to side. "Kiss me, please," I beg.

His grasp shifts so both hands are on my ass as he leans in and kisses me. Tongues tangle and teeth collide; it's messy and sloppy, and so damn good.

Pressure in my pelvis and a fluttering against his cock have me whimpering into our kiss. His pace picks up. His grip on my ass will inevitably leave bruises, but it only adds to my oncoming orgasm.

It hits me hard. I suck in a breath as he thrusts deep and holds there.

"Fuck," he gasps.

We collapse against the door, catching our breath.

His grip loosens. "I'm sorry I held you too tight."

"I'm good, I promise." I sigh, completely content.

He spins us around, walking to the couch and sitting down with me still on him.

"Today was one of my favorite days." Fingertips run along my spine.

"Mine too. I'm so fucking proud of you." My eyes fill with tears.

"Thank you, baby. But you know what I'm looking forward to?" he says with nothing but love and happiness in his eyes.

"What?"

"The rest of our lives together. This isn't the end of anything. It's the beginning of the best thing that's ever dropped into my lap. You downing a gin and tonic will forever go down in history as a turning point in my life."

I laugh at his assessment. "Who knew a forced vacation would completely change my life."

"I love you so much. Thank you. For today, for being with me, for making me better every day." He looks me in the eye.

"I love you. I don't think I could handle … everything without you. This last year has been scary and full of so much change, and there's never been a day where I wondered if I could really handle it all. Because of *you*, Beckett Davis. You make me feel like anything is possible." The tears now fall steadily.

"You ready to start forever together?" He smiles.

"Is that a proposal?"

"No, you'll know when I'm proposing, baby." He tickles my side.

"I can't wait."

Epilogue
BECKETT

Sitting on the balcony in Idaho, I pat my pocket for the fiftieth time. The ring I've had since Bahrain is in there. Somehow, I always knew it would happen here, but if an opportunity was perfect, I wanted to be prepared.

We got here two days ago after a trip to Paris for the FIA Prize Gala. I had to collect my Drivers' Championship trophy and eat my weight in bread before we could relax for Christmas.

"How are you not freezing your ass off?" Sydney says from the doorway.

I look down at my joggers and sweatshirt, all Legacy branded. *Guess I'll have to get new clothes for next season.*

"It's like taking an ice bath." I shrug.

"Yeah, no thanks. Breakfast just got delivered," she says over her shoulder, already moving back into the warmth.

"I'll be right in."

Patting the ring box, I know the time is right. I could wait until Christmas day, but I don't want to wait any longer. And if I can convince her to marry me while we're here, I wouldn't be mad.

Breathing in the cold air, smelling the fresh layer of snow on the ground, I stand up and head inside.

"You ordered an obscene amount of food, Beckett, jeez." She's lifting cloches, seeing the variety of choices.

"Wanted options," I say quietly before walking up behind her and wrapping my arms around her stomach. "Hi." I kiss her temple.

Spinning in my arms, she gives me a soft smile. It's the one she has when she's her happiest, most content. "Hi right back, hot stuff."

"I love you." I clear my throat as the words get stuck. "I love you so damn much. I've thought about this for so many months. What the right way was, what would make you the happiest."

"What are you talking about?"

"Life does this funny thing where it throws huge wrenches into your life. Sometimes it's for the better, and sometimes it challenges you. You, Sydney Johnson, we're a little of both."

"Beckett..."

"That first year here was... God, it was so good. And *fun*. I can't remember ever having that much fun. And then we left, and I thought I lost the best thing to happen to me in ... forever." I search my memory. "And then Christmas, right here in this suite, became our tradition by some good grace. I got my second chance. And I promised myself I wouldn't throw it away."

"Please," she whispers with tears in her eyes.

"Marry me," I whisper. "You are everything good in my life. You are the best part of me, and I don't want to wait any longer."

"What took you so long?" she says through her tears.

Laughter bursts from me. "I don't know, baby. We had a lot of shit going on in the last year."

"Fair," she says through a watery chuckle.

"What's your answer, baby?" I'm starting to feel unsure.

"You didn't ask." She arches an eyebrow even with tears in her eyes.

"Sydney Johnson, will you marry me? Put up with my over-ordering food at every meal? Teach me how to not be a racer anymore? Let me make you so fucking happy?"

"Yes. Yes, times a million." She laughs through her tears, pressing a kiss to my lips.

***

sydney

Best Christmas ever.

As I'm snuggled against Beckett, I sigh, catching a glimpse of the ring now sitting on my finger—a simple solitaire but large enough to be seen in Texas. The man went overboard. I'm not sure he knows how to do it any other way.

This year has felt like every major type of natural disaster mixed with climbing Mount Everest. It's been a hard year, but it's been more fulfilling than any other in my thirty-five years, adding a sense of accomplishment to every area of my life.

My rheumatoid arthritis is mostly under control unless I push myself too far. My new job is going fairly smoothly, considering everything that needs to be done. And Beckett is officially mine.

"What are you sighing about?" Beckett asks.

"Nothing in particular. Just … content. Happy. God, I'm so happy, Beckett."

"It's weird, right? To be this happy?" he asks.

"I think I just never knew it was possible to actually be this happy, you know? Like, life was good, but I didn't realize it could be *this* good."

"Yes, exactly!" He snaps his finger.

"You still haven't opened up your Christmas present," I observe.

"That would involve you getting off of me, so I think I'll wait until later."

"No." I lightly slap his chest.

He groans at the loss as I climb off of him. I've been eager for him to open this since he surprised me with the proposal, and I can't wait any longer. Grabbing the box from under the tree, I bring it back to the couch and hand it to him.

He carefully unwraps it, and the ever-familiar wooden box greets him. "We're going to run out of stuff for them to make." He chuckles.

"You might be right. This took some creative work."

Opening it up and removing all of the protective foam, he looks up at me with a question in his eyes.

"You beat me to it."

"Beat you to…?"

"Proposing." I smile.

He pulls out the gorgeous piece of glass—a simple rectangle, but the colors make it look like a watercolor painting. Etched into the glass are two simple words: *The Davises.*

"Sydney..."

"We need a new wall feature in our office." Since we need to redo it so we both can work from home.

"You're so fucking perfect." He gingerly wraps the sign back up. Once he sets it on the table, he pulls me to him and peppers every inch of my skin he can reach with kisses.

Giggling, I cup his head and hold him to me. "I love you," I tell him.

"I love you too, Mrs. Davis. You better get on that wedding planning because I'm feeling very impatient."

"I think I can make something happen."

Two weeks later, still in Idaho, our friends—who are also our family—join us in a small ceremony in the snow. There are perks to having endless resources at our fingertips. Sadly, Daisy and Luka couldn't make it, for obvious reasons, but everyone else is here.

I become Mrs. Beckett Davis as light snow falls around us, in the place where a chance meeting at the bar led us to our forever.

He's changed my life in more ways than I can count, and as he kisses me for the first time as a married couple, I'm excited for our future. The possibilities are endless, and as long as I have him by my side, I know without a doubt, it'll be the best life.

Also By

Ainsley and Ledger

For the Thrill of It
Willow and Oakley

What You Broke
Rina and Arlo

Redefining Strength
Lennox and Roxie

Be sure to join my newsletter to stay up to date on new releases and all other things me!

http://www.samanthamthomas.com

If you enjoyed Serendipity, please think about leaving a review! I would be so grateful to you!

Acknowledgements

To Michelle: The one I bitch to every day, who deals with me with I'm in the sticky middle and freak out that I can't ever write a book again. Thank you. You keep my imposter syndrome in check almost single handedly.

To Kait: You are a light in not only my life, but the book world and I'm so thankful to have you in my life.

To J: Girl... I wouldn't get through edits without you. Or writing for that matter. Our friendship is one of my favorite things.

Tara: Thank you so much for beta reading!

Casey: I absolutely love talking to you. You go above and beyond to support a little author like me and I am so thankful for your friendship.

Nina: You've single handedly made my books something I can be so incredibly proud of. You aren't just and editor, you're a wonderful person and a better friend. Thank you.

Hubs: Did our long-distance start inspire this book? Absolutely. It was a hard couple of years, but we made it, and I wouldn't want to do life with anyone else.

To my dear readers: I don't have the words to thank you enough. You keep me going, you give me a boost with every single message and I'm so grateful to you. This career can be hard and isolating, but you all have shown me love and support that I didn't think was possible. Thank you.